TAKE A CHANCE ON ME

Take a Chance on Me

MEGAN BYRD

ARDENVILLE PRESS

To Adam,
costar of my real-life romance

1

JULY

Rachel

I LET OUT a long breath while my eyes ping around the store in search of somewhere to channel all this energy pulsing through my body. Usually the sight of row upon row of dark wooden shelves filled with books has a calming effect on me. No such luck today. My foot taps out a frantic beat from my place behind the checkout counter. It must be louder than I realize because my co-worker, Brett, gives me a death glare. I shoot him an apologetic smile and grasp my thigh with both hands until my foot stills. My hundredth glance at the clock lets me know I've still got another forty minutes of work. I groan. My fingers drum against my leg while I will the clock hands to turn faster.

The thud of books on wood draws my eye to the customer in front of me. I smile and make small talk while ringing up the purchases, glad for the momentary distraction. Finally, the anticipated hour arrives. I rush to the employee lounge, more than ready to grab my things and make a hasty exit. Thayer and I have a date tonight.

I'm meeting him at The Crustacean, the swankiest seafood restaurant in Asheville. The pricy menu means it's usually reserved for big celebrations, so I'm anxious to find out what's worth the cost. My mind whirs with possibilities. Maybe he finished his manuscript early and wants to take a tropical vacation. I wouldn't mind a little beach time with my guy. My heart stumbles when my brain raises another idea. Is he going to propose? I mean, we've been together for a year and we're not getting any younger. I'm twenty-seven, which isn't old, but he's almost thirty-five. Maybe he's ready to take the next step in life. Settle down, have a few kids.

Am I ready for that? Do I love him? I definitely care deeply for him, but neither of us has said those three big words. Maybe that's what tonight's about—a declaration of love. Yeah, that seems more probable than a proposal. Though if things keep progressing like they have been, I could see that in our future.

I retrieve my purse from my locker, shut the door, turn, and startle at the face staring at me. I clutch my chest before scowling and swatting the shoulder of the person in front of me. "Brett! Don't do that!"

He laughs. "It never gets old."

I take deep breaths to steady my pulse. "You are the *worst*."

Brett grins wider. "You know you love me, Rachel."

I narrow my eyes even further, but then Brett tilts his head and flutters his lashes at me and I break, my frown lifting into a reluctant smile. "You nearly gave me a heart attack."

"Sorry about that. Where are you rushing off to?"

"I'm meeting Thayer at The Crustacean."

Brett whistles. "Fancy. What are you celebrating?"

I shrug. "I'm not sure yet. I'll let you know tomorrow."

Out in my car, I immediately crank up the air conditioner. It feels like a sauna in here after sitting all day in the blistering sun. I glance in the rear-view mirror to make sure I don't have any errant makeup after my long day at Page Turner Books. I love working there, but you'd be surprised how sweaty you can get lugging books around the shop and setting up displays. Or fidgeting like you've consumed half a dozen energy drinks. I grab my emergency deodorant from the center console and reapply. I add a spritz of perfume just in case. I want to put my best foot forward for whatever's happening tonight. Satisfied, I retrieve my phone to pull up directions to the restaurant. I have a text from Thayer which has me smiling before I even open it. My joy is short lived.

Thayer: I have to cancel tonight. Sorry.

I don't have any missed calls from him so it's probably not an emergency. A sense of dread still pools in my stomach. I press the phone icon on the screen to call him. I run through the possible scenarios. Something happened with his mom. Something happened to Shep, his lovable Labrador. My heart twists at that thought. That dog's definitely wormed his way into my heart. Though, he didn't have to try hard. I'm a pushover for all animals. Perhaps there's a work emergency, though what kind of emergency would there be during summer on a college campus? My mind immediately jumps to a shooting.

When the call goes to voicemail, I hang up and pull up the news. I search "Warren Wilson College," my heart in my throat, but the only result is an announcement of the graduating class back in May. I send a text, hoping he'll see it and respond soon.

Rachel: Is everything okay? Please respond ASAP I'm worried.

I wait for a few moments, and then my stomach grumbles. Sorry, tummy, no crab legs for you tonight. Guess that means leftover chicken salad at the apartment. I start the car and drive home, willing my phone to sound with a message from Thayer.

I'm curled up in my pjs and most of the way through *You've Got Mail* before my phone gets a message alert.

Thayer: I'm fine, just a thing at work.

My shoulders relax, and I chuckle with relief.

Rachel: So good to hear. Are we rescheduling The

Crustacean?

Thayer: About that…

I watch the bubbles dance as he types, wondering what he's going to say. Which of my theories is correct? None of them, it turns out.

Thayer: I don't think we should see each other anymore. I'm swamped with this book deadline and summer classes. I don't have time to sustain a relationship as well.

My heart plunges to my gut. *What?!* Where is this coming from? I call him, hoping I can better understand what's going on over the phone, but it goes immediately to voicemail. Did he just decline my call? I try one more time just in case it was a finger slip. Nope, not an accident. My face heats and the back of my neck tingles. Is it getting hot in here? I pull on the neck of my pajama shirt and flutter it, creating a small breeze. I type out a text.

Rachel: What's going on Thayer? Can we talk about this?
Thayer: It's not you, it's me. I think this is best for everyone involved.
Rachel: Please call me. I don't understand.

Bubbles appear and disappear several times, but no message ever comes. What in the world was that? Thayer broke up with me over text after a year together? *Who does that?* I need someone to help me process everything. I dial Abbie's number. Thankfully, she picks up after the first ring.

"What's up, little sis?"

I roll my eyes at her greeting, not like she can see it, but then burst into tears.

"Whoa, Rach, what's wrong?"

I take a few deep breaths and manage to get a few shaky words out. "Thayer…broke up…with me."

"What? When? How? Why?"

My response is a wail and more tears. I grab the box of tissues off the coffee table in front of me. They were reserved for the end of the movie, but I need them now. I swipe one under my nose and then grab another one which I press against my eyes. My phone chimes with a video chat request from my sister. I accept it and tear up again at Abbie's sympathetic expression.

"Rachel, I'm so sorry."

Abbie continues to speak softly to me until I'm recovered enough to speak again. "We were supposed to go to dinner tonight, but he canceled and then dumped me over text."

Her eyes narrow. "That snake. I always knew you were too good for him."

"Abbie," I groan. "I'm not ready to trash him. Besides, what does that say about me that I dated him?"

Abbie gives me a stern face and uses her bossy, no-nonsense voice. "You are a kind, loving person who always sees the best in people and lifts them up. He saw that and took advantage, the low life."

"Abbie, I'm serious. Stop with the name calling."

"Fine." She slumps against her chair and huffs out a breath. "But let me know when you're ready, because I've got a bunch more. I honestly don't know what you saw in him."

I give her a pointed look. "Still not helpful."

She schools her face into a penitent expression. "Sorry. Want me to come visit this weekend? We can watch Meg Ryan movies and eat chocolate."

"No, but thanks for the offer. I'll be okay. Just need time to process. And maybe stay away from men for a while."

Abbie chuckles. "Glad to see you've decided to join the dark side."

I can't help but smile. "You're so dumb."

"Yeah, but you love me."

"I do."

When we hang up, I decide I can't stomach seeing someone

else's happily-ever-after, even if it is fictitious, so I turn off the movie and head to bed. Maybe things won't look so bad after a good night's sleep.

2

Tom

THE SOUND OF the front door shutting spurs me out of my bedroom and into the living area. Julie kicks off her shoes, drops her bags at her feet, and drops onto the couch. My sister's obvious exhaustion kicks up sympathy in my chest. I walk behind the back of the couch, place my hands on her shoulders, and knead her muscles. She groans and drops her head back.

"Have I told you lately how much I appreciate having you here?"

I chuckle. "Not this week, but I've definitely gotten the message."

She sits up and turns her body so she can grab my hands with hers. "Seriously, Tom. You have been a lifesaver. Every day you help in the store is a blessing."

I squeeze her hands. "You know, you should probably hire more help. Maybe someone to manage the store who can take some responsibility off your shoulders."

She rolls her eyes. "You sound just like Emily."

I shrug. "She sees the same things I do. You're working yourself to death, Jules. It's okay to have help, you know."

"I know. That's why you're here."

"It's a first step, but you know I'm only temporary. I *do* have another job that requires me to travel for long stretches of time.

You need someone reliable, someone for the long haul."

Julie sighs and slumps back into the couch. "Yeah, yeah. Speaking of which, when do you leave again?"

"Next week. I'll be in South Africa for a week or two."

"Will Jeff be there?"

My smile widens. "Yeah. I can't believe I haven't seen him since December."

Julie frowns. "I'm sorry you've had to be here instead of at the competitions."

"Hey, no, I'm happy to help. That's what siblings are for, right? Besides, it's not like I missed going somewhere new. I've been to all those places multiple times and I'll probably see them next year." Julie looks unconvinced. "I'm serious. I'm more than happy to help, and Asheville is growing on me as a city. No beaches, but the mountains are gorgeous."

That seems to reassure her. "I miss living by the beach sometimes too. Speaking of which, are you ever planning to move back to Huntington Beach? You'd be able to see your best friend all the time if you did."

My chest twinges. I miss getting to hang out regularly with Jeff, but I still see him at surfing competitions, so it's not like my moving away cut off all contact. I just couldn't handle all the reminders of what I used to have. I shake my head to dislodge the unpleasant thoughts. "No, I don't think so."

Julie seems to notice the shift in my mood because she changes the subject. "Weren't you supposed to hear back about your submission for National Geographic soon?"

"Yeah, today actually."

"And?"

I try to keep a straight face, but fail miserably. "And I won."

Julie leaps up and wraps her arms around my neck. "Congratulations!"

I hug her back, allowing myself to indulge in the joy of my accomplishment. "Thanks."

"What picture did you submit?" I open up the email on my phone and hand it to her. "This is amazing. I can see why you won. You're so talented."

She returns the phone, and I study the photograph for a moment. It shows a surfer underwater with his board, a wave crashing over the surface above. The water under the wave is turbulent and looks almost otherworldly. It really is stunning, though seeing Johnny MacKenzie's face and remembering everything that happened kills my joy. We used to be good friends. Me, Jeff, and Johnny started the pro circuit at the same time and rooted for one other, joining forces as the newbies against the old pros. It felt like a sacred brotherhood that would stand the test of time. But then my world collapsed, and it turned out our bond wasn't as tight as I'd imagined. I click off my phone screen and look up at Julie, hoping my face doesn't betray my thoughts. "Do you need me to work tomorrow?"

"Yes, please."

"Great. There's dinner for you in the oven."

Julie grins. "Thanks, bro. You're the best."

"And don't you forget it." I wink even though my mood is still somber. No need to burden my sister with things she can't do anything about.

3

AUGUST

Rachel

MY SHOULDERS BOB in rhythm to "Party in the USA" playing over the store speakers. I'm grooving and singing along, giving my all to my one-person show in the storage room. The song reaches the chorus and I throw my hands up just like Miley sings, my whole body moving to the beat. I turn to the doorway and freeze when my eyes meet Brett's. He smirks and shakes his head before turning away and walking down an aisle. Of course, *he'd* be the one to catch me.

My arms drop to my sides. Embarrassment floods through me for allowing the music to carry me away while I'm working. Chastened, I turn back to my task of loading the cart to restock the books on the floor. A stack with an unfamiliar cover catches my eye and I pick one up for closer inspection. I thought Christine McMahon's latest book was coming out in October, not August. It makes sense now why she has a book signing in the store next month. I open the front cover and read the jacket flap. I'm intrigued by the premise and mentally put it on my to-be-read list. I promised myself I wouldn't buy more books until I've finished the embarrassingly large stack that covers my nightstand and part of the floor. *Books for book club don't count,* my mind reminds me. I grin, grateful for the loophole I've allowed myself with the book ban. I wonder if the ladies would agree to read a contemporary book for group. I'll ask them tonight. I add several copies of the new book to the cart and push it out onto the floor.

Miley's song ends and it's briefly quiet, but as soon as I hear the first call from Beyoncé to all the single ladies, I just can't help myself. I give the cart a shove and hop my feet up onto the legs, swinging my hips to the beat while I hum along. The cart starts to wobble and my stomach drops. Is this the busted cart? I'm positive I chose a good one earlier. *Wait a minute.* My eyes narrow when I remember I traded carts with Brett an hour ago. He'd asked me to finish stacking his books so he could visit the restroom. Did he purposefully stick me with the bad cart? Probably. I don't have a work husband. I have an annoying work brother.

I put one foot down to tame the wobble, but the weight shift worsens the cart's shake. A man steps into the aisle in front of me. My throat closes. *Oh no!* I drag both feet along the floor, desperate to stop the cart. I wrench the handle left. "Look out!" I yell, locking eyes with the customer. His surprise turns to alarm when I lose my footing and my legs slide under the tipping cart. I release my grip on the cart. My back hits the floor and I have enough sense to throw my arms up over my face and squeeze my eyes shut before I'm pummeled by a mountain of hardbacks.

There are a few thuds to my torso and thighs, but nothing like I was expecting. I open one eye to find the cart standing upright. I open my other eye, pull myself up to a sitting position, and survey the ground. Where's the avalanche of books? Why isn't the cart crushing my legs?

A hand reaches over the cart toward me. I follow the length of the tanned, muscular arm up to a broad chest in a well-fitted green t-shirt. My gaze continues up until it stops on the handsome face of a man with short, dark hair, brown eyes, and full, frowning lips. "Are you okay?"

My face heats immediately. My eyes dart away from his face and focus on his proffered hand. I take it, standing quickly. I straighten my shirt, brush off the seat of my pants, and take a deep breath to gather myself before meeting his eyes again. "I'm fine. Did the cart hit you?"

He smiles. "No. You stopped it just in time."

I cringe. "I'm really sorry about that. I'm not usually so reckless."

I bend down, pick the books up off the floor, and replace them on the cart. My face is still flaming, but I try to get back into professional mode. "Do you need help with anything?"

The customer opens his mouth, but before he can speak, Brett comes barreling out from the back of the store.

"I found it!" Brett says, triumph in his voice. "I knew we had a Tahiti travel book somewhere. Not sure how it ended up in the Africa section."

Brett hands the book to the customer.

"Thanks," the man says. He tips the book toward me. "Looks like I'm all set."

"Great," Brett says. "I can check you out over here."

The man turns to me and grins. "It was nice almost running into you."

My cheeks burn even hotter. "Yeah, right," I mumble.

My gaze follows the man until he exits the store. He doesn't look my way again and I'm astonished to feel a tug of disappointment. Why am I always so awkward? Especially around cute guys. I sigh. It is what it is. I turn, push the cart across the floor, and start placing books on shelves and displays.

Brett returns from the counter and helps me with the display. "What was that all about?"

"What was what?" I say, hoping Brett didn't witness me almost mow down the customer.

"It seemed a little tense between the two of you. Do you know him?"

"Nope. Never seen him before."

"Really? He seems familiar to me."

I shrug and return my attention to the cart. I tune back into the music, trying to forget about my most recent embarrassment. Just call me Awkward Annie. Only don't really, because my name's Rachel. Thankfully, the playlist works its magic and in a few minutes I'm grooving to the music again.

"What's put you in a good mood?" Brett says, pulling a few books from the cart.

"What are you talking about?"

"You're humming. You hum when you're happy."

"Do I?"

"Yeah. What tune is that?"

I look at him like he's crazy. "It's what's playing right now."

He shoots me an affronted look. "You know I don't listen to pop music willingly."

I roll my eyes. "I know. You like songs where the band screams indecipherable words."

"*I* know what they're saying."

I huff out a laugh. "Sure you do. It's 'The Best Day of My Life.'"

"It is?"

"Yeah."

"Why's it the best day of your life?"

I sigh, shaking my head. "No. It's the name of the song, Brett."

"Oh."

"But today is the best day of my month, at least."

"Why's that?"

"Because it's Classic Chicks day!"

Brett shakes his head. "Seriously? I was hoping you had some actual exciting news, like you have a date or something. A book club should not be the highlight of your month."

"You know how much I love books, Brett. Besides, Thayer and I just broke up. I'm not ready to date again."

"It happened a month ago."

"Three weeks," I say, glaring at him.

"That's practically a month."

"We dated for a year. It's going to be awhile before I'm ready to get my heart smashed again."

"Maybe your next relationship will end in happily ever after."

I roll my eyes. I feel further from a happily-ever-after than ever. "That'd be great, but it's not likely."

"Wow. Cynical much?"

I shrug. "I guess that's what happens after a string of terrible relationships."

"You've had one bad relationship."

This is actually number two, but no one in Asheville knows about my college boyfriend. I'd like to keep it that way. "It was pretty bad. And getting dumped over text was no picnic either."

Brett gives me a skeptical look. "Sounds like an excuse to me."

I huff out a breath and throw my hands up, frustrated he's not on my side. "Fine. Think whatever you want."

Brett's face softens, and he places a hand on my shoulder. "Breakups suck. I'm sorry. I just want you to be happy."

I pat his hand. "I appreciate that, but right now I just need my friends." I turn back to the cart and grab more books.

"I understand. It's too bad, though."

My head whips around at his teasing tone. There's an impish grin on Brett's face. "Why's that?"

"I saw how that guy looked at you."

"What guy?"

"The one you almost hit with the book cart."

I groan. "You saw that?"

"I did. That was a close one."

"I know. Not my best move. Or my smoothest."

"Well, you succeeded in getting his attention at least."

"Yeah, with the worst first impression ever."

Brett shrugs. "Whatever works, right?"

Hopefully, Brett will forget my gaffe in a few days. Most likely, I'll find some other way to embarrass myself, which will make today's event seem paltry. At least the entire store wasn't witness to my near-assault of a customer with a book cart. Just Brett. Well, and the cute guy, but I doubt he'll step foot in the store again after almost being flattened by yours truly.

One of Brett's earlier comments flashes through my mind. "Wait. How did he look at me?"

"Let me put it in your language. Like he'd just stumbled upon a first edition of *Pride and Prejudice*."

My heart flutters at his words, but then I remember where the information is coming from and am immediately wary. "Yeah, sure."

"No. I'm serious."

"Well, it doesn't matter. Like I said, I'm not ready to date again."

Brett purses his lips. "Okay."

"I'm serious."

"Whatever. I saw you staring after him when he left."

I roll my eyes and turn away so he doesn't see me blush. *Ugh.* See? Annoying brother.

4

Rachel

I'M PUTTING THE finishing touches on the refreshment table, but turn when a shoe squeaks behind me. Susan, one of my book club members, enters the room.

I smile warmly. "Hi, Susan. Where's Lori?"

"She's coming separately tonight. She needed to stop by her house and let the dog out."

"Oh, okay. Well, help yourself." I sweep my arm toward the table like one of the models on *The Price is Right* showing off a fabulous new prize. It seems appropriate since the truffles I bought for tonight are award-winning.

Susan points to a white truffle with light brown powder on top. "Oooh, is this new?"

"Great eye. That one has a milk chocolate center with Chai tea spices, a white chocolate exterior, and a dusting of cocoa powder and cinnamon. It's called the Taj Mahal. The one next to it with curlicues on top is called Blackout. If you like dark chocolate, you'll love it. It's my new favorite."

"You know I do." Susan picks up a plate and sets a Blackout on it. "I see you also picked up a Jitterbug just for me. I really do think the espresso gives me a little buzz."

I smile, pleased Susan noticed the gesture. "I want to keep you happy so you keep coming to Classic Chicks."

"I don't need bribing. I love this group."

A very tan woman in a flowy floral dress and leather sandals glides in the door, a lei around her neck. "Aloha, ladies."

"Deb," I say. "So great to see you again. How was Hawaii?"

"Fabulous, just fabulous! I was having so much fun, I almost didn't come back, but then I started missing my grandbabies and knew it was time. You gals *must* go sometime. It's like a facelift for your soul. I feel relaxed and rejuvenated."

"That's quite an endorsement," Susan says.

Voices float in from the hallway. "It sounds like the rest of our crew is here," I say.

Two women appear in the doorway, talking in excited tones.

"Hey, Lori and Anna," Susan says. "Why are you so worked up?"

"You won't believe what just happened," Lori says and turns to Anna.

Anna presses her hands together in excitement. "I saw Lori walking on the sidewalk when I got out of my car, so we started walking here together. When we turned onto Haywood, there was a large group huddled on the sidewalk outside of Bluebird restaurant. Lori squeezed through the crowd, pulling me with her until we could see in the window. Guess who we saw."

I venture the first guess. "Taylor Swift?"

"No."

Susan tries next. "George Clooney?"

"Nope!" Lori crows, her eyes dancing.

"Just tell us!" Deb says.

"Mark Darcy!"

Susan, Deb, and I exchange confused looks before Deb asks the obvious question. "How is a fictional character in Asheville?"

"Not Mark Darcy," corrects Anna. "Colin Firth."

"Oh!" we say in unison.

A dreamy expression crosses Lori's face and she sighs. "If I wasn't happily married..."

"Must I remind you Colin Firth is also married?" Anna says.

"Minor details." Lori waves her hand to dismiss Anna's comment. "Anyway, how exciting, right? A famous actor here in our town."

"I wonder why he's here," I say.

Susan shrugs. "Maybe he's shooting a movie."

"Well, whatever the reason, I hope to run into him again," Lori says, wiggling her eyebrows.

The rest of us roll our eyes. Lori's an Anglophile and romance junkie who has probably watched *Bridget Jones's Diary* and *Love Actually* dozens of times. I know for a fact she watches *Pride and Prejudice* every year. The Colin Firth version, of course.

It's time I got us back on track. "Now that we're all here, let's begin our discussion of August's book, *Jane Eyre*."

"I know we're the Classic Chicks and have many wonderful books to choose from," I say as we're wrapping up the meeting, "but I was wondering if perhaps we could deviate slightly from our normal format for a month."

"What do you have in mind?" Susan says.

I take a deep breath, suddenly a little nervous at suggesting a change to the group's usual book selection. "Christine McMahon is going to be here at the bookstore to read and sign copies of her new book in September. It's the day after our book club meeting and I thought we could all read it, discuss it, and then attend her event together the following evening. What do you think?"

I look around the room at each woman's face. Lori and Susan appear thoughtful. Anna scowls. She's the one I'm most concerned about nixing my idea.

Deb smiles at me. "I think it would be good to mix things up a bit, keep our group from getting stale." I smile back at her. I can always count on Deb to be up for something new.

"I'm game," Lori says.

Susan nods. "Me too."

Everyone's gaze swings to Anna. "Well, it'd be breaking from the norm since it's not a classic," she says. Her lips purse and her eyes narrow before she breaks out in a grin. "However, I loved Christine's first two books and would be interested to know if her third is just as wonderful. Let's do it!"

I exhale. My plan worked. I love beating the system. It doesn't matter that I created the no-book-buying rule in the first place. Besides, I'll get around to my other books, eventually. Even as I think it I know I'm kidding myself. "Great. Thank you all for your willingness to be flexible. We'll plan to go back to a classic for October. I appreciate you and look forward to our discussion next month. Oh, and please let the group know if there are any more Colin Firth sightings!"

I wake early the next morning in need of a jog in the cool morning air. On my way through the lobby of my apartment building, I spot a missing pet flyer. It's a cute orange-and-white-striped cat with big green eyes who apparently lives on my floor. My heart twinges with sympathy, and I send up a silent prayer for its safe recovery.

I take my usual route to Wolfe Ridge Park, where I can run the half-mile path around the playground and large green space often used for soccer or Ultimate Frisbee games. Ultimate looks kind of fun, but the idea of trying to throw a Frisbee across an entire field in front of other people intimidates me. I'm not a sporty person like my sister.

Speaking of Abbie, I wonder what she's doing right now. Odds are she's waking up to a beautiful sunrise over the Atlantic Ocean, maybe even jogging on the beach before she heads into work at the College of Charleston. She's the athletic trainer for the women's basketball program.

Abbie goes after her goals with tenacity and a never-quit attitude. It's how she'd ended up as captain of her volleyball, basketball, and softball teams during her junior and senior years of high school. Her hard work and dedication to sports, coupled with her natural athleticism, resulted in a college scholarship.

I'm proud of my sister and her successful pursuit of her dreams. Sometimes I wish I was as fearless as Abbie. I've had my moments. In high school, I submitted a proposal for a weekly teen advice column to my local newspaper, which was accepted. I was Reliable Rachel for two years. I once called into a radio station and karaoked a Taylor Swift song for backstage passes and a limo ride to the concert. Of course, those instances were B.C.—Before Chris, my college boyfriend. I shudder. A pervasive heaviness creeps into my mind. I shake my head and pick up my pace to outrun the emotions that are emerging from a place deep in my heart that I keep locked up tight.

5

Tom

SADIE TROTS BESIDE me into Wolfe Ridge Park. There aren't any other dogs around and I'm glad. We cut our last visit short when a small dog wouldn't stop nipping at me and Sadie. The dewy grass seeps into my sneakers, but I don't mind. I remove Sadie's leash and hold up the disc. "Are you ready, girl? Do you wanna catch the Frisbee?" The chocolate lab dances around my feet, ready to play. "Okay, go!"

I fling the Frisbee across the green space and it arcs gracefully through the air. The dog rushes after it, leaping and catching it in her mouth. She trots back to me and drops the Frisbee at my feet. I grin. "Too easy, huh? Let's try a little further."

I throw it harder. Sadie takes off like a shot, chasing it down. I let my gaze wander around the park. There's a lone runner on the path about twenty yards away. She comes closer and I read the front of her t-shirt. *I'd rather be reading.* I chuckle. Yeah, that's how I feel about running, too. I track her progress along the path as she heads back toward the playground at the far end of the field.

Sadie returns with the Frisbee, and I decide to test my arm's strength. I throw it as hard as I can and feel a sense of satisfaction as it sails fast and far across the grass. Sadie sprints after it, but the Frisbee drops to the ground and rolls onto the paved path a few yards ahead of the runner. The woman stops when she reaches the disc. She bends down and picks it up, looking around. I wave my arm.

Sadie reaches the woman and circles around her, tail wagging wildly. The woman pets her, scratching behind her ears, and I know Sadie's just found her new best friend. She sits down in front of the woman, her face lifted, obviously enjoying the attention. I'm debating whether to walk over to them, but then the woman stops petting Sadie and holds out the Frisbee to her. Sadie takes it, turns, and trots back toward me. I wave my thanks and she waves back before resuming her jog.

Sadie nudges my leg, and I tear my gaze from the woman. I take the disc from the dog and launch it. She races after it, determined to catch it this time. She leaps high in the air and closes her teeth around the disc. I shout and pump my fist in the air, thoroughly impressed with Sadie's skill. My gaze searches the path again for the woman. When she passes by, something about her is familiar. Maybe I've seen her here before?

When the woman jogs my way again, I make a split decision and walk toward the path to intercept her. "Hey." I hold my hand up in greeting, but quickly pull it back down and stuff it in my pants pocket. That was lame.

Her brown hair is pulled back into a sleek ponytail, but there are curly wisps sticking out above her ears. The baggy shirt hides her figure, but black yoga pants show off nice legs. Her pink lips curve down at the corners and glisten with moisture, possibly perspiration. When I look back up at her face, tears course down her cheeks. Compassion for the obviously distressed woman floods my heart. "Hey," I say again more gently, "are you okay?"

The woman stops, her eyes skittering away from my gaze. "Oh," she says, looking at the ground. She wipes her eyes. "Yeah, I'm fine."

"You sure?"

"I'm okay, really."

It doesn't feel appropriate to push the subject, so I let it go. I wrack my brain for something to ease the tension. She looks up at me and time stops. I've seen those startling blue-green eyes before. I glance down at her shirt and it hits me.

"Hey," I say in my most casual voice, "you work at the bookstore."

Surprise flits across her face before her features scrunch together, her narrowed eyes searching my face.

I remove my hat to give her a better look. "I'm the guy you almost ran over with a book cart."

Her cheeks flush, and she looks away. "Sorry about that. I'm usually more careful."

"Hey, don't worry about it. I now have a near-death experience at a bookstore in my story arsenal. How many people can say that?"

She scowls. "Near-death experience? You're much too muscular to be felled by a few books."

I grin, pleased by her observation. "I didn't know you noticed my physique, but yes, I suppose that's true."

Her blush deepens. "I...that's not...you..." Her mouth snaps shut, and she crosses her arms over her chest.

I'm enjoying seeing her flustered but I don't want to embarrass her. "I'm just teasing you. I'm Tom, by the way."

She hesitates for a second before speaking. "Rachel."

"Nice to meet you, Rachel."

She shifts her weight from one foot to the other and looks off into the distance. "I should finish my run."

I'd like to keep talking to her, but she's obviously dealing with something so I don't push it. "Oh, okay."

Rachel takes off along the path and I return my focus to Sadie, though my body remains aware of her presence in the park. She makes two more laps before leaving the park. When Sadie comes back with the Frisbee, I grab her leash from the grass. "Let's head back home, girl."

6

Rachel

I JOG AWAY from the park, mortified that I've had another embarrassing encounter with the cute guy from the bookstore. Have I mentioned he's cute before? Well, it's true. He's got a dimple in his cheek that appears when he smiles and I like it. Now I have a name to go with that delicious dimple. Tom. It suits him.

I scrunch up my face, remembering how rude I was to him. I get defensive when I'm feeling vulnerable, but he doesn't know that. And somehow I've seen him only in awkward situations. I just can't win. Oh well. It's probably for the best since I'm on a dating hiatus.

I shake my head, exasperated with myself. I can't believe I was crying over a dog. Seeing Tom playing with his dog reminded me of Thayer's dog. Shep and I had spent many weekend afternoons together throwing a tennis ball, often in this very park.

Shep was so affectionate and accepting, a calming presence for me. Sometimes he'd cuddle up next to me on the couch and lay his head in my lap when I'd hang out at Thayer's house. Now those memories are all that remain. My emotions were already volatile thanks to thoughts of Chris. I hate that memories of him still bother me so much. Shouldn't I be over something that happened years ago? Remembering that I won't see Shep again was the last crack in the dam holding back my tears.

I'm so focused on rehashing the unexpected grief I'd felt at the park that I don't realize where I am until I smell the inviting aroma of freshly baked bread wafting out of Dough Knots. *Geez, Rach, get it together.* I turn around and walk back down the block toward my apartment. I pass the alley next to my building and catch an orange blur out of the corner of my eye. I turn in to investigate. There are two big green dumpsters overflowing with black garbage bags. Plenty of cover to hide behind, but whatever I glimpsed was small, probably an animal. Just in case, I pull my phone out of a pocket, unlock it, and type in 911. Surely I'll have enough time to hit the call button if there's real danger. I sound just like one of those dumb movie characters who runs toward the murderer, but I can't help it. An animal in need is my kryptonite.

Extra cautious, and very conscious of my thundering heart, I tiptoe to the first dumpster not wanting to scare whatever's back here. I peer around it but see nothing. I walk lightly to the next one. There's an orange and white cat huddled between the dumpster and the wall. It looks up at me with big green eyes and my heart melts.

I crouch down and call softly to it while stretching my arm out, palm up, and inching slowly toward the cat. The cat's body is tense and I'm worried it's going to dart away before I can reach it. I take another small step and the cat's tail fluffs up. "Oh, poor kitty, are you scared? I won't hurt you. Let me help you."

I continue to speak in soft, measured tones while creeping closer to the cat. I stop a few feet away, keeping my arm extended. After a minute, the cat takes tentative steps toward me and sniffs my hand. It then rubs its cheek against my fingers. I flex my fingers and scratch the cat's chin. It pushes its head into the palm of my hand and purrs. I grin and rub the top of the cat's head, working my fingers all the way down its spine. "You must belong to someone in our building," I say, keeping my voice soft. "Let's find your owner, okay?"

I pick up the cat, cuddling it to my chest so it feels safe. The cat stiffens momentarily before relaxing against my body. A problem reveals itself when I reach the building's entrance. My building key is in the waistband of my shorts and my hands are full. I'm puzzling out my next move when the door swings open in front of me. I step through, apologizing to the woman who's startled at my quick appearance.

"Sorry. Thank you!"

I look down at the cat. "Let's find the flyer and get you home."

I walk to the bulletin board, but it's bare. "I guess we're going to have to knock on doors. I'm pretty sure you belong on the third floor. Maybe you can help me figure out which apartment is yours." I roll my eyes because I'm talking to a cat.

I climb the stairs and use my foot to knock on the first door. There's no answer, so I move across the hall. An exhausted-looking man opens the door a crack. Embarrassment pings through me when I realize that I might have woken him up. "I'm sorry to wake you."

The man shakes his head. "You didn't wake me. This is my new look. No one's getting much sleep around here with a newborn."

"Congratulations on your new baby. I'm sorry you're not sleeping, though."

"Not your fault. Can I help you?"

"Is this your cat?"

He shakes his head. "We don't have a cat."

"Okay, well, sorry to bother you. Hope you get some sleep soon."

The man shuts the door without responding.

"Zero for two," I say out loud. "I hope you're not actually a stray. Though a furry roommate wouldn't be so bad."

The cat's content in my arms, so I'm pretty sure it has a home. I walk down to the next door and knock. There's shuffling inside, but no one opens the door. After another minute of staring at the closed door, I shrug. "Well, maybe they saw you and knew you weren't theirs. Onward."

I cross the hall to my last neighbor's door. "I hope this is it."

I knock on the door. While I wait for someone to answer, I glance down at the doormat under my feet. A cat with a grumpy face stares up at me. Above its head are the words, *It's about time you got home.* I chuckle. This has to be the right place. I hear a bolt slide back and then the door swings open. A woman appears in the doorway. She has white permed hair, purple-framed glasses, and a pink sweater with the outline of a cat and the words *Cat Person* written on top.

Her face lights up when she sees the cat. "You found Mitzy!"

I smile, happy to have found the right home, and extend my arms out. She reaches up and takes the cat from my arms, cuddling it to her chest.

"Thank you, thank you! Mitzy, where have you been? I've worried myself sick!" She hugs the cat and then looks up at me again, her eyes brimming with tears. "Where did you find her? I've been so upset thinking about what might have happened to her. You're my hero."

I duck my head, embarrassed by the woman's praise. "I found her in the alley around the corner. It was nothing."

She frowns. "It's not nothing to me. Come in. Let me get you something to drink."

"Oh no, you don't have to—"

"I insist. You did a wonderful thing and now I want to express my gratitude."

I look down at my running attire and crinkle my nose. "I'm kind of sweaty. I wouldn't want to stink up your apartment."

The woman bats away my protest. "Nonsense. Don't even worry about it. Come in. Please."

I suppose I can humor the woman for a few minutes. I don't work until noon, so I have time. "If you insist."

She steps inside and motions for me to follow. The door

closes behind us. I reach the kitchen and feel a sense of déjà vu. The apartment layout is just like mine, but flipped like a mirror's reflection. Well, and the décor is different, obviously. Her kitchen table looks like solid wood with years of use, unlike my white Ikea one. The woman feeds the cat and pats it on the back. She then straightens up and looks at me. "Okay, now, what can I get you? Tea? Coffee?"

"Water would be great."

"Sure." She pulls two glasses from a cabinet, fills them with ice and water, and points me toward a chair at the table. "Have a seat, dear. We haven't properly met, have we? I was so excited at seeing Mitzy that I completely forgot my manners. I'm Louise Shaw."

I smile. "I'm Rachel Price. Nice to meet you."

"I haven't seen you before, Rachel. Did you move here recently?"

"I moved into the building last month, but I've lived in Asheville for five years."

"What do you do for work?"

"I'm a clerk at Page Turner Books on Haywood."

Louise's eyes light up. "I love that place! I usually stop in at least once a month, but I don't recall seeing you in there."

"Well, it's a large store and I don't work every day. What brought you to Asheville?"

Louise gets a wistful look on her face. "My husband, John, and I always talked about taking a trip here to see the Biltmore Estate. We never made it happen but, after he died four years ago, I stopped deferring my dreams and came to visit on my own. I loved the town so much that I moved here. I haven't regretted it for one second."

I frown, place a hand over Louise's, and squeeze gently. "I'm sorry about your husband. I'm sure you had a wonderful love story."

Louise smiles. "We did. Sometime I'll tell you about it." She pulls a handkerchief out of her shirtsleeve and dabs at her eyes.

"I can't wait to hear it. Do you have any children?"

"No, it's just me and Mitzy, which is why I'm grateful you found her. She was an anniversary present from John the year before he died."

My heart pangs in sympathy. "I see why she's so important to you. I love Mitzy's name, by the way. Is it significant?"

"When she was a kitten, she had enormous paws, and the white contrasted so much with her orange body that she looked like she was wearing oven mitts. Hence, Mitzy."

I chuckle. "That's cute."

Louise clears her throat. "What about you? Do you live alone? I probably should have asked sooner, but where in the building do you live?"

"Oh, my goodness! I'm so sorry. I should have introduced myself better. I'm next door in 3C. I live alone. No pets."

"What brought you to the area?"

My cheeks warm. "It's a little complicated. The best way to phrase it is that I needed a fresh start. Asheville is far enough from home, but not so far that visiting becomes a pain. It also seems to be a great environment for writers."

Louise perks up. "You're a writer?"

"I want to be."

"Where do your parents live?"

I exhale, glad that Louise didn't delve any further into that topic. "Atlanta. Well, Acworth, a suburb of Atlanta."

"Do you have any siblings?"

"Two, both in South Carolina."

"It must be nice having everyone live in the same region."

I nod. "It is. We usually meet at my brother's house in Greenville for the holidays. It's most central for everyone. Plus, he's the only one of us with kids, so it's easier for their family."

Louise smiles. "Pardon my forwardness, but you're a pretty woman so you probably have a boyfriend, right?"

"My last boyfriend and I just broke up, actually."

Her lips curve down, and her eyes convey compassion. "Oh, I'm sorry. Was it serious?"

I shrug a shoulder, trying to seem nonchalant but tears wells up in the corners of my eyes for the second time that morning and I internally chastise myself. It seems ridiculous that I'm getting emotional over Thayer. "We were together for a year."

Louise puts a hand on my arm. "Endings are always hard, dear. Even when we know it's for the best. You're still young. Take your time. Find someone who supports your dreams and can make you laugh. The years fly by with someone you genuinely adore. At least, that was my experience."

I paste a smile on my face and nod, afraid the tears will spill if I try to speak.

"I'm a good listener if it helps to talk about it."

I wipe my eyes with my fingers and swallow the lump in my throat. "Thanks, Louise. I really appreciate that."

Maybe I will feel better if I share it with someone. I take a few deep breaths to get myself under control and dive in. "Thayer and I met at one of his book signings. He'd written a book about the history and evolution of the library. The topic interested me, so I showed up to the event at the Pack Library."

I glance at Louise. She nods encouragingly, so I continue.

"I approached him afterward, asking if he'd answer a few additional questions. I was instantly attracted to his curly blond hair, bright blue eyes, and the smattering of freckles across his nose. I thought his black-rimmed glasses and the plaid scarf hanging jauntily around his neck made him look like the quintessential English professor. He suggested we go down the street to Hill of Beans and talk over coffee. We talked for hours about books and only stopped because the cafe closed. Thayer asked for my number and then texted me the next morning asking me to dinner that evening."

"It sounds like you had a lot in common," Louise says.

"We did. His passion for books and writing hooked me. Truth be told, I kind of hoped some of his confidence would rub off on me, but, unfortunately, it didn't."

Louise stays quiet, and I continue with my sad tale. "We talked almost daily while we were dating and spent several evenings a week face-to-face. Thayer insinuated once or twice that he saw our relationship going the distance.

"Recently, he seemed overwhelmed trying to fit in writing time on top of his daytime classes and weekly evening writer's workshop. The deadline for his fourth book is in a few months and it's been weighing on him. He arranged dinner at The Crustacean one evening. I assumed we were celebrating something. Instead, he texted to cancel and then said he didn't think our relationship was working out and it was best if we went our separate ways."

"What did you do?"

"I called him but he didn't answer, so I sent a text asking if something had happened. His response was essentially 'it's not you, it's me.' And that was it. I haven't heard from him since."

"That seems a little harsh."

I shrug and swallow, hoping to get rid of the tremor in my voice. "I guess that's how it goes sometimes."

"Did you love him?"

"No, I don't think so. I did care for him, though."

She reaches across the table and pats my hand. "Of course you did, dear. I can tell you're a very kind person."

"Thanks."

So much for Louise's theory. I don't feel better now that the story's out. I feel embarrassed and awkward. I shoot to my feet. "I should probably go. I need to clean up and eat something before work."

"Okay, dear. It was very nice to meet you. Thanks again for bringing Mitzy back to me. You'll have to come over for a thank-you dinner sometime soon."

I smile, my embarrassment easing slightly. I feel like a

cherished family member when Louise calls me 'dear.' "That would be lovely, thank you, Mrs…I mean Louise."

I walk next door to my apartment, closing the door gently behind me once I'm inside. I lean against the backside of the door and exhale. Whew. What an emotional morning. I hope the rest of today isn't like this. I shake out my limbs and neck to release some tension and head to the bedroom.

7

Tom

THERE'S A THRONG of people at baggage claim when I arrive. I roll my neck and shoulders to dislodge some kinks acquired during the long flight from Los Angeles. Hands clamp down on my shoulders and work on the knots in my muscles. It feels so good, my shoulders relax under the touch. A groan escapes my lips when a thumb finds a sore spot. The hands fall away from my shoulders.

"I can't believe you'd let a stranger touch you like that."

I turn, a grin spreading across my face. "Jeff, I knew it was you."

He narrows his eyes. "Sure you did."

"It's good to see you."

His frown flips up into a smile, and he pulls me into a bear hug. "Welcome to Tahiti, Tommy Two-Tone."

I groan, this time from displeasure. "You're never going to let me live that down, are you?"

Jeff grins. "Of course not."

"Maybe I should start calling you Jumpy Jeff, then."

Jeff's smile morphs into a scowl. "That's a low blow, bro."

I smirk, glad to have dirt on him, and turn back to the conveyor belt in search of my bag. "So, how's it looking out there?"

"Man, the conditions are gnarly. It's going to be a good time."

I smile at Jeff's enthusiasm. "That's great. How are you feeling about the competition?"

"It's going to be tough. Johnny Mac is right behind me. If I can make it deeper than him in the competition, then I'll be able to keep a comfortable lead."

I nod, feeling a twinge of jealousy. Part of me misses the adrenaline of competing. "I'm sure you can do it. You're on fire right now. I'll do my best to get some great shots of you this week."

"Maybe I can use one to give out with autographs for all of my adoring fans."

I laugh. "Yeah, sure. You don't want to disappoint all those surfer chicks."

"No, never." Jeff winks. "Anyway, I bet you're tired of all things airplane. Let's head to Teahupo'o and get some ia ota."

My mouth waters just thinking about the marinated tuna mixed with vegetables and coconut milk. "Sounds like a plan, man." I spot my suitcase and pluck it from the belt. "I'm all set."

Jeff slings an arm across my shoulders and steers me to the car.

I lean back in my chair to get more comfortable, my hand rubbing over my stomach. "Oh man, I'm so stuffed. I think we ordered too much."

"I don't know, Tom," Jeff says. "Which of our dishes should we not have ordered?"

I think through our meal of shrimp, fish, pork, pineapple, and a delicious fruit pudding. "I see your point. I rescind my last statement."

"As well you should. This place has the best food in town."

My head nods in agreement. "It's pretty amazing. I always

love when August rolls around and I know I'll find myself back here where I can enjoy the food."

Jeff tilts his head and gives me a cautious look. "So…do you still miss all this?"

"Yeah. Asheville's a foodie town, but it can't beat the real deal."

Jeff shakes his head and looks at me expectantly. "I wasn't asking about the food. I was talking about surfing."

His words churn up memories from what feels like decades ago, but are only a few years old. Paddling out to the line-up, anticipating the next wave, being stoked after a solid ride. "Yeah, I do." The guilty look on his face makes me press on to relieve his distress. I can't let my pain derail his career too. "But that will never change the fact that I'm happy for you and proud of how well you're doing." A sudden pang of melancholy threatens to choke me. Time to change the subject. "How's Lisa?"

Jeff lights up. "Lisa's great! She couldn't come because her sister's getting married in a few weeks and she's been helping her make sure everything's ready. They're going to fittings, making sure the flowers are perfect, assembling party favors." He scrunches up his nose. "You know, all that fun stuff."

I laugh. "Will there be little packages of bubbles with your and Lisa's name on them sometime soon?"

"No way. We'll have miniature surfboards, not bubbles! What about you?"

"I don't care what party favors you have."

Jeff laughs. "Nah, man, I meant are you seeing anyone?"

I look away. "No."

"It's been two years."

"And?"

"Maybe it's time to get back out there." I open my mouth to respond, but he holds up a hand to stop me. "I know Bethany did a number on you. I can't imagine how rough it was breaking up on top of everything else, but it doesn't mean you should give up on relationships altogether. Give someone else a chance."

I know he's trying to be kind, but his words sting. "Easy for you to say. You found the last good one."

"Nah, you know that's not true."

I won't convince him otherwise so it's time to end this line of conversation. "Whatever. I'm ready to go if you are."

"Sure. You could use some rest. You look rough, man."

I chuckle. "Thanks for not sugar-coating it for me, Jeff."

"Hey, that's what bros are for."

The next morning I'm out at the beach just after sunrise, going through my equipment. I nod at the other photographers when we catch eyes. I recognize most of them from previous events. I turn my camera to the lush green mountains behind me and take a few shots. I also point it down at the dark sand on the beach, using my pale toes for contrast.

I run through my checklist: set the focus and aperture, fully charged batteries in the cameras, empty memory cards, backup batteries and cards for each camera in a waterproof pocket. Satisfied the equipment is ready, I pull out a bottle of sunscreen and start applying it to my face and arms.

I notice a few head shakes from the other guys, but they don't have to face a nagging sister if they come back sunburned. Julie's very adamant about proper skin care, especially since our uncle died of melanoma a few years ago. She makes sure everyone in our family sees a dermatologist and has researched the most effective sunscreens. She even emailed a chart detailing specific activities and how often to reapply. A bit of overkill, but losing Uncle Bill was a colossal blow for her, so I understand the overabundance of caution for her other loved ones.

The surfers are just making their way down to the beach, so I visit the water's edge and dip my feet in. I close my eyes and sigh. There's nothing quite like the feel of water splashing over your toes while your feet sink into soft, wet sand. The salty air infuses my lungs with every breath. The sun warms my face and my shoulders relax. The sound of feet down the beach and into the water breaks my meditation, telling me it's time for warm-ups.

I open my eyes and head back up the beach to grab my gear before finding Chuck, the guy who drives the jet ski while I take pictures. I climb on the back and we edge past the surfers, heading out to the break. I smile, remembering how calming yet energizing the paddle out feels. The anticipation of catching the first wave, but also ruminating on past runs and deciding what to try today.

I tap Chuck's shoulder and he throttles down so I can take some photos of the waves and double check that everything looks good. I find Jeff already behind the waves, sitting on his board and taking it all in. When his face turns my direction, I hold up a hand. He grins and lifts his chin in response. In the next instance, his focus has switched to the swells in front of him and he takes off. I lift my camera and take a few photos as he gets to his feet and drops down the front of the wave. My heart thuds as he rides back up the wave before cutting down again. Longing floods through me for the experience of riding a wave with such precision. I have to shake my head so I don't get lost in my own thoughts. I get a few more photos before Jeff finishes his ride.

He looks my way and throws up a shaka sign with his hand which I toss back. I have to swallow down the jealousy I feel that Jeff still gets to do something I love. It's not his fault my career's over. Besides, if there's anyone who deserves to be champion, it's him.

I tap Chuck again, motioning to a spot closer to the action. He nods, starts the jet ski, and drives me to a new spot. I push down my yearning and regret and get back to work.

8

SEPTEMBER

Rachel

A SLOW WORKDAY allows me to sneak in pages of *The Secret Ingredient,* this month's book club read. The sound of the bell over the front door breaks into my thoughts of sous-chef Tami's loveless marriage to Luther and whether I, too, would have fallen for pastry chef Jasper's smooth-talk and flirtations. I mark my place with an old receipt before closing the book.

I look up from the checkout counter and see a familiar face heading toward me. Short brown hair, brown eyes, clean-shaven face, athletic build. *What's he doing here?* Didn't he get my telepathic message not to return to the store? And what's his name again? Tim? Todd? Teddy? Something that starts with a T. He stops in front of me. My fast-beating heart betrays my anxiety, but I don't think he can tell anything's wrong. He smiles and I have to will my lips to curve up, so I don't glare at a customer. Must maintain my stellar employee reviews.

"Rachel, right?"

"Yes. And you're… Tim, maybe?"

The small downward curve of his lips tells me I'm wrong. Not that I'm staring at his lips. "You're close. It's Tom."

I wince. "Right, Tom."

"Don't feel bad. I double-checked your name tag when I came

in."

"Oh." My hand flies up to the rectangular bar attached to my shirt. "Of course."

He says nothing else but continues to smile at me. Why is he here? Better figure it out so I can get rid of him. Too much time in his presence might weaken my defenses and I can't have that. I clear my throat. "So, Tom, can I help you?"

"Yes. Do you have travel books for France or Hawaii?"

"I'm sure we have both." I search the store for another co-worker to pass him off on, but there's no one nearby. Rats. I guess it's my duty. "Follow me."

I step out from behind the counter and lead him down a hall made up of parallel rows of seven-foot-tall bookshelves. The back of my neck feels warm and I wonder if it can feel Tom's gaze. I take a left at a break in the shelves followed by a sharp right before coming to a halt in front of our travel section. Tom turns to the side to avoid crashing into me and bumps into the bookshelf behind us. "Oof."

"Oh, I'm sorry. I stopped too fast, didn't I? I forget customers don't know the store as well as I do." I school my face into one of concern to cover the smile that wants to pop out. I didn't mean for him to hit the shelf, but I'm not sad about it. It's nice to have the tables turned so I can witness him in an embarrassing situation for once. "This is our travel section. It's divided into U.S. and international travel. Each section is in alphabetical order. Where in France are you traveling?"

"I'm going to the coast, near Biarritz."

I turn back to the shelf and run my hands along the France travel books. "It looks like we have nothing specifically for the coast. Your best bet would be a book that covers all parts of the country."

I choose one with a blue spine, pull it out, and open up to the table of contents. I find Biarritz in the index and open up to the proper section. "Does this look like what you need?"

He takes the book and peruses a few pages. "Yes, this'll work."

I turn back to the shelf, mumbling aloud as I look through the U.S. travel section. "Alaska, Arizona, California, Colorado, Florida, Georgia, Hawaii." I motion for Tom to come closer. "We have a few books about Hawaii. One on volcanoes, one on water activities like snorkeling and surfing, and a few general sightseeing books."

He takes a step forward. His arm brushes against my shoulder when he reaches up to grab the water sports book. Heat zings through my shoulder and I'm momentarily stunned. What is happening? My body is a traitor. Tom flips through the book until he freezes, his eyes wide. After a moment, he blinks out of his stupor and snaps the book shut. He returns it to the shelf and grabs a large blue one. "I think this one will work just fine, thanks."

I'm tempted to ask if something's wrong, but decide to stay professional and distant. I'm more than ready to get him out of the store. "Is that all you need?"

"I'll be taking a few trips soon, obviously." He holds up the books in his hand. "Do you have any recommendations for fiction?"

As much as I'm ready for this encounter to be over, I can't pass up an opportunity to give novel recommendations. "What kind of fiction do you enjoy? Mystery, horror, fantasy, historical, suspense, detective novels?"

"I like books that are adventurous, like searching for a lost city or a buried treasure."

I'm not surprised. He seems like the adventurous type. "Something like Indiana Jones, but in book form?"

Tom's eyes brighten. He gives me a wide smile and my heart somersaults. "Yes, exactly like that! Does that exist?"

"Yes. There's an author who has a series of novels, each trying to find an ancient city's lost treasured artifacts. They've received very positive reviews."

"Great. Can I get one of those?"

"Sure." I lead him past the travel section, turning down a narrow aisle of books with small lights twinkling overhead, before proceeding into a cave-like room.

"Wow," Tom says. "This is cool."

I look around the space, trying to imagine how it looks to Tom. The walls and bookshelves are midnight blue, making the colorful book spines shine against the dark background. There are two club chairs on a shaggy gray rug in the center of the room with a small round table between them that almost begs for someone to sit down and crack open a book. "Yes, this is a unique bookstore. I come in here to recharge before I have to turn on again." I realize too late that I'm sharing something personal with Tom. Maybe he didn't catch my slip.

He tilts his head and quirks his lips to the side. "Turn on again? Are you a robot?"

I scream silently in my head, feeling my cheeks warm with embarrassment. When will this interaction be over? "No, just an introvert."

"If you don't like people, why work a job where you have to interact with them so much?"

I release a breath, willing myself not to roll my eyes. "I didn't say I don't like people. I *do* like people. It's just that too much time with people saps my energy. I love this job. I love being surrounded by books and helping people find books they'll love. This is practically the best job ever." Why do I feel the need to defend myself to Tom?

He grins. "Wow, you're quite passionate about books. Why isn't it the best job ever?"

"Um…" My hesitancy doesn't dissuade him. In fact, it seems to intrigue him.

"Is your dream job super embarrassing like being a jam taster?" he says, a challenging look in his eye.

I scoff. "What's a jam taster? Surely that's not an actual job."

"You know, you love jam and get a tremendous thrill from

tasting new flavors. I'm sure someone gets paid to do that."

I shake my head, but can't stop the smile from forming on my lips. "No, definitely not."

"Then you want to be the curator of a museum filled with stuffed animals and dolls."

An image of a room full of ceramic dolls with vacant eyes staring straight ahead enters my mind and I stick out my tongue in disgust. "No. That's weird and a little creepy."

He claps his hands together and I startle at the loud pop they make. "A dolphin trainer at an aquarium!"

Where is he getting these guesses? "No, not one of those, either. It sounds kind of fun, but then I'd smell like fish all the time."

Tom lifts his hands palms up and shrugs. "Well, I'm all out of guesses. Will you please tell me?"

I study Tom's face. Why is he so insistent about this? If I tell him, will he finally go away? "You really want to know?"

"I do."

"Okay, fine, but don't make fun of me."

"Why would I do that?" His eyes widen. "You *do* want to run a doll museum. I knew it!"

I can't help laughing. "Oh, my gosh. For the last time, no!"

He looks at me expectantly, and I sigh. "My dream job is writing books."

"Why would I laugh at that? That's an exceptional dream." My cheeks burn. How can one tiny shred of encouragement affect me like this? "What genre books do you want to write?"

Might as well be completely honest. "Adventure."

He straightens, his mouth curving up into a smile. "That's great. What's stopping you?"

I shrug, not wanting to reveal to a practical stranger that my lack of talent is the impediment. Instead, I turn and point toward a shelf. "Anyway, here are the books I was talking about. The Lost Treasures series by William O'Mara. The first one is *King John's*

Jewels. I'd start there because the series has the same main character and each book builds on the previous one."

When I look back at him, he catches my gaze and holds it. "Okay. I'll take it."

I break eye contact first and grab a copy of the novel. "Great. Follow me back to the front and I'll ring you up."

At the register, I hand him his bag of books. Tom smiles at me, his eyes crinkling at the corners. "Thanks for your help, Rachel."

When he's gone, I cover my still-warm cheeks with my hands. That wasn't quite as terrible as our previous interactions. I opened up a small part of myself to a cute guy and didn't die. I also learned he's funny and kind. And seems to enjoy reading, which is always a check in the pro column. I mull over the last few minutes before pulling my book back in front of me. I'm eager to see how it ends, but for some reason my mind keeps returning to Tom and the way his enthusiasm for my author dream made my heart flutter.

9

Tom

I'M LOST IN thought as I head away from the bookstore. I want to know more about Rachel's desire to write, but her discomfort was crystal clear. There's definitely a story there. Perhaps if I continue to run into her, she'll open up to me. My heart thumps its agreement in wanting to spend more time with Rachel, and I squash the implications. Despite my heart's eagerness, I'm not ready to open myself up to getting hurt again.

My mind flashes to the photo I'd seen in the water sports book in the bookstore and I shudder. I hope Rachel didn't notice my shock. I'd flipped through it, hoping to see a picture I'd taken of surfers at Pipeline. Instead, I encountered a photo of me in the barrel of a wave my championship year. I can still remember the high of that amazing year. Too bad the next one felt like being smashed against a coral reef. Oh, to relive that perfect year again. It's impossible, but a guy can still dream, right?

I'd been dating Bethany—an amazing, supportive, beautiful woman. She was a sponsor rep, but also my biggest fan. She'd tackle me in a congratulatory hug each time they called my name as the winner and we'd celebrate with a delicious meal at an amazing restaurant.

I proposed after earning the world title. I felt untouchable. And then the accident happened. The night that changed my entire world.

I shake my head to get rid of the depressing thoughts. I'm older and wiser now. I can't change the past. Time to focus on the future.

I stop walking, reach into my bag, and pull out the fiction book Rachel recommended. I flip it over and read the back copy. It sounds interesting. If I like it, I'll return for the sequel and maybe run into her again. I enjoyed teasing her about her dream job, even if it did end a bit awkwardly. I respect her passion for books and adore her beautiful smile. I wouldn't mind seeing more of it.

I catch my train of thought and grimace. Jeff and his lovey-dovey relationship has gotten into my head. I'm happy for Jeff, but the sting of Bethany's betrayal still feels fresh. I know all too well how painful it is to watch the future you've planned get smashed to bits like a surfboard flung against the rocks by a merciless wave.

Is it possible to find lasting happiness with another person? Maybe, but my heart's still in recovery mode. I should stay away from Rachel. Her presence tempts me to throw caution to the wind, and I'm just not ready. Decision made, I drop the book back into the bag and resume walking.

10

Rachel

I SHOULDN'T BE surprised by the number of people in the store. I'm obviously not the only one who loves Christine McMahon's books because she's a bestselling author. Apparently, a lot of them live in Asheville and are here tonight.

I smile at customers as they approach my table to grab a cup of punch and a cookie. I wish we could give out truffles from Little Shop of Sugar. Maybe I can convince my boss to talk with the chocolate shop's owner about a discount. We could set up a display near the register to promote the shop. I make a mental note to talk to Sarah later in the week.

"Hi Rachel!"

I snap out of my thoughts and look up into the smiling faces of the Classic Chicks. "Hey ladies! Glad to see you. Are you excited?"

"Of course we are," Deb says. She waves a piece of paper in the air. "I have my question all set to go if I get picked." She finishes with an exaggerated wink.

I grin. "That's Brett's job tonight, so you'll have to get in good with him."

"Oh, okay." Deb looks around. "Where is he?"

"I think he's back with Christine. I doubt you'll see him until it's time to start the event."

She deflates a little. "Well, shoot."

"If you stay to get your book autographed, maybe you can ask her your question then."

Deb nods. "That's true."

"I'm glad you suggested this," Lori says. "I think we should read more contemporary books. I want to read *Ayesha at Last*. I hear it's a fresh take on *Pride and Prejudice*."

"That sounds interesting," Anna says.

"I've heard it's good," Deb says.

Lori pins me with her eyes. "Do you think we could read it instead of *The Age of Innocence* that we decided on yesterday?"

I shrug to appear casual, but I'm always game to read an Austen adaptation. "That's fine with me. Is everyone else okay with that?" The women nod. "Okay, then it's settled. Read *Ayesha at Last* for October's meeting."

Another excuse to buy a book I've had my eye on. Excellent! My conscience pricks me. I shouldn't use book club to feed my insatiable book-buying habit, but I wasn't the one that suggested it this time. Though perhaps I could find a happy medium and start suggesting titles from the pile on my nightstand to the group. It might help get me back down to a manageable size. I'll consider that for next month.

"Of course, we'll have to come up with a new name for the group now," Deb says. "Classic Chicks just won't do unless we're referring to being old ladies."

The group laughs.

"How about the Lovely Book Ladies?" Anna says.

"I know," Lori says. "The Brainy Book Babes."

"Ladies of Literature," Susan suggests.

Deb wrinkles her nose. "That makes us sound all hoity-toity." She raises the plastic cup in her hand and sticks her pinky out like she's having high tea.

"Keep thinking and we'll discuss it next month," I say. I incline my head toward the line forming behind the women. "We need to give others a chance for some punch and cookies."

"Oh, yeah. Sorry," Deb says.

Susan waves as they leave the table. "We'll save you a seat."

Christine reads an excerpt from her book, and then Brett opens up the floor to questions. Someone in the crowd asks the author where she gets her ideas and inspiration from. Another person asks if she's already working on another book. Christine nods and shares the plot basics. When Brett points to Deb's waving arm, I put my hands together in a gesture of thanks and give him a grateful nod. He winks at me and I groan. He thinks I owe him now.

Deb stands up. "How did you get started in the writing industry and was your first published book the first one you wrote?"

I perk up, very interested in the answer. Christine smiles before answering.

"Excellent questions. When I first began my career, I wrote short stories. I sent them to magazines that I enjoyed. I received several rejections, of course, but had my first piece published in *The Pacific Press* magazine. I didn't get paid for that one, but I received exposure. Eventually, I began receiving small checks for my work. After a few years of regular submissions, an editor who read my short stories asked if I'd consider writing a full-length novel. He wasn't interested in my first story, but published the second one. I now have three books with them and a fourth underway. The first book I wrote probably won't ever be published, but I kept at it and found success."

I sit with this new information. It's reassuring to be reminded that it's hard work for everyone and instant success is rare. I shouldn't give up after the first rejection. But how do I distinguish whether a "no" means "not-right-for-our-organization" or "you're-a-terrible-writer?"

I'm still dealing with my relationship rejection, and that only lasted a year. How would I hold up under professional rejections over a dream I've had since I was a kid? I'm not ready to lay my writer's heart out for people to smash. But will I ever be?

"That's the end of our question-and-answer session," Brett says. "In a few minutes, Ms. McMahon will sign books. Refill your cup or grab another cookie while we get set up."

I blink, surprised. I missed all the questions after Deb's. How long was I distracted? I stand up from my chair and walk to the autograph table. I'm in charge of keeping the line moving and organized, and this crowd is larger than we expected. The crowd is cordial, and the signing goes smoothly, which allows my mind to bounce between Christine's words and my fear of rejection.

11

OCTOBER

Tom

THE SUN BLINDS me when I step out of the airport in Biarritz, France. I raise my hand to shield my eyes and smile when the warm breeze ruffles my shirt. It seems unseasonably warm for the beginning of October, but I'm not complaining. It's going to be another glorious trip to another amazing country.

I make my way to the taxi station and give the driver the address of the house in Hossegor. I lean back against the cracked leather seat and close my eyes. I startle awake when the car stops. I look out the window and smile. We've pulled up to a familiar white wall partially covered in lush vegetation with the red Spanish tile roof of a house beyond it.

I pay the driver, grab my bags, and get out of the cab. The front gate is open so I step through, looking up at the house. Memories from previous visits bombard my mind and my heart hitches when I remember that this time differs from the others. I force the thought out of my head and move toward the front door. Before I reach the porch, the door swings open and out steps Jeff, smiling from ear to ear. "About time you made it, bro."

He pulls me into a bear hug, and I drop my bags so I can wrap my arms around him. When we step apart, I notice the short woman with curly blond hair standing just behind Jeff. "Lisa, hi! I didn't know you'd be here. So great to see you." I step forward for a hug.

"Hey, Tom. I'm glad you made it here safely."

"I'm glad to be here. How was your sister's wedding?"

Lisa sighs wistfully. "It was a beautiful wedding and a gorgeous honeymoon in Fiji. I wouldn't mind taking a trip there someday." She looks at Jeff and winks.

"Wherever my lady wants to go, we'll go," Jeff says, kissing her. It lasts long enough for me to feel awkward so I clear my throat. Jeff laughs, then grabs my shoulder and pulls me into the living room. "Bedrooms are the same. Make yourself comfortable and then we'll go eat."

I smile. Some things never change. "It's always about food with you, isn't it?"

"Of course! The only reason I surf is to visit exotic locales with great food and burn enough calories so it doesn't look like I live to eat."

"Is Le Scaphandre still open? I could really go for some of their seafood."

"It is, and it's just as good as I remember."

"I guess you've already been there?"

Jeff grins. "Maybe once or twice."

"We can go somewhere else."

"No way, man. You requested it and I love just about everything on the menu. I could eat all my meals there."

"And he would, too," Lisa says, patting Jeff's flat stomach, "but some of us like a little more variety in our diet."

"Great," I say. "I'm starving. I ate nothing on the plane in anticipation of the food here."

"A man after my own heart," Jeff says.

After a delicious dinner of rice and seafood, we head down toward the beach, walking along the Quai de la Plage promenade. Roche Ronde, a huge rock that juts out of the water, is barely visible through the darkening sky. The lighthouse in the distance appears as a tall, white beacon.

"How's your family doing, Tom?" Lisa asks.

I glance over as she grabs Jeff's arm and weaves their fingers together. This act of intimacy stabs my gut. I look away and try to swallow down the longing that's clawing its way up my throat. "They're doing well. My brother's still in New York. He's now an editor at Quill Books Publishing. He's been dating a woman named Serena for about a year and they seem happy. Julie's business is thriving in downtown Asheville. She's following in our uncle's shoes and winning awards for her truffles."

Lisa arches an eyebrow. "Did you bring any of these award-winning truffles with you?"

"I did." Jeff opens his mouth and I hold up a hand. "And my parents are loving being back in Huntington Beach. Which I know you already know, since they said they saw you the other week."

Jeff grins. "Yeah. I didn't realize they moved back into your old house."

"They rented it out when we left Cali. I guess they knew the Asheville move wasn't permanent."

Jeff gets a faraway look. "That house holds so many great memories for me."

His words spark something in my brain. "Speaking of memories, remember the first time we stayed at the house here?" Jeff looks confused so I continue. "With the ice?"

His eyes sparkle, and he laughs. "Oh man, Milo!"

Lisa perks up. "I don't think I know this story. What happened?"

Jeff straightens and turns toward Lisa. "The fridge's ice machine had issues. The owner left a note, but Milo didn't see it. He went straight to the fridge with a cup and pressed the button for ice."

Jeff looks at me, and I continue the story. "I yell to Milo to stop, but I'm too slow and we hear a terrible grinding sound from somewhere inside. Milo releases the button, but the sound doesn't stop. Suddenly, ice shoots out of the door. Milo tries to catch it with his cup, but soon it's overflowing."

Jeff jumps in. "So Tom, thinking quickly, flips up the bottom of his shirt to catch the ice. Meanwhile, I'm standing there frozen in shock. My brain finally kicks in and I reach behind the fridge and unplug it. The grinding stops, but ice is everywhere."

He looks back at me, and I pick up the story. "The ice in my shirt is giving me chills, so I dump it in the sink. My shirt is soaked, so I toss it aside and continue cleaning up."

"And now, the best part," Jeff says, eyes dancing. "Milo's girl walks into the kitchen and slips on some ice. Tom catches her before she hits the floor, but then I crack up because, with Tom shirtless and Steph flushed from the heat, they looked like the cover of a romance novel!"

I smirk. "Yeah, Milo did *not* appreciate you saying that."

Jeff chuckles and shakes his head. "No, he did not."

"You two have a lot of marvelous stories from your surfing days together," Lisa says.

Jeff winks at me. "Of course. We're board bros for life."

I laugh. "Board bros! I'd forgotten about that."

"What's board bros?" Lisa asks.

Jeff looks at me. I shrug.

"It's just something dumb from our teenage years together," Jeff says. "When we'd lounge on the beach between wave sessions, we'd talk about life after surfing, how we could still stay close to the water even when we weren't competing. We said we'd open a surf shop and school together in Huntington Beach and call it Board Bros."

Lisa squeezes Jeff's arm. "That's sweet. Do you think that's something you'll actually do?"

Her question sobers me, and the smile drops from my face. "I haven't been able to surf since my accident, so I can't train students."

Jeff claps me on the back. "Tom's got his photography business now. He's figured out his own path for staying in the surfing circle."

"But what about you? What will you do after?" Lisa says.

Jeff shrugs. "I don't know. Maybe I'll still open a shop. We'll see. Right now I'm focusing on the things I love—surfing and you."

"I love you, too, Jeff." She tilts her head up toward Jeff and they kiss.

I give an exaggerated groan. "Alright, you two, get a room."

"Speaking of relationships, anything to report on that front, Tom?" Jeff says.

I shake my head. Not this line of interrogation again. It's bad enough I have to be the third wheel to their love fest. Why are couples so adamant about fixing up single people? Do they feel bad for us? They shouldn't. I've been perfectly happy being solo for the past couple of years. Well, until recently. A certain someone makes regular appearances in my thoughts, though I'm not quite ready to tell anyone that. "That's a stretch of a segue. And no."

"Not even a hint of something?"

A small smile crosses my lips before I realize what's happening. I quickly school my face into a disinterested look and flick my eyes to Jeff. I'm busted.

"I saw that, man. What is it?"

I release a breath, considering what to say. "I've seen a woman around Asheville a few times. She has these really pretty blue-green eyes. But she doesn't like me, so it doesn't matter."

"Why do you say that?"

"Whenever I see her, she seems annoyed with me."

"What did you do?"

I glare at Jeff. "Nothing."

"If she's always annoyed when you're around, it seems like you've made some sort of impression on her. Probably an accurate one." Jeff snickers.

"Haha," I say, my voice flat. "Thanks for that." I'm done with this conversation. And all of those lingering looks I'm catching between Jeff and Lisa. "I'm gonna head back to the house. Enjoy the rest of your walk." And your sweet love story that I'll probably never have.

12

Tom

THE SUN'S JUST peeking over the horizon, but I'm already at the water's edge, assessing the weather for the day's competition. I pick a spot on the sand to set up my gear. It's possible to shoot everything from the beach, but I also like to capture some close-ups of the action so I'll probably spend some time on the jet ski again today. I snap a few photos of my surroundings—the rocks, people strolling along the beach, the funky turret house that juts out over the water. The first surfers appear on the beach and I snap a few shots of them waxing their boards, checking leashes, and studying the waves.

I sigh and lower the camera. I close my eyes and listen to the waves slapping the shore, imagining the salty spray pelting my arms and spitting on my face as I slice through waves, my hand trailing along the wave's wall. That part of my life is over now, I remind myself. No matter how much I wish to be back on a board riding monster waves, it'll never happen. I suppose it's kind of a silver lining that I can fully appreciate the skill levels of the surfers I photograph, but part of me will probably always long to paddle out to the break line, straddle a board, and look for the perfect wave.

The surfers paddle out to onto the water. I take some photos of the surfers' warm-up runs. Maybe I'll capture something I can sell to sponsors. The surrounding buzz increases in volume and I look around. The crowd on the beach is growing as people seem to realize there's a competition happening today. I smile, nostalgic for the days when the crowds came to see me. I loved trying to wow the crowds with something they'd never seen before. Knowing that's now impossible might be the hardest thing for me. The smile slips from my lips. I take a deep breath, allowing the sea air to infuse my lungs. My shoulders drop a few inches and my facial muscles relax. At least the beach still calms me.

The sun warms my back, reminding me it's time to lotion up before I become too distracted. Once I'm sufficiently coated, I set up the beach umbrella Julie gifted me just before I left. It feels like overkill, but I know she'll ask about it. I grab my phone from my pocket and take a selfie, making sure the photo includes the umbrella and my zinc-coated skin. I text it to Julie, knowing that she'll appreciate it. Then I grab my camera and mentally shift into work mode.

📷

Before I know it, the week is nearly over. I'm itching to experience something new and make memories unrelated to surfing so, on my last day, I pull the travel book from my suitcase. My thoughts turn to Rachel and her confession at the bookstore. What's keeping her from pursuing her dream of becoming an author? I know all about what happens when you aren't able to pursue your passion.

I really struggled the first year after my career ended. I know I didn't make it easy on my family and friends. To be fair, I was dealing with a lot. The physical therapy was pretty tough, but I'm an athlete so I'm used to working my body hard. What I wasn't ready for was the compounded grief of losing my fiancée on top of my career. I know it's best that I learned the truth about Bethany's fickle feelings for me before marriage, but it still stings. I truly loved her. It was especially crushing when she started dating

Johnny MacKenzie not long after we broke up.

I can't imagine Rachel doing something like that. Of course, I don't really know her that well. I know I think it's cute the way her cheeks turn pink when she's flustered. The knowledge that I can tease her and get that reaction elicits a smile from me. I wonder if it would be possible for us to be friends. A knock on the door interrupts my musing.

"Hey," Jeff says, pushing the door open. "You up for doing some exploring today?"

I hold up the book. "I was just thinking the same thing. Know anywhere good, or should we consult the travel guide?"

Jeff shrugs. "Let's look in the book. I know nothing about this area other than surfing and places to eat."

I open the guide to the section for where we're staying. "Let's see. We could visit the Musée Basque et de l'histoire de Bayonne. "

Jeff waves away the suggestion. "Nah. Not a museum."

"Okay. We could actually go visit the lighthouse instead of just staring at it from a distance like we usually do. It has two hundred fifty-eight stairs and superb views of the Basque country, so the book says."

He shrugs. "Meh."

I turn a few more pages. "Okay, here's something—the Rocher de la Vierge. According to legend, a divine light guided anglers in a storm to shore. They installed a statue on the rock in tribute. There's a pedestrian bridge to the site, and it supposedly has 'awe-inspiring panoramas of the coastline.' You can apparently see Spain from there."

"That sounds rad. Let's do it. Meet out front in five"

When I'm sunscreened and have my water bottle, I head out the door. I take a sip but nearly choke when I see the giant green bucket hat decorated with white flowers on Jeff's head.

He smacks me on the back. "Are you okay?"

I nod and point at his head. He touches the brim of the hat. "It'll protect my neck from the sun." He lowers his voice. "Lisa got it for me the last time we were in Oahu. I kinda gotta wear it to show her I like it.”

“Oh, man.” I shake my head. “I don't miss that part of being in a relationship.”

“She's worth it. I'd gladly wear a flamingo costume while I surfed if it makes her happy.”

Jeff's words sober me. Longing for someone to love as fiercely as Jeff loves Lisa stirs in my gut.

The walk from our house takes half an hour. I enjoy the views of the coast along our journey. I could probably stare at the water for hours, if not days. When we finally make it to the rock, we cross the bridge and shuffle past the crowd to the far railing. It almost feels like we're at the edge of the world. A wave crashes into the rock and the spray shoots into the air. A few droplets hit my arms and I laugh. Beside me, Jeff raises his arms out to the side. I look over at him, and he gives me a playful grin. “I'm flying! Tom!”

I shake my head, chuckling. “At least I'm the guy in this scenario.”

Jeff laughs. “I don't mind being the hot, rich woman.”

I nod, conceding his point. “True.”

We spend the next few minutes in silence. The brilliant blue-green water sparkles around us. The tall green hills to our left might be part of Spain, though there's no way to verify. The lighthouse is a speck on our right. I take deep breaths, enjoying the warm sun and cool mist from the occasional wave spray. My body feels relaxed and limber from the walk here. Everything feels perfect. And then Jeff speaks.

“Speaking of women, what else can you tell me?”

I groan. Why is he so interested in me dating again? “Honestly, there's nothing to tell. If I ever date again, you'll be the first to know. I promise."

"Have you seen her in any of the same places?"

He just won't let it drop, will he? "Let's head back."

Jeff remains silent as we retrace our route north again. If he's trying to wait me out, good luck. I'd rather deal with some awkward silence than have this conversation.

"So…" he finally says.

Fine. I give up. I'll give the man what he wants. "I've seen her at one of the local bookstores twice."

"I don't remember you being a big reader."

"I went in both times for travel books. Now that I'm not surfing, I thought maybe I'd have time to explore the cities between shooting the event."

"Based on our current activity, I'd say you're correct. Was she also looking at travel books?"

"No, she works there."

Jeff gives me a pointed look. "You returned to the store where you know she works."

I roll my eyes. "I wasn't trying to run into her, if that's what you're implying." Though I won't admit that I've had that thought recently. I grin when the memory of our first meeting floats into my head. "Actually, the first time I saw her, she nearly ran into *me* with a cart full of books."

Jeff turns to look at me. "Oh really? And this is the first I'm hearing about it? You've been holding out on me."

I wave away his words. "Not really."

"So what happened the second time? Did she try to cut you with bookmarks?"

I look at Jeff like he's crazy. "What? No, weirdo. She showed me to the travel section."

"The same travel section you visited on a previous occasion for your Tahiti book?"

I know what he's getting at. "It's an enormous store with a unique layout that's easy to get lost in. You'd understand if you saw it."

"Sure." Jeff doesn't sound convinced, but he's a bit of a romantic, always looking for love in everyone's lives. Even when it's not there.

"She also gave me a good recommendation for a fiction book. I just finished it. It's like an Indiana Jones movie, but in book form. You can borrow it if you want. It's part of a series. I'm planning to get the next one when I get a chance."

"Mm-hmm. And you'll return to the same bookstore for that purchase?" Jeff raises an eyebrow.

"Well, I know they have it in stock." I smile sheepishly at Jeff, knowing he's going to read more into my comment than intended.

"Seriously man, this is good. I'm teasing you, but you should take a chance. You never know, something good may happen."

Could something good happen between me and Rachel? Maybe, but there's also the possibility of getting hurt and I won't let that happen again. "I'm not ready. I got burned pretty badly last time."

"I know, man, but you can't hide your heart away forever."

I definitely can, but I won't say that to Jeff. "Oh! You'll never guess what I saw at the bookstore."

"Books?"

I ignore his response. "When Rachel was showing me travel books–"

"Rachel, huh?"

I frown. I hadn't meant to spill that bit of information. "Yes, her name's Rachel. Anyway, I was flipping through a book on water sports in Hawaii to see if any of my pictures might be in it and there was one of my perfect ride on Pipeline."

"That's awesome, man."

I wince at the memory of my reaction. "Yeah, but I froze when I saw it. It felt like a sucker punch to be reminded of my old life out of the blue."

"Do you think *Rachel* noticed?"

"I don't think so." I narrow my eyes at Jeff. "Why are you saying her name like that?"

His grin is teasing. "Like what? I think *Rachel* is a lovely name."

I shake my head, defeated. He's never going to drop this Rachel thing now.

13

Rachel

THE BELL OVER the door to Little Shop of Sugar chimes when I step inside. I inhale the sweet cocoa scent that permeates the store. This might be my second favorite place in town. The bookstore being my top pick, of course. I get in line behind a man who's already at the counter. He rattles off his order and then pulls a phone out of his pocket. His thumbs tap away at the screen, his body curled over it like a question mark.

"Sir, I can check you out over here," the clerk says from the register a few feet away.

The man continues tapping away on his phone. The clerk clears her throat. "Excuse me, sir? You're all set to check out."

The clerk appears frustrated, so I move into action. I step forward and tap the man on his shoulder. "Um, excuse me–"

The man flinches, spins around, and pins me with a glare. "Don't touch me."

I draw back, my cheeks pinking with embarrassment. "I…I'm sorry, sir. I didn't mean to scare you. The clerk is ready for you at check out."

His furrowed brow deepens. "You didn't scare me. It's rude to touch other people without permission."

"Yes, you're right. I'm sorry."

The man harrumphs, then walks over to the cash register. He

pulls out his card, hands it to the cashier, and resumes typing on his phone. The clerk finishes the transaction, but the man is oblivious. "Your card, sir," she says.

This is ridiculous. How do we get his attention off his phone without touching him? An idea pops into my head. It's silly, but it just might work. "Aah. Aaaah. Aaaaah. Aaaaaah. ACHOOOOOO!" I use my whole body to sell the fake sneeze.

The man looks up from his phone. When he sees it's me again, a disgusted look crosses his face. My cheeks are on fire, but I did a good deed.

"Your card, sir," the clerk repeats. The customer turns back to the register and straightens his posture. He takes the card from the clerk and grabs his purchases from the counter. He walks toward the door, brushing against my arm as he passes. "Some people should stay home when they're sick. Gonna infect us all."

My hackles rise. *He* thinks that *I* have no manners? Is he really that clueless? I release a huffy breath and turn to the clerk, who is hiding a smile behind her hands. When the bell chimes and the door thwaps shut, the tension breaks and we both laugh.

I take a step toward the display counter but freeze when I notice a second clerk behind the counter. And not just some random person, I realize with growing horror. It's Tom. And he's smirking. He's everywhere I go. Did he witness my performance? I'm surprised my skin isn't actually on fire as hot as it feels.

I don't want him to see that I'm flustered, so I inhale deeply, release it, and casually cross the remaining distance to the counter. "I guess you saw all that, huh?"

Tom's eyes shine, and a lazy smile unfurls on his lips. "I sure did."

I lower my gaze to study the chocolates in the display case.

"Hey, don't feel embarrassed. You were just helping Emily out and trying to save the man's dignity. Obviously, he couldn't see that."

"Yes, thanks," Emily says.

I nod to her and then look back at Tom. "So, this is where you work?"

"Sometimes."

"I never would have guessed."

"This is my sister's store. I help when I'm in town."

My eyes brighten. "Your sister owns Little Shop of Sugar?! She's my hero. Her dark chocolate pistachio caramels are to die for!"

Tom chuckles. "You sound like quite the connoisseur."

I can't help nodding enthusiastically. Books and chocolate are my favorite conversation topics. "I am. I pick something up from here every month for my book club meetings. I've gotten all the other members hooked on the truffles."

Tom's eyes sparkle with mirth. "Well, on my sister's behalf, thank you for the enthusiastic endorsement and consistent patronage."

"No problem. It's definitely my pleasure." Something niggles at my brain and I mentally rewind the conversation. "Where do you work when you're not here slinging chocolate?"

Tom grins. "Slinging chocolate, huh? I kind of like that. It makes me sound like a tough guy from the Wild West, only instead of guns that shoot bullets, mine discharge chocolate candy." He lifts both of his hands up, extending each index finger and thumb, then blows across the top of his fingers. He then tips an imaginary cowboy hat at me. "Ma'am."

I roll my eyes, but my mouth quirks up into a smile. "Wow, you have quite an imagination." I study him, struck again by how handsome he is. There are flecks of amber in his eyes near the pupil that I missed before. He smiles under my scrutiny and that delectable dimple makes an appearance. Strong, defined arms extend from the sleeves of his t-shirt. I wonder if there's also a muscled torso hidden underneath. Maybe I was too quick to judge him. A throat clears, breaking my appraisal, and I realize I've been silent and staring for too long. "Sorry. Did you say something?"

Tom smiles, displaying his dimple once again. "No."

I straighten my spine and shake my head to dislodge the sexy thoughts about Tom from my head. "Anyway," I say, "you haven't answered the question about what else you do for work."

"You're quite persistent. If you must know, I'm a photographer."

I wasn't expecting that. I would have guessed personal trainer or some other physical job based on his sculpted body. "That sounds interesting. What kind of photographer? You don't seem like someone who does weddings or babies."

Tom quirks an eyebrow. "Should your assessment offend me?"

I shrug. "You just seem like someone who would photograph sports or cars or something super manly."

"Sounds like you're stereotyping me, but I can't be mad because you're correct. I take pictures of athletes."

"How did you get into that?"

The bells over the door sound. A large group enters the store, their conversation filling the space. "Maybe I should help you with your order before someone jumps in line," Tom says.

I sigh, disappointed in the disruption to our conversation. I glance at my watch. "Yes, definitely. My break's almost up."

I rattle off the list of standards I get for book club meetings. "Do you have any seasonal truffles today?"

"We have pumpkin-flavored white chocolate truffles and maple syrup-infused semi-sweet truffles."

"I'll take one of each."

"Julie's also trying out a new Halloween-themed flavor called Bump in the Night. It's three kinds of dark chocolate with a hint of mint."

"You had me at 'three kinds of dark chocolate.' Add two of those to my order."

"A dark chocolate fan. Me too."

"Something we have in common. What's your favorite truffle

here? Mine's Blackout."

Tom tilts his head and is silent for a few moments. "Blackout's a good choice, but I'd have to say my favorite is Ancient Treasures."

"Is that the one with cayenne pepper on it?"

"You sure know your truffles."

I shrug. "I may come in here more than I'm willing to admit. I don't like spicy things, though, so I've never tried it."

"It really isn't that spicy. There's a bit of heat initially, but it blends in with the dark chocolate and becomes a really pleasant flavor meld."

"Hmm. I don't know if I believe you."

"Fair enough, but I promise I wouldn't steer you wrong. My sister may own this shop, but I'm no slouch in the confectionery department."

"I'll have to take your word for it." I check my watch again. "Gotta get back across the street."

Tom rings me up while I scrounge through my purse for my wallet. I hand Tom some bills. When he returns my change, I drop it into the tip jar. Feeling a little reckless, I wink at Tom when he looks up at me. "For the excellent service today."

I stuff my wallet back into my purse. Tom extends the bag to me, but holds onto it until I look at him. "Your receipt is in the bag." He winks and then releases his grip.

What does *that* mean? I'll analyze his words later. "Thanks. See you around."

14

Rachel

WHEN I REMOVE the chocolates from the bag, the receipt comes with them and flutters to the ground. I pick it up. Blue ink bleeds through the back. I flip the receipt over and find a note.

Try it and let me know what you think. —Tom

He's included a phone number.

"Try what?" I say.

I stuff the receipt in my pocket and arrange the chocolates on a plate. I hope the seasonal flavors are good. My hand stills over a dark chocolate truffle with a sprinkle of red powder on top. I know at once that it's an Ancient Treasures truffle, and that I didn't order it. Then it clicks. Tom's note.

I smile. Maybe my flirting worked. "How sweet."

"What's sweet?"

My head snaps up. I spin and find Lori just inside the door. "Oh, you know…" I rack my brain for a plausible explanation and draw a blank. "Uh…these chocolates from Little Shop of Sugar. Sometimes I think they're almost too good."

"Yes, they are delicious. You certainly do spoil us, Rachel." Lori looks around the empty room. "I'm obviously early. How can I help?"

"Would you mind setting up the chairs?"

"Sure." Lori sets her purse on a table and heads toward the

stack of chairs against the wall.

I return the Ancient Treasures truffle to the bag. I'll sort that out later. Warmth spreads through my body as my thoughts turn to Tom and his cute dimple. I wrap my arms around my shoulders and squeeze.

"Why are you so happy?" Lori says.

I freeze, the smile dropping from my face. Oh my gosh. I'd forgotten I wasn't alone. I drop my arms and turn around, trying to look casual, even though my cheeks are advertising my embarrassment. "Oh, nothing especially. It's just been a good day. And there's a book discussion with wonderful company happening soon which I love."

Lori smiles. "So true. I love Classic Chicks day. It's the highlight of my month."

"That's sweet of you to say."

The three other members arrive together, laughing and smiling. Their enthusiasm is infectious and I'm grinning from ear to ear in seconds. I love these women. I'm so glad they're all part of the club. I clap my hands to get everyone's attention. "Welcome, ladies. The refreshments are all set up, so grab a plate, have a seat, and let's figure out a new name before we discuss this month's book."

"I've got my top two," Susan says.

"Let's hear them," Deb says, popping a truffle into her mouth.

"I think we should either be the Book Babes or the Literary Ladies."

"I like the alliteration," Lori says. "I think I'd go with Book Babes. Literary Ladies seems a little stuffy and formal. Book Babes makes us sound like we're young and hot."

The group chuckles.

"I like your reasoning," Deb says. "I'm voting for Book Babes."

"Wait a minute," I say. "Before we vote on these two, let's see if anyone else has a suggestion." Anna, Deb, and Lori shake their heads at me. "Well, I have one. It's not alliterative, but I still think it's fun, considering where we are. What about the Page Turners?"

"I think it sounds more like a band name than a book club," Anna says.

"It's cute," Deb says, "but I'd still prefer to be called a babe."

I shrug. "That's fine. I like alliterative names too. What does everyone else think?"

"Book Babes," Anna and Susan say together.

"Alright, Book Babes it is. Now, let's dig into *Ayesha at Last.*"

I eye the Ancient Treasures truffle on the coffee table from my spot on the couch. Dare I try it, knowing that the first thing to hit my tongue will be the cayenne pepper? I reach over and pick up the receipt with Tom's note and phone number. A small thrill shoots through me at the obvious flirting. It's been awhile since anyone's hit on me. I kind of miss it. It's flattering to feel wanted, especially when it's by someone I find attractive.

I hop up from my seat, pour a large glass of milk in the kitchen, and carry it back to the couch. I take a deep breath and pick up the chocolate. Here goes nothing. My teeth pierce the outer shell and sink through the soft center.

I chew slowly. The spice pricks my tongue, and I raise the glass to my lips. Then the smooth, slightly bitter taste of the dark chocolate overpowers the heat. My body relaxes, and I set the glass down. Surprise and delight mingle together. I pop the rest of the truffle into my mouth and relish the heat followed by the cooling effect of the rich chocolate. Tom was right. My eyes lock on the full glass of milk on the table. I shake my head, a silly grin on my face. I'm glad Tom wasn't here to witness my theatrics. I stick the milk back in the fridge and get ready for bed.

When I wake the next morning, I consider texting Tom to

give him my assessment of his favorite truffle, leaving out the part about the milk, obviously. He captured my attention, which I assume is the motive for his actions, so it seems only fair that I play along. But he's still a stranger. He could be a controlling creep for all I know. Sure, he seems thoughtful, but so did Chris initially. I know I shouldn't use Chris as the plumb line for every other guy, but it's hard when he was my first serious relationship. Should I give Tom the benefit of the doubt? Provide the opportunity for him to prove me wrong? Or right?

A knock on my front door breaks my train of thought. I'm not expecting anyone, so I pad over to the front door in silent, socked feet and look through the peephole. A cloud of white curly hair and a rainbow-hued scarf are visible. I open the door and greet my visitor with a genuine smile. "Hello, Mrs. Shaw."

"Hello, Rachel. And please call me Louise. I brought you some freshly baked pumpkin bread." She holds out a multi-colored ceramic plate with half a loaf of bread sealed in plastic wrap.

"Thank you, Louise, but it's not necessary."

"Of course it is. You found my precious Mitzy and I'm forever in your debt."

"You've already brought me an angel food cake, double chocolate cookies, and half of a spiral ham. You've given me more than I deserve."

Louise bats a hand at me. "Pshaw. Mitzy is my only family now that John's gone. I don't know what I'd do without her."

"I'm glad to have been able to help." I open the door a little wider. "Care to come in for a slice of pumpkin bread?"

"No, dear, I can't. I've got too much to do." She pauses, scanning me with her eyes. I realize I'm still in my pajamas with no bra. I cross my arms across my chest in a sudden bout of self-consciousness.

"I'm having a dinner party in two weeks. You should come."

Her comment catches me off guard. "Who, me?"

"Yes, you. I'm having a few friends over and I think you

would enjoy the gang. It's quite casual. It's at seven o'clock the Monday after next."

I narrow my eyes. Something about this feels fishy. "This isn't an excuse to set me up on a date, is it?"

Louise laughs. "No, dear. We're all over fifty. There's no way I'd set you up with someone that old."

"Well…"

"Do you already have plans?"

My instinct is to lie, but Mrs. Shaw has such a kind, trusting face. I feel bad just thinking about being dishonest with her. "No, I don't. I can come."

Louise's face lights up and she claps her hands together. "Great! I look forward to seeing you."

"What can I bring?"

"You don't need to bring anything."

I give her my best puppy dog eyes. "I want to."

She nods. "Something for dessert, then."

"I have the perfect recipe."

"Excellent. Bye, dear."

I close the door but am now feeling antsy. Perhaps a run will help me decide whether to text Tom. A few flirty text messages might be fun and give me a little added excitement to my life. My conscience pricks me with the reminder that I've chosen a hiatus from dating. I sigh. A run is just what I need to provide some clarity. I change into exercise clothes, find a hat to block the sun from my face, grab my keys, and head out the front door.

15

Tom

SADIE AND I are taking advantage of the surprisingly nice weather by playing at the park. We're becoming quite the Frisbee dynamic duo. It almost makes me want to get my own dog, but my current travel schedule makes pet ownership impractical. Thankfully, Julie lets me play with her dog whenever I'm in town.

After an hour of playing fetch, I'm ready to go until I spot a woman jogging around the park. Is it Rachel? My heart quickens with anticipation of another opportunity to be near her. The woman's too far away to identify. If it is Rachel, why hasn't she texted me yet?

A new thought springs to mind. Maybe she threw away the receipt before reading it. A definite possibility. I rarely keep up with my own receipts. I should have written on the bag. No, that would have been too obvious. Even if she missed the receipt, the truffle I slipped into her bag should have been impossible to ignore. It's the perfect excuse to talk to her.

I watch the woman as she rounds the curve in the track and begins jogging in my direction. She has the same slim body type. A hat hides her hair and the top half of her face. I toss the Frisbee toward her. Sadie takes off in a sprint, desperate to catch it. It arcs over the path and lands in the grass beyond.

I jog toward the path, calculating in my mind the best angle to run into her. When we're about five feet apart, I see a smattering of freckles across her nose, but the bill of the hat still shields her eyes. I don't remember if Rachel has freckles. I clear my throat to see if she'll look up. It works and I smile when my eyes connect with the familiar blue-green eyes. Rachel's eyes widen in surprise and she stops in her tracks. I smile, hoping to put her at ease. "Hey there," I say, trying to sound like I didn't orchestrate everything.

She fidgets with the hem of her shirt and looks everywhere but at me. "Hi."

Oh, no. Did I read her wrong? Am I now some weirdo stalker in her eyes? "I'm sorry if I startled you. I was chasing an errant Frisbee. I thought I saw you, so I wanted to say hi."

Rachel turns in the direction I'm pointing. Sadie's trotting toward us with the yellow disk between her teeth. "Looks like your dog found it."

"Looks like it."

Rachel still won't meet my eyes and her cheeks are slightly pink. It could be from the exertion of running, but I kind of hope it means she's happy to see me. My desire to know how my gesture went over, or didn't, as I'm more and more concerned may be the case, is making me fidgety. Might as well get it over with. "Did your book club enjoy the chocolates last night?"

She looks up at me, her eyebrows scrunched together like she's puzzling something out. "They did. The pumpkin and Bump in the Night were both hits. I received requests for more if they're still available for the next meeting."

"That's great! I can't give you an answer, though. It's Julie's decision." I pause, then try again. "Did *you* try anything different last night?"

"I assume you're referring to the Ancient Treasures truffle you slipped into my bag?"

She doesn't sound enthusiastic about the surprise. "I am. Did you try it?"

"I did."

I wait for more, but she's silent, her blank face not showing what she's thinking. "And…?"

She scowls, puts a hand on her hip, and straightens herself to her full height, which is still a few inches shorter than me. "*And* it about burned my tongue off!"

My mouth falls open. "What?! Oh no! I'm so sorry, Rachel. I must have given you a bad one."

My insides swirl like a whirlpool and I'm in danger of drowning. My grand gesture is a complete flop. She probably thinks I was trying to make a fool out of her. How can I fix this? I close my eyes and rub my forehead, feeling a headache forming just behind my temple.

A giggle breaks into my panicked thoughts. I open my eyes. Rachel's lips are pinched together but turn up at the corners. When she meets my eye, she loses control and emits a hearty belly laugh.

I frown, confused by this turn of events. Then it hits me. She's teasing me! My shoulders drop and I'm relieved to see that I don't appear to have screwed anything up. What a fun surprise that she can give as good as she gets. I release the breath I didn't realize I was holding and smile. "You had me really worried for a minute."

"I'm sorry if I caused you any distress. The opportunity presented itself and I just couldn't let it pass by."

"I understand. However, you still haven't said whether you liked the truffle. If you say no I will be heartbroken as it's my absolute favorite."

"Lucky for you, I did like it. The spice and the richness of the chocolate really blended well together. Though I must admit, I poured a full glass of milk before I tried it, just in case."

I laugh, warmth spreading through me at her admission. "I don't blame you."

Rachel leans down and pets Sadie. "How's fetch going?"

"She's wearing me out!" I take the disc from Sadie and hold it out to Rachel.

She blocks it with her hand. "Oh, no. That's okay."

"Are you sure?"

"I'm definitely sure."

Rachel's words are so resolute that I'm immediately intrigued. There's something she's not saying. "Have you thrown a Frisbee before?"

Color rises to her cheeks. "You caught me. No, I haven't. If I tried, I'm afraid I'd just embarrass myself."

"It's really not that hard. Your wrist generates most of the power. I can teach you if you'd like."

She shifts her weight between her feet and looks away. "I don't know."

"Please, will you try? If I'm a terrible teacher, you can quit, but I think you'd really like it."

I sound pathetic to my own ears, but I'm enjoying being around her. If I can convince her to try, that gives us more time together.

After a few moments, she nods. "Alright. The truffle was good. Let's see if you can go two for two."

"I'm feeling the pressure. Better warm up." I shake out my limbs and crack my neck.

Rachel cocks her head to the side and gives me a skeptical look. Her forehead crinkles. "Am I supposed to do that too? Because I'm not gonna."

I laugh. "No, I'm just being silly. Okay, so first things first. Hold the Frisbee with your thumb on top, your index finger along the side, and the other three fingers touching the underside like this."

I grip the Frisbee and hold it out toward Rachel, twisting my arm around so that she can see all sides. She nods. I walk her through the steps for positioning the body, demonstrating as I go. I release the Frisbee and it sails in a long, smooth, straight line. Sadie takes off after it. "How does that seem? Not too hard, right?"

Rachel huffs out a breath. "Yeah, it *looks* easy, but I've never been all that great in the sports department."

"No? You look like an athlete." I gesture to her body and then freeze when I realize what I'm doing. "I mean, uh…" I close my mouth because it's now filled with my foot.

Rachel laughs and my embarrassment eases. "Thank you for that. No, I was a nerd in high school. Reading bowl team and writing for the school paper were my activities. My sister was the athlete."

"You have a sister?"

"And a brother."

"No kidding. Me too."

"Something else in common."

We smile at each other until my knee gets bumped and I look down. "Sadie's back." I take the Frisbee from her and wipe it on my shirt. I don't know how Rachel feels about dog drool. "You ready to try?"

"I guess. But don't laugh at me."

I put a hand to my chest and affect a terrible Southern accent. "Meeeee? No, I would never…" I bat my eyelashes for effect.

Rachel chuckles and pushes my shoulder playfully before taking the Frisbee. "You're silly, Tom."

My heart squeezes at the sound of my name on her lips. I clock the sensation of her hand on my shoulder. This Frisbee lesson is turning out to be a brilliant idea.

"Am I holding it right?" Rachel's question breaks me from my reverie.

I spot the opportunity to get closer and take her wrist in my hand, making a show of inspecting it from every angle. Her skin is soft and warm. "Yep, you look like a pro."

Rachel rolls her eyes. "Okay, what's next?"

"Your feet placement."

She adjusts her stance. "Like this?"

"Perfect. Now for the arm motion. It may be helpful to practice moving your arm in and out before you actually release the disc. Get a feel for the motion. That's pretty good. Make sure your elbow doesn't move much and practice snapping your wrist a little once your elbow is straight."

"This feels weird."

"Release the Frisbee and I'll gauge what tweaks need to be made."

Rachel extends and retracts her arm a few more times, her face a mask of concentration, before letting the disc fly. It hooks right and hits the ground about fifteen feet away. "Ugh, that was terrible."

I'm quick to reassure her, not wanting her to give up so soon. "No, that was actually pretty good for your first try. The disc's trajectory showed me a couple of things that are easy fixes. We can try it again."

Sadie returns with the disc and sits down at Rachel's feet. "See," I say. "Sadie thinks you can do it. Let's try again. This time I'll help you. Position your hand on the disc…good. Set your feet up…excellent. Now, I'm going to help you practice with the arm motion. Your throw was to the right, which means your elbow probably moved. Aim the disc up when you release and it will travel farther."

Rachel scowls and opens her mouth, but I hold up my hand to stop her from speaking. "I forgot to tell you about aiming up for lift. That's my fault. I *am* a first-time instructor, though, so maybe cut me a little slack?" I wink at her.

Rachel turns her head, but I still catch her smile. "Sure, Teach," she says. "What do I do now?"

"Bring your throwing arm up and straighten it out like you're aiming for your target. Good. Now, I'll guide your hand with mine so you can experience my throwing motion, okay?"

She pauses in her actions and studies me for a minute. "Alright," she says.

I try not to let my excitement show and command my legs to move at a leisurely pace. I approach her from behind and gently cradle her hand in mine, noting how well they fit together. I angle my arm parallel to her, adjust my feet to the outside of hers, and then place my free hand at the top of her hip. She sucks in a breath. "What…what are you doing?"

Is she affected by my proximity? I don't hate the thought of that. "It's a counterbalance, so we don't topple over when we release the Frisbee."

I hold my breath as I wait for her response. Finally, she nods. "Okay."

With our positioning, it almost feels like we're preparing to dance. Our bodies are hovering next to each other. If I leaned forward an inch, we'll be touching from shoulder to thigh. I catch a light, fruity scent and wonder if it's her shampoo. Coconut maybe?

"Are we going to throw the Frisbee or just stand here like frozen dancers?"

Rachel's voice snaps me out of my trance. I blink and shake my head. Whoops. Get it together, Haynes. "Now we pick a target. How about that tree in the distance?"

She sighs. "I can't throw that far."

"We're not trying to get it there. That's just the direction we want our frisbee to go. Now bend the arm in and then snap it forward, trying not to move the elbow. Just practice a few times."

I push her arm in toward her body with my own. Our elbows fit snugly together. I pull her arm out as quickly as I dare without worrying that I'll hurt her. "Now is when you'd let go. Okay, let's try the real thing."

We move through the sequence together. Rachel lets go of the disc and it sails straight for about thirty feet before dropping to the grass. Rachel claps her hands together, breaking my hold on her wrist. "That was much better," I say. "How did it feel?"

She takes a step away from me, and my hand falls from her waist. "It felt different. I definitely didn't keep my elbow pointed at my target last time."

"Ready to do it alone?"

I plead silently for her to seek my assistance a bit longer.

When she nods, disappointment thuds in my gut, but I try not to let it show on my face. "Alright, Ms. Independent, go for it."

Rachel stills and then looks at me with narrowed eyes. "What did you just say?"

"I said, 'Go for it.'"

"Did you call me Ms. Independent?" Her voice is frosty.

My heart rate ratchets up like I'm staring into the face of a monster wave. I'm afraid I'm about to get pummeled. Did I offend Rachel somehow? I swallow the thick lump in my throat. "Yes, but I was just teasing."

Her lips curve down into a scowl. "There's nothing wrong with a capable woman. Why do men desire needy women? Don't they want an equal partner?"

"Whoa." I hold up my hands. Mayday, mayday! I need to diffuse this prickly situation pronto. "Rachel, if I offended you, I'm sorry. I meant nothing negative by my comment, I promise. I like successful and accomplished women. I don't need to be a woman's everything to feel manly. Frankly, that's too much pressure."

She releases a heavy breath. "I'm sorry, Tom." She looks down and digs into the grass with the toe of her shoe. "I didn't mean to take my frustration out on you. You're just trying to help and I blew it out of proportion. I'm sorry."

"Hey." I take a step toward her. "I'm sorry on behalf of whoever made you feel that there's something wrong with being able to take care of yourself."

I bend down to catch her eye. "Rachel, I think it's great that you can take care of yourself. You should be proud. I know several people from high school living in their parents' basements. Wait. You aren't living in your parents' basement, are you?"

"No," she says, her lip curling up faintly. "They don't even have a basement."

I swipe my hand across my forehead. "Whew, I'm glad. I was afraid I'd stepped in it again."

She smiles at me, and I feel like I just won the lottery. "Nope.

Not this time, at least."

"Well, good."

A warm fuzzy sensation builds in my chest. I have the sudden urge to lean a little closer. I wonder if Rachel's also feeling drawn toward me. I take another step forward. My shoe hits something soft, and a yelp sounds from below. I've kicked the dog. Pet sitter of the year, right here, folks. "Sadie girl! I'm so sorry. I didn't see you down there. Are you okay?"

I bend down and rub her back and sides. I check her paws and everything seems fine. She wags her tail. I give her a vigorous scratching of her back and sides. Her tail moves faster. Sadie turns her head and her tongue is all over my face. "Aaaaaggghhh, Sadie!" I turn my face away and stand up. Rachel laughs.

"Yuck!" I groan and lift the bottom of my shirt to wipe the dog drool from my cheek and forehead. The laughter halts, replaced by a sharp intake of breath. Concerned that something's wrong, I lower my shirt to assess the situation. Rachel's ogling my exposed stomach. What an interesting development.

I let go of my shirt and watch as Rachel's eyes make a slow journey up my torso to my face. I give her a wink and her cheeks turn the brightest shade of pink I've seen yet. I'm certainly not mad that she obviously appreciates the hard work I've done to stay in good physical condition. I consider letting her off the hook for about a second but can't resist trying to see if she can blush even deeper. I quirk an eyebrow. "Like what you see?"

"I…I'm sorry. I didn't mean to…Um, you look very nice."

Rachel slaps a hand over her mouth and squeezes her eyes shut. Her cheeks are practically magenta. "I…I mean…uh…oh, I'm so embarrassed."

"I'm just teasing you." I touch her arm and she meets my eye. I just can't help getting one more dig in. "Though I can't say I'm sorry to know that you think I look very nice."

She opens her mouth to speak, but quickly shuts it again.

"What, no snappy retort?"

"Nope. I admit defeat. You win."

I relent, turning the focus back to my own awkward situation. "I actually think *you* won because you aren't the one with dog slobber all over your face."

Rachel wrinkles her nose. "Yeah, that's probably true. Okay, I win."

"What?" I say in mock outrage. "You're stealing my victory?"

"Hey, you didn't want it. A win's a win in my book."

She winks at me, and I can't help but grin back. I love a playful woman.

"Well, this was fun," she says, breaking eye contact, "but I need to clean up."

"Are you working today?"

"I am."

I wish our time together could stretch indefinitely. "Cool. Hey, we didn't actually get much Frisbee practice in. Would you like to meet again? I can give you my number so you can reach me."

"Um..." Her cheeks flush again. "Was that your number on my receipt?"

She *did* find it. "It was."

"I guess I've got it, then."

"Great. I can bring Sadie so we'll have a disc retriever on hand."

She smiles and turns to go, but then looks back at me. My heart surges, hoping maybe she'll decide she doesn't have to leave just yet. "What's your last name?"

"My last name?"

"To add you to my contacts."

"Oh, sure. It's Haynes."

"Like the t-shirt brand?"

"No, with a Y. H-A-Y-N-E-S."

"Thanks."

"And what's your last name? Or shall I call you Rachel the

Mysterious?"

"Price. Spelled normally."

"Okay, so P-R-Y-C-E, then?"

She shakes her head at my lame joke. "See you, Tom."

"Bye, Rachel."

My eyes follow her out of the park. My heart thuds in my chest. Oh, man. I really like this woman. What am I going to do?

16

Rachel

MY MIND IS a tornado of thoughts while I jog toward my apartment. The surprise truffle was definitely flirtation on Tom's part. I can't deny that he's cute, but he definitely seems like someone who's broken a heart or two and I'm just not ready for that possibility. He also knows I have his phone number and wants me to use it.

Do I take him up on his offer of Frisbee lessons? I certainly don't mind the way he teaches. I quite enjoyed the feel of his hand wrapped around my own. I can't deny that my body had a reaction to his touch.

My flare-up earlier at being called independent makes me cringe. He slammed right into one of my sore spots. Chris was the guy who'd called me independent like it's a bad thing. My competence somehow made him feel emasculated. If Chris wants a woman who'll do everything he says and worship him like some kind of hero, I'm glad we're through. That'll never be me. Besides, I'm fine on my own. I don't need anyone to complete me or tell me what to do. My only regret is that I didn't end things myself.

Tom seemed adamant about not wanting a woman who loses herself in him. Maybe we're more compatible than I give us credit for. Sure, he likes to tease me, but I teased him back, and he didn't seem threatened or annoyed. In fact, he seemed to enjoy it. I must admit I also found our verbal sparring invigorating.

He's also undeniably handsome. The dimple that flashes when he smiles, the sparkle in his dark brown eyes, and that toned stomach! Where did he get abs like that? He's probably a fitness buff. I really hope that isn't the case. I'm not a gym-goer at all. However, Tom complimented my form, so I'd say I'm doing just fine without regularly visiting a fitness center where guys with enormous arms and skinny legs grunt and grimace while they curl heavy weights.

Okay, okay. I know I'm stereotyping gym-goers. My bad. Besides, even if Tom goes to the gym, he obviously has a well-rounded routine because his muscles are defined but not abnormally large, and his legs looked plenty muscular and strong.

When I reach the steps of my apartment building, I'm chagrined to realize that Tom has dominated my thoughts all the way home. I barely know him, but thinking about his toned body and drop dead gorgeous smile causes my heart to beat a little faster. Am I positive I'm not ready to date again?

Up on the third floor, I spy Mitzy sitting on the mat outside Louise's door. "What are you doing out here?"

I pick her up and she rubs her head against my cheek. This cat officially has me wrapped around her furry little tail. I knock on Mrs. Shaw's door. "Just a minute" comes from inside. I scratch under the cat's chin while I wait. Metal scrapes against metal, and then the door swings open. Louise smiles at me and then her mouth drops open when her gaze swings down to my arms. "Mitzy! What are you doing out here?"

I hold the cat out to her. "I was coming back to my apartment and saw Mitzy sitting on your doormat."

"She must have escaped when I borrowed sugar from a neighbor." She snuggles her face into Mitzy's fur before looking back up at me. "Thank you for rescuing her. Again."

"I really didn't do anything."

"Of course you did, and I'm grateful. Come inside for a cup

of coffee." She shifts the cat to her side and opens the door wider.

"Um…okay, sure, but just for a minute."

Louise bustles around the kitchen while I take a seat at the table. Mitzy saunters over and rubs against my leg. When she looks up at me with her big green eyes, I bend over and scratch along her back. When I stop, the cat jumps up onto my lap and curls into a ball.

"Oh my goodness!" Louise says. "Mitzy must really like you. She rarely does that with anyone but me. I think she knows you're her guardian angel."

"I was just doing what anyone else would do. I love animals and would hate to see something bad happen to your sweet cat."

She brings two mugs to the table and sits down. "What have you been up to this morning?"

"I just got back from a run at the park."

"How was that?"

My mind zooms to the park and Tom, and a blush warms my cheeks. "I, uh, ended up throwing Frisbee for a bit with a guy and his dog."

Louise smiles and I steel myself for the inevitable inquisition.

"That sounds lovely."

I release the breath I was holding, surprised to find myself a tiny bit disappointed she didn't ask for more details. Do I really want to talk to someone about Tom even though I know nothing can happen? I'm a mystery even to myself. I glance at the clock and nearly spit out my coffee. Is it that late already? I stand up quickly. "I'm sorry, Louise, I didn't realize the time. I have to go clean up and get to work."

Louise nods. "Thanks again for looking after Mitzy."

"Anytime. See you soon."

"In two Mondays, if not before!"

I'm halfway to the door when I stop and turn back toward her. "What?"

"For the dinner party."

I'd forgotten all about that. I'm not excited to meet a bunch of strangers, but I don't want to disappoint Louise by canceling. I'd better put it in my phone calendar when I get home so I don't accidentally flake. At least I'll have Mitzy on my side.

"Right, the dinner. I'll be there."

17

Tom

COLD AIR BLASTS me when I step into the terminal. I fish my phone out of my backpack and take it off airplane mode. It buzzes immediately, letting me know I have messages and emails I missed during the six-hour flight from California. Scrolling through my texts, I stop at one with an Asheville area code and click on it.

Unknown Number: Hey Tom, it's Rachel Price. Have you used your travel guides yet?

My heart leaps in my chest, and I smile. She texted me! That's a good sign. I quickly type a response.

Tom: Great to hear from you. I used the France guide last month. I actually just landed in Honolulu and the Hawaii book is in my bag in case I have time to sightsee.

I wait for three dots to appear, though I'm not sure how long ago she sent the message. I check the local time and realize it's after midnight in Asheville. *Duh, Tom. She's probably asleep.* I finish checking my other messages, then slide the phone into my pants pocket. I sling the backpack over my shoulder and head toward baggage claim with a lightness in my step.

📷

My alarm blares, startling me awake. I grab my phone off of the nightstand and stab at the screen to turn it off. My eyes focus on the screen and my heart skips a beat when I see Rachel's name.

Rachel: Exciting! How long are you in Oahu? Hawaii's on my bucket list.

I grin and do the time zone math in my head. Six-thirty here translates to eleven-thirty in Asheville. A reasonable time to respond.

Tom: Ten more days.

An hour later, I'm getting my stuff set up on the beach when my phone buzzes in my pocket. I pull it out and click on the new message.

Rachel: A week and a half! Sounds like quite a vacation. I bet it's so warm and beautiful there. Have some fun for all of us poor suckers stuck back in cloudy, beachless Asheville!

My thumbs fly across the screen.

Tom: I promise it's not as glamorous as it seems. I'm here for work.

Sarcasm radiates from her next text.

Rachel: Oh, poor Tom, forced to spend days on a beautiful, sunny beach listening to the waves, smelling the salty air, getting wonderfully tan, and eating fresh seafood. I promise I'm not one bit jealous.

I can't deny she has a point, but it's so much more enjoyable teasing her.

Tom: I'm so glad that you see the struggle and demands of such a dreary job. I appreciate your compassion. Though I have to admit I'd rather be here in late October than just about anywhere else.

I laugh when she sends back an emoji face with its tongue sticking out.

Tom: What are you up to today?
Rachel: Just work and then dinner with my neighbor.

Fingers of jealousy wrap around my neck. Who is this neighbor she's having dinner with? Is it a date? Dare I find out? I dare.

Tom: Where are you going?
Rachel: It's at their house.

My throat constricts. I'm not enjoying this conversation topic at all, but I should be supportive.

Tom: I hope they're an excellent cook.
Rachel: I guess I'll find out. I'm more nervous about meeting a bunch of strangers than the food, to be honest.

My brow furrows. It's a group dinner? Maybe she's been seeing someone for a while and is meeting his family tonight. I never asked if she's single. This is why I don't date. Time to cut my losses and move on.

Tom: I'm sure you'll be fine. Time to get ready for the day's competition.

Rachel: Okay. Hope it goes well!

I lock my phone and shove it back into my pocket, my mood darker than it was a few minutes ago. I pick up one of my cameras and look through the lens, making sure it's adjusted properly. I do the same with the others. I hope the routine of work will distract me from my gloomy thoughts.

18

Rachel

LOUISE'S PARTY STARTS in a few minutes and I'm sitting on the couch scrolling through social media. It's awkward meeting people for the first time, so I'm delaying it as long as possible. My saving grace is the knowledge that her apartment is as small as mine, which means a limited guest list. Her table only had six chairs, so perhaps that's what I should expect. I can handle meeting four strangers.

I check the time. It's officially seven, so I take one last look in the mirror near my front door, pick up my dessert, and head next door.

A tall, older gentleman holding a half-full wineglass opens Louise's door. "Hello!"

I flinch at his boisterous greeting. "Hi. I'm Rachel. From next door. I'm here for Louise's dinner party."

The man motions me in. I duck my head and pass through the doorway into the kitchen. Louise pulls a dish out of the oven and sets it on the stove. She turns around and smiles when she sees me. She points to the container in my hand. "Just set that anywhere, dear, and grab a glass of wine. I'm sure Reggie will help you."

"Okay."

The man who answered the door is in conversation with an elegant-looking woman with long silver hair and a thin middle-aged man with a bald head and tortoiseshell glasses. The woman seems vaguely familiar. I approach the group and give a self-conscious wave. "Hi. I'm Rachel, Louise's neighbor."

The tall man tips his glass. "I'm Reggie." He points to the woman. "This is Nora, and that's Don."

"Nice to meet you all."

The side table boasts a couple of open bottles of wine. I grab a glass and pour myself some of the white. I could use a little liquid courage. I take a sip and study the other guests. Reggie's gesturing wildly with his hands while talking to Don. Nora has moved to the couch. She smiles at me, so I join her, mentally preparing myself for small talk. I hate small talk. "So, Nora, how do you know Louise?"

"We both take Tai Chi at the YMCA."

"That sounds fun. Have you lived in the area long?"

"I've been here for fifteen years."

"Wow. What brought you here?"

"I like the relaxed atmosphere and the mountains. I used to live in Los Angeles. Asheville is the complete opposite of that, which I wanted."

I nod. "I can imagine."

Louise enters the room and claps her hands twice, successfully getting our attention. "Okay, ladies and gentlemen, the food is ready. Please fill your plates and find a seat at the table."

We chat amiably during our courses of Caesar salad and spinach lasagna roll-ups. When we've had our fill, Louise ushers everyone to the living room. I offer to help clean up in order to avoid more small talk, but she waves me out of the kitchen.

"Isn't there anything I can do?"

She spots my container and lifts the lid. "Take these into the living room and dish them up to everyone."

Not quite what I'd hoped, but at least I can fill my mouth with rich, gooey goodness to avoid talking. I carry plates into the living room and serve brownies to the other guests. Reggie takes a bite, closes his eyes, and groans in pleasure. "These brownies are amazing. What's in them?"

"There's caramel and pieces of dark chocolate in the middle," I say.

"Fantastic," Don says. "What do you call them?"

My cheeks color. I didn't think my dessert choice through. "Knock-You-Naked Brownies."

Reggie guffaws. "The perfect name! You must give me the recipe." I nod. Reggie gives me a look I can't decipher. "You're an attractive young woman. Are you dating anyone?"

I choke on my bite of brownie. Is he hitting on me? Surely not. He's got to be at least my parents' age.

Louise joins us in the living room, and I hand her a brownie while trying to figure out what to say. She sits next to me and pats my arm. "What are we talking about in here?"

"Reggie just asked Rachel about her dating life," Don says.

Louise turns to me with a sympathetic look on her face. "You don't have to answer that."

I straighten up, appreciating her kindness. "No, it's fine." I look at Reggie. "To answer your question, I'm very single by my own choice."

Reggie's grin turns sly. "Does that mean there's someone who's interested in you, but you keep turning them down?"

My brain flashes on Tom, and my eyes widen. "What? No. Definitely not."

He smirks. "Oooh, there's a story. Do tell."

My gaze is suddenly riveted on my brownie. My face is on fire. I know I have to say something. "Um…" I shake my head and try again. "It's really not much of a story. I've run into the same guy a few times around town. He's cute, but I just got out of a relationship and am not ready for another one."

Nora gives me an encouraging smile. "You know, sometimes the best things that happen to us are the ones we don't expect."

I don't have a response to that, but thankfully Reggie moves on to another subject. When the dinner party's over, I linger for the opportunity to talk with Louise. I busy myself putting corks on half-full wine bottles and taking the empty ones to the recycling bin in the kitchen. Finally, it's just the two of us.

Louise smiles. "Your brownies were delicious. That melding of the dark chocolate and caramel really excites the taste buds, doesn't it?"

"It sure does." I decide to bring up what's been on my mind all evening. "Nora looks familiar to me. I know this seems crazy, but would I know her from somewhere?"

"You might. She's an actress."

Everything slots into place. "Eleanor Jenkins! I love her movies. Especially *Little Saint Nick*. I've watched that one every Christmas since I was a kid. My favorite part is when she nearly discovers Nicholas Clouster's true identity."

Louise laughs. "She'd be delighted to hear you say that, though she doesn't like people fawning over her. She's just Nora at our suppers."

"I get it. I won't say a word." I mime turning a key in an imaginary lock over my lips.

"Thank you. I knew I could count on your discretion."

"Is your dinner party a regular thing?"

"We've had supper together once or twice a month for over three years. It's usually here at my place, but sometimes someone else will volunteer to cook and we'll go over there. We're all single, so it helps us feel like we're part of a family."

Compassion wells up inside for Louise and her friends. "I understand wanting to have family where you live. Since my parents live in Georgia and my siblings live in South Carolina, we're not impossibly far away from one another, but it would still be nice to pop over to someone's house spontaneously. We schedule well in advance so everyone can meet up." Maybe I belong in this group after all.

"Yes, it's tough. We do what we can, right?"

I nod and stifle a yawn.

"It's getting late. Go on home and get some rest. Thanks for coming over and bringing dessert."

"Thanks for having me. It was lovely to be with such charming people tonight."

Back home, I feel the urge to share my experience with Tom. It's afternoon where he is, so I know I won't wake him.

Rachel: I survived Louise's supper club!

Tom: Supper club? I thought you were having dinner with your neighbor.

Rachel: That's right. She hosts a regular group dinner. I was the youngest by at least twenty years, but it was still fun.

Tom: Glad you enjoyed it.

I'm trying to come up with something else to say to continue the conversation, but I realize I'm actually pretty tired.

Rachel: Thanks. I'm exhausted. Off to recharge!

19

NOVEMBER

Tom

PEEKING IN THE front window of Page Turner Books, I find Rachel standing at the register reading a book. She's perfectly framed by the red, yellow, and orange leaves taped around the edges of the store window. Her plaid shirt completes the fall scene and has me looking forward to spending Thanksgiving with my family in a few weeks. I move down the sidewalk to the entrance and push the door open. The bell dings to announce my arrival.

I keep my eyes on Rachel to see the moment she recognizes me. Her lips turn up into a radiant smile. My stomach flips and I smile back. I can't believe I was so quick to give up on whatever is developing between us. Guess I'm still gun shy after last time.

"Hi, there." *Lame, Tom.* I pull the gift bag from behind my back and set it on the counter. "I brought you something."

Rachel's hands cross over her heart, and her smile widens. "A gift for me? What is it?"

I hold back a chuckle. She's adorable. "Why don't you open it and find out?"

Her cheeks turn pink. "Right. That's what you do with gifts."

She removes the tissue paper, sticks her hand inside, and pulls out the rectangular item. She reads the packaging and then looks at me, her eyes shining. "Dark chocolate, my favorite! That's so sweet of you." She hugs the chocolate bar to her chest and shimmies her shoulders.

Her reaction is well worth my effort. "If you can't go to Hawaii, why not have some Hawaii brought to you?"

She reaches out and squeezes my shoulder. A jolt of heat surges through me. Did she feel that too? "Thank you so much, Tom. I really appreciate it."

I shrug, playing it cool, but inside I'm leaping for joy. We grin at one another until Rachel looks away. It's time to announce the real reason I'm here. I clear my throat. "I was wondering if you'd be interested in having dinner with me. Maybe Friday, if you're free?"

Rachel meets my gaze again, her lips scrunched together. I realize I'm holding my breath while waiting for an answer. Thankfully, I don't have to wait long. "I am free Friday. That would be nice."

I straighten up, my facial features relaxing. "Great! How about Gli Amanti at six? I hear it's pretty good."

"I have to close up on Friday. Can we say seven instead?"

"Sure. Do you want me to pick you up?"

"No, that's okay. It's not a far walk from here."

"I don't mind." I especially don't mind the idea of getting to spend more time with her.

"I insist."

I'm only slightly disappointed since we officially have a date. "Okay. I'll see you Friday." I turn toward the door.

"Thanks again for the chocolate," Rachel calls after me.

20

Rachel

NERVOUS ENERGY RADIATES through my body, making my skin feel tingly. Tonight's my date with Tom. I haven't had a first date in over a year, and that was just coffee. I still can't believe I even agreed to dinner. I don't feel ready to put myself out there, but he brought me chocolate and looked so earnest, I just couldn't bear to disappoint him.

Choosing an outfit last night was a struggle. I wanted something nicer than everyday wear but also practical for work. I decided on a knee-length long-sleeve black dress that fits me well but isn't too tight. I'm in flats right now since I'm on my feet all day at the bookstore, but have heels in my bag for later. I even took the time to curl my hair today.

I can't stop thinking about the fact that Tom got me a gift while he was away. It's a small thing, but seems significant. Does it mean he's been thinking about me when we're apart? I've been eating the chocolate bar one small piece at a time to savor it. The first bite was heavenly, just the right amount of bitterness. It might rival the stuff Tom's sister makes.

"Hot date tonight?"

Startled, I turn and find Brett standing right behind me at the checkout counter. "What?"

He gestures to my outfit. "You never wear dresses to work,

so…"

My cheeks pink. "You caught me."

"I knew it! Is it anyone I know?"

"Maybe. He was a customer in our store a while back. You helped him pick out a book on Tahiti."

Brett furrows his brow and then shakes his head. "Sorry, I don't remember."

I sigh, knowing exactly how to jog his memory. "He's the one I almost hit with a book cart."

Brett grins. "So injuring customers leads to dates for you, huh?"

I scowl at him. "You know it was an accident, and I didn't hurt him."

"I'm just teasing." He bumps my shoulder with his own, and my brow smoothes out. "Where are you going?"

"We're meeting at Gli Amanti."

Brett whistles his appreciation. "Fancy and romantic. The guy's got style."

"Is it? I've never been."

"It means 'The Lovers' in Italian, which definitely lends a romantic vibe. Inside are candlelit booths perfect for private conversations. Or whatever." He nudges me with his elbow and winks.

I roll my eyes. "We hardly know each other. He isn't thinking like that."

"I'm just saying."

Brett leaves me to help a customer who's just come in and I'm left with my thoughts. What if Tom is interested in romance? Am I ready for that? What do I really know about him? I know he's attractive. He's also thoughtful, kind, and fun. If I'm honest, I wouldn't mind getting to know him better. A song pops into my head and I hum while I work, excitement for the evening ahead building inside.

Arriving at the restaurant ten minutes before seven, the brisk wind hurries me inside. Tom's not here yet so I order a glass of wine at the bar. A man two seats over gives me a withering look and I realize my fingers have been tapping the counter. I clasp my hands together and move them to my lap.

When my wine arrives, I take a sip and think about work to settle my nerves. We're gearing up for a book signing next week with Darlene Cherry. I can't wait to meet her. I've loved all of her books and have been reading the newest one during slow times at work. I'm trying hard not to buy more books, so this is my newest compromise. I should just bring books from home to read, but I'm a sucker for the way Darlene crafts a story and this one's incredible. Maybe I'll be able to ask Darlene some questions about how she got started as a writer. Maybe hearing more authors' beginning stories will give me the confidence I need to take a step forward with my own work.

I lift my glass and find that it's empty. When did I finish it? Tom's conspicuously absent. I pull out my phone and see that it's already seven twenty. He's late. My eyes widen and my heart stutters with anxiety when a new thought hits me. Have I been stood up?

I'm considering my options when the front door bursts open and Tom rushes in, eyes darting around the restaurant. His gaze finds mine, and he hurries over to the bar. He's panting. "I'm so sorry I'm late. I had to walk Sadie, and she was in a leisurely mood. I dropped her back off at home and started walking here. I was going to text you, but I left my phone at the house. I ran as fast as I could. I'm sorry to keep you waiting."

His eyes reflect a mixture of remorse and hope. I decide to give him a break. "It's fine. I was just enjoying a glass of wine."

Tom exhales. "Thank you for being so understanding." He looks around for the hostess stand. "Shall we get a table?"

I place some money on the bar and stand up. "Sure."

My stomach knots up once we're seated in a round booth. The curved walls and high bench backs block out other tables, making it feel like we're the only people in the restaurant. The dim lights positively scream intimacy. What's Tom's purpose for this evening? My eyes dart over to him, but he's studying the menu. Brett's gotten in my head. Just relax, Rachel. Easier said than done.

21

Tom

DINNER IS DELICIOUS. Rachel orders eggplant parmesan while I have chicken marsala and fettuccine. We share appetizers of calamari and caprese salad, which are both outstanding. Gli Amanti is now high on my list of best restaurants in Asheville. "That was amazing. How was yours?"

Rachel smiles. "So wonderful. I won't need to eat again for a week."

I laugh. "I was going to say we should get dessert, but I'd probably explode."

"Me too."

"How about an after-dinner walk instead?"

"That sounds perfect."

I motion for the check, and soon we're strolling down the sidewalk. Rachel's face is a tapestry of joy as she takes in the lighted trees and shop windows on Patton Avenue. At one particularly intricate display, she sighs. "I love the Christmas season. Everything is so festive and bright."

I nod, but I'm definitely not as into it as she is. Christmas decorations don't really do it for me. Get me on a beach with stellar waves and I'm sure I'd have the same awed expression on my face. "Yes, it's very nice. It doesn't bother you they put all this stuff out before Thanksgiving?"

"No. I wish Christmas was longer." She turns toward me. "You said you spent time with your best friend while you were in Hawaii. Does he live there?"

"No. He lives in California. He's a surfer, so I see him at a lot of the events I work."

"Is that how you two met?"

My heart rate kicks up as my brain flashes a warning sign. "We've actually been friends for a long time. We met as kids when I lived in California."

"Did your friend get you into the surfing photography business?"

I'm at a crossroads. I can either lie or tell the truth. Her trusting face deserves the truth. "I used to surf, too."

Her eyebrows shoot up. "You did? You don't sound like a surfer."

I give her a wry grin. "Yeah? And what does a surfer sound like?"

Pink starts creeping up her neck to her cheeks and I smile bigger. "Um…not…I mean, you might sound like a surfer. Maybe I'm stereotyping again. Sorry."

I bump her shoulder with mine. When I pull back, I can still feel heat where we touched. "I'm just teasing you. I know what you meant. My parents sent me to a private school that didn't allow the use of slang, so I learned to only use it when I was at the beach and the habit continues more than a decade after I finished school."

"Why'd you switch from surfing to photography?"

I swallow over the lump that's formed in my throat. This had to come up sometime. Just get it over with. "I was in a car accident that shattered my leg and caused nerve damage to my foot. I couldn't surf after that."

Her face crumples into concern. "You couldn't surf at all?"

"I can get on a board and ride a wave, but the damage to my body severely blunted my skill set. I can't compete with the pros anymore."

She places a hand on my forearm, which I don't hate. "Tom, I'm so sorry. That sounds terrible."

I shrug, hoping she doesn't sense my struggle. "It is what it is. I still get to hang out with old friends while seeing the world, so I can't really complain."

She links her arm through mine and squeezes it to her side, briefly resting her head against my shoulder before releasing me. My chest warms from her tenderness. We walk in comfortable silence for a few minutes before she looks up at me. "Have you always enjoyed taking pictures? Was it something natural for you?"

I smile, happy to be back on a more comfortable topic. "Yes. We moved to California when I was in elementary school and I struggled to make friends. My dad gave me a cheap point-and-shoot camera which I took to the beach and photographed everything—waves, birds, people, piers. I soon realized I enjoyed watching the surfers the most and tried to capture my joy through pictures. My parents noticed my new love and upgraded my camera for my birthday. I learned everything I needed to get outstanding action shots and have been fond of sports photography ever since."

"It sounds like you're almost as passionate about photography as I am about books."

I frown. "Almost? Why not equally?"

"Well, I don't see a camera on you now, whereas I…" She reaches into her tote bag, pulls out a book, and gives me a challenging look.

"You've got me there." I like her spunk. I see an opportunity and take it. "Since we're talking about careers, tell me more about your desire to be an author."

Her smile drops, and she turns away. The warmth leaves her voice. "What do you want to know?"

Looks like I've found a touchy subject. "Have you written any stories or published anything?"

"I've written a couple of short stories and three books for a fiction series, but no, nothing published."

I'm impressed to hear how much she's done, published or not. "It sounds like you have several promising projects. Have you submitted your work anywhere?"

"No, I haven't."

"Why not?"

Rachel shrugs and fidgets with the strap of her tote, still not looking in my direction. "They're not ready yet. More like rough drafts. They need a lot of work before someone else can see them. Besides, I don't know that anyone would want to read what I've written. It's probably not even good enough writing to be published. It's mainly just been a hobby for me."

"I think you've accomplished a lot already by getting as far as you have. I'd be quite interested to read something you've written."

"That's kind of you."

I steal a glance in her direction. Her body language reminds me of a turtle hiding in its shell. My heart twists at her downcast expression. How can I change the mood?

I place a hand on her shoulder and step in front of her. She stops and I place my other hand on the opposite shoulder. I wait for her to meet my eyes, so I know she's listening. "Rachel, you are a smart, fun, and thoughtful person. I'm sure you have wonderful, exciting stories in that brain of yours that others would love to read. I don't know why you're downplaying your abilities, but I think the world will miss something great without the opportunity to enjoy your writing."

Her face is stone. "I appreciate that, Tom, but with all due respect, you don't know what my writing is like. It might be horrific and then you'd have to eat your words."

Her words hold a challenge. One I'm more than willing to accept. "Then let me read something so I can make an informed decision. I'll either rescind my statement or pummel you with more words of praise for your genius."

Rachel tilts her head and furrows her brow.

I try once more. "Come on, take a chance on me."

She huffs out a breath. "Fine. I'll work on one of my short stories and let you read it, but if it's awful, let me down gently and never ask me about my writing again. Deal?"

"Those are some high stakes."

Rachel puts a hand on her hip. "Deal or no deal?"

I hold up a finger. "Just a sec. What happens if I like your story?"

Her eyes widen like the thought hadn't occurred to her. "What?"

"Well, if I don't think it's great, I can't ask you about your writing again. If I think it's amazing, do I get to read more? Will you submit it somewhere?"

Rachel's face scrunches like she's in pain. "I suppose I could polish up one of my novels for you to read if you like the short story."

It's not quite what I want, but it's something. "That works for me."

Rachel narrows her eyes. "I'm sure it does. Though it feels unfair that I'm sharing something so personal with you and you're not doing the same."

I tilt my head in thought. She's not wrong. "That's a valid point. Do you have something in mind?"

"What if you go through your photos and select a favorite one to show me? I haven't seen your work yet."

"I suppose that's fair. Okay, deal."

Rachel nods once. "Good."

"There should be a timeline. I'm worried you may keep putting me off and I'll never get to read it."

Rachel looks at me sheepishly. "Dang, you caught me. I thought I'd have a loophole. How about three weeks from now?"

"What about one week?"

"Two?" she says through gritted teeth.

"Two it is." I extend my hand.

"You want to shake on it?"

"Yeah, let's make it official."

She huffs out a breath. "Fine."

She gives me a weak shake and quickly pulls away, but not before I feel something electric pass between us. Was it just me, or did she feel something too? She looks surprised, so maybe. "What should we do now?"

"I guess I should head back to my apartment?"

"Why's that?"

"I have some writing to do."

I grin. "That's the spirit. May I walk you home?"

It's a short walk to her apartment. At the stairs out front, I debate leaning in for a kiss, but I've probably already pressed my luck for the evening with the writing thing. I watch her go inside, and then turn back down the block for my trek home. I'm excited about the opportunity to read Rachel's work. This has been a great evening. I whistle the rest of the way home.

22

LEANING AGAINST MY closed apartment door, I release a sigh. That was an interesting evening. First, I was afraid I'd been stood up. Then I worried it was too romantic. Now I'm feeling disappointed that Tom didn't try to kiss me when he dropped me off. What was the purpose of walking me home, then? Just being thoughtful, I guess. My emotions are all over the place.

Reality slams into my chest, and I gasp. I agreed to let Tom see my work. I can't believe I got suckered into that deal. Haven't I experienced enough humiliation around him? Pressure builds in my chest. *Calm down. Breathe.* Two weeks is manageable if I don't procrastinate.

I remember an exercise my therapist taught me to do whenever I feel overwhelmed and panicky. I close my eyes and try to picture myself succeeding in this task. I take a few deep breaths to clear my mind and conjure up a scenario.

I give Tom the story and watch his expressions change appropriately at each scene while he reads. He laughs at the right moments and gasps in surprise at the unbelievable twist. When he finishes, he looks at me with admiration in his eyes and tells me how wonderful it is. He smiles so big that his dimple pops. Then he leans toward me. I close my eyes as I lean toward him, anticipating the moment we close the distance between us.

Just as our lips meet, something tickles my side. My eyes fly open and I jump away from the door. The sensation comes again and I realize it's the phone in my tote that's still on my shoulder. I shake my head to clear the fantasy from my mind. I'm a little embarrassed at where my thoughts went. *Get a grip, Rach. It's just a story. He may say he likes it. It won't make him fall head-over-heels for you.*

I set my tote down on the kitchen counter and rifle through it until I find my phone. It's a message from Brett. Of course, he'd be the one to ruin my daydream.

Brett: Can you cover the morning shift for me on Tuesday?

I check my schedule.

Rachel: Yes. Everything okay?
Brett: Fine. Just have an appointment. Thanks!

I make my way to the bedroom, turning off lights as I go. I complete my bedtime routine and slide under the covers. My phone buzzes on the nightstand and I pick it up, anticipating another message from Brett, but I'm wrong.

Tom: I had a great time tonight. Looking forward to reading your story!

My grin turns to a grimace. There's no getting around sharing my work now. Well, that's a problem for Tomorrow-Rachel. Tonight-Rachel is going to bed to possibly dream of a cute, brown-haired man with a sexy dimple. But first, I should reply to his text.

The next morning, I wake up on a mission. I inhale my breakfast of dry cereal and then sit down in front of my laptop. Opening my

"Work in Progress" folder, I consider which of my short stories to work on. Tom likes action and adventure, so maybe I'll show him the one about the missionary couple in Costa Rica who tries to stop the illegal hunting of jaguars and stumbles upon the treasure of an ancient civilization. Yeah, that sounds good.

I open the document and read through it, changing grammatical errors as I go and making notes of any inconsistencies I spot. It's in decent shape, but it needs more action in the middle to keep up pacing. I stare into space, hoping for inspiration on what to add to make it more exciting. After an hour with little progress, a change of scenery is needed to give me some new ideas.

On my way down the stairs, I meet Louise on her way up, carrying several bags of groceries. "Can I help you with your bags?"

Louise smiles. "You're on your way out. I don't want to be a bother. I can manage."

"I'm just going on a walk. I can help you first."

"I'd appreciate it."

I take a few bags and we climb the stairs together. Inside Louise's apartment, I set my bags on the counter. "There you go."

"Thank you, Rachel. You're too kind."

"It's no problem."

"Where are you walking?"

"The park. I'm working on a short story and it needs some more action. I thought maybe getting outside would help me figure out how to achieve that."

"That's exciting. What's the story for?"

"I'm sharing it with Tom."

"Who's Tom?"

"Tom's the guy I mentioned at your supper club."

Louise's eyes light up. "That's exciting."

"I suppose. I'm a little nervous. No one's read my work in a while."

"Why not? You seem very smart. I'm sure it's wonderful."

I frown. "The last person who read my work said it was trite and juvenile."

She pats my arm. "Well, what do *they* know?"

"*They* are an English professor and published author, so, a lot."

Louise waves a dismissive hand in front of her. "Maybe your style just wasn't for them. Not everybody likes the same genre of books. That's why there are so many." She places her hand on top of mine. "Even professional critics disagree about the same book."

Her statement gives me pause. I hadn't really thought about that. "I suppose that's true."

"Let me know if I can help." Louise gives me a warm hug. "I'm hosting another supper club on Monday night. Will you come?"

I can't think of a good reason not to and it's better than eating dinner alone in my apartment. "Is it okay if I show up a little late? I'm closing at work."

"Of course. Don't worry about bringing anything. I've tasked Reggie with dessert this week."

"Okay. See you Monday."

I walk downstairs and turn right outside of the building toward the park. A few laps around the path might help knock some exciting action scenes loose from my brain. Yes, a part of me also hopes to run into Tom, even though I just saw him last night. Maybe we could resume Frisbee lessons. I wouldn't mind feeling his muscled torso against my back or his hand engulfing my own. The thought gives me tingles.

I'm surprised at how busy the park is when I arrive. There are parents kicking soccer balls with their kids, a few people riding bikes around the path, and a drone flying above the field. I don't see any dogs, which means no Sadie or Tom. One less distraction, I suppose.

What should I do with my characters? The poachers could kidnap one half of the couple who later escapes. Or they kidnap both people and trap them somewhere. Perhaps they're in a cave with a hidden entrance, or hoisted up into the treetops with no means of escape. But then, how would someone rescue them? I switch from a walk to a jog while considering potential solutions.

On my second lap, goose bumps rise on my arms and there's an eerie tingling sensation on the back of my neck. I swivel my head, trying to figure out the source of my unease. People are staring in my direction. I'm getting concerned. I glance behind me and stop cold.

Hovering a few feet behind me is the drone. It has a GoPro attached to it. I'm officially creeped out. I turn and take a step toward it. The drone lifts up out of reach and zooms off. I follow its path until it lands in the grass a few feet away from a man in black track pants, a blue hoodie, and a ball cap tucked low on his head holding a controller in his hand.

I jog over to the drone, annoyed and unsettled. I'm glad for the crowded park or there's no way I'd have the nerve to approach the guy. He's bent over his drone, his back to me when I arrive. I clear my throat to get his attention and my voice shakes a little when I speak. "Were you following me with your drone?"

The man turns, revealing his face. His sheepish smile shows off a familiar dimple in his right cheek. My stomach flops and my knees weaken as fear turns to relief.

Tom stands up. "You caught me."

"You really freaked me out." I take a few deep breaths to slow my galloping heart. "I thought I'd gained a stalker."

Tom touches my shoulder and locks eyes with me. "Rachel, I'm sorry I scared you. I should have considered how my actions would appear to you. I'm glad to see you, though."

I'm happy to see him too, but not ready to admit it. "Where's Sadie?"

"Sadie and the drone don't get along. The one time I flew it around her, she almost broke it when she grabbed it out of the air. I didn't know she could jump so high." He shakes his head.

"What's the drone for? Just having fun?"

"I'm trying to see how well the GoPro functions with it. I'd like to get some aerial pictures of surfers, and the drone would give me a whole new view of the action."

"Aren't you concerned about all of that equipment being so close to water?"

"I thought about that. I bought a waterproof drone, and the camera has a waterproof case."

I toe the grass with my sneaker, unsure of how to continue the conversation. I'm feeling a little discombobulated standing so close to him. I can smell a hint of cologne and I like it. I look at Tom and he smiles. Can he tell what I'm feeling? "Well, I guess I should get going. Be sure to keep that drone away from others or you might get arrested for harassment."

"Yeah, I'm very sorry. I'll try to think before I act next time."

I turn and jog toward the park gate. An idea slams into my brain and I freeze. A drone! Someone could fly a drone and find the stranded couple. Perfect! I give myself a mental high-five, silently thank Tom for the idea, and head back to my apartment.

23

Tom

I'VE SPENT THE majority of my day at Little Shop of Sugar trying to plan a second date with Rachel, but am drawing a blank on activities. Julie steps out from the back and I decide to pick her brain for ideas. "What's there to do here that's Christmas-themed?"

She looks up, surprised. "I thought we were all spending Christmas with mom and dad this year."

I nod. "We are, but I'm here right now. This seems like a great city for getting into a festive spirit."

"Okay. Well, let's see. There's the Nutcracker ballet. The Biltmore, obviously."

"What does the Biltmore do?"

Julie looks at me like I've sprouted a second head. "You haven't heard about the Biltmore?!"

"I mean, I know it's a mansion belonging to the Vanderbilts, but that's not really Christmassy, is it?"

"Oh, Tom." Julie shakes her head in disbelief. "The Biltmore has the ultimate Christmas experience. They decorate the entire house, including putting up over fifty Christmas trees inside. You can take evening candlelight tours with live music and get your picture taken with Santa."

I whistle. "Wow, that's a lot of trees. It seems excessive."

Julie pulls out her phone and taps at the screen before turning it to face me. I see an enormous tree, at least thirty feet tall. It's decorated from top to bottom with colored bulbs, ornaments as big as my head, and overflowing with presents at the base. I have to agree that it looks pretty impressive. "Okay, that looks quite spectacular. I bet that's not a cheap ticket, though."

"It's not, which is why I haven't been in years, but it's definitely worthwhile. If you want a similar cheery atmosphere for less, check out the Arboretum. They do a Winter Lights display in their gardens that you can walk through."

"An outdoor walking tour, huh?"

I imagine walking hand in hand with Rachel through a maze of lights. She looks at me, adoration in her eyes. I smile and lean toward her. She matches my lean, and—

Julie's voice shatters the daydream. "That's not something one does alone. Nor are you known for getting into the Christmas spirit. Is there someone you're thinking about taking?"

"Yes."

"Who is it?"

I try to keep my voice level. I don't want Julie getting too excited. "Just someone I've met here in Asheville."

"That's cool." Julie's response sounds casual, but I know she's holding back excitement.

The front door swings open, bringing in cold air and a few people. It turns into a steady stream of customers through lunch and into the afternoon. Julie and I work in tandem, doing our utmost to meet the needs of each person in line. I'm helping the umpteenth customer of the afternoon when I hear a familiar voice.

"I'd like four Blackouts, please."

I turn, and there she is talking to my sister. I'm thrilled to see her, but also a little nervous about Julie meeting her so soon. I try to focus on the next customer in line, but now that I know Rachel's nearby, I can't stop sneaking glances in her direction. I finish helping the customer and turn to find Rachel standing right in front of me.

"Are you here for some chocolate?" *Duh, Tom. Of course, that's why she's here.*

She smiles and holds up one of the store's bags. "Blackouts, my favorite."

"Is it a special occasion?"

She leans in toward me and speaks in a low voice. "It's motivation to work on my story."

"You're bribing yourself?"

She places a hand on her chest, feigning offense. "Of course not! I'm *motivating* myself."

I can't help the smile spreading across my face. She's so cute. "Okay, sure. Completely different. My mistake."

Her playful grin lights me up on the inside. "I'm glad you agree. Anyway, I have to get back to work, but wanted to say 'hi.'"

"I appreciate that. Enjoy your truffles."

After she leaves, I feel eyes boring into the back of my head and turn. Julie's staring at me with a smirk on her lips. "Who was *that?*"

I can't keep a straight face. I'm too happy. "That's Rachel."

"Is she the one you mentioned earlier?" I nod. "She seems nice."

"She is. And she loves your store. She's in here at least once a month picking up goodies for her book club meetings."

"Then I like her very much."

I laugh. The bell over the door chimes again. My heart somersaults hoping that it's Rachel, but, of course, it's not. *Get your head out of the clouds, Tom.*

24

Rachel

IT'S A FEW minutes before seven when I arrive home. I drop my tote on the counter and change into more comfortable clothes before I grab my phone and keys to walk next door.

Reggie greets me, wineglass in hand. "Rachel, hi. Come in."

He leans in for a hug. I learned at the last dinner this group is fond of hugs and air kisses. The latter makes me feel silly, but I can survive pressing cheeks with Louise's friends for an evening of fun conversation and good food. It's nice to have something to look forward to besides book club.

"Hi, Reggie. What are you drinking tonight?"

"It's the limited edition Christmas White from the Biltmore collection. It's just delightful. I tried it at a tasting and knew it was the perfect wine for this holiday season. The label's even festive. Come on over and I'll show you."

I wave at Nora and Don when I enter the living room, and then take the wine bottle Reggie holds out. The label depicts the Biltmore house during sunset, with snow-covered hills, a pond, and a few evergreen trees.

"That's quite a pretty picture." I hand the bottle back to Reggie. "Now, let's see how it tastes."

Reggie grins and pours me a glass. I smell it, and take a small sip. "What do you think?" Reggie says.

I glance toward the sofa where the others are and find that they're also watching me. Color rises to my cheeks at the attention. "It's quite good." I smile at Reggie and lift my glass in a toast. "Excellent choice."

Louise comes out from the kitchen. "Hello, Rachel. Glad you could make it. Okay, gang, the food's ready. You know the drill."

Reggie offers his hand to Nora, helping her up from the couch. Don makes a beeline for the kitchen, clinking glasses with me as he passes. We fill our plates with chicken enchiladas, black beans, and rice and join the rest of the group at the table. Reggie regales us with stories of his adventures in Italy on wine tours and sightseeing expeditions. He has everyone laughing with his tale of trying to haggle with a local vintner.

When we're resettled in the living room, Louise brings over a plate of cookies. "These look delicious," I say.

Reggie looks at me with a teasing glimmer in his eye. "Well, they won't knock you naked, but I think they're still pretty good."

I laugh and take a cookie, trying to think of a clever retort while I chew. "I don't know. These are pretty tasty. You could call them Knock-Your-Socks-Off cookies."

I wink at Reggie, and he chuckles. "Touché."

There's a lull in the conversation and I notice the furtive glances my way. "What?"

Reggie turns to me. "Have any updates on the guy you mentioned last time?"

I swallow the bite of cookie in my mouth and groan. "Seriously, guys?"

"Rachel, if I had any love life to speak of, believe you me, I'd be shouting it from the rooftops," he says.

I know they don't mean any harm. Might as well get it over with. "We went to dinner last weekend."

"So romantic!" I can almost see the hearts in Reggie's eyes. "And then what?"

"That's pretty much it. He walked me home."

"Did he kiss you?"

"No."

"Well, that's disappointing." Nora smacks Reggie on the shoulder. "Ow! What was that for?"

Nora gives him a withering glare. "There's nothing wrong with taking it slow."

Reggie turns to me with a contrite smile. "I'm sorry."

I shrug. "It's okay. To be honest, I'm a little disappointed myself."

Reggie guffaws.

"Tell them about the story you're working on," Louise says.

Don perks up. "You're a writer?"

I wince, rankled by the title I don't yet deserve. May never deserve. "Not exactly. I've written some fiction, but it's just for fun."

"Would you like to write for more than fun?"

I take a deep breath for courage to speak the truth. "Yes. I've wanted to be an author for a long time."

"Does this relate to the guy you're seeing?" Reggie says.

"Always about the romance, huh, Reggie?" Nora says.

"What? I *love* love." He shrugs and looks back at me.

I shoot a look at Louise to learn whether she filled them in behind my back but she shakes her head. I suppose there's no harm in telling this group. "Actually, yeah. I've agreed to show Tom one of my short stories. We agreed on a deadline, next Friday. I'm a little nervous because I haven't shared my work much and I'm afraid it's terrible."

"Do you think you could share your story with us when you're finished?" My heart speeds up at Nora's request.

Reggie nods. "We'd love to hear your story. Bring it to the next supper club."

"I don't know." I'm struggling just knowing Tom's going to read it. Do I want four more sets of eyes on it? "What if it's awful? Besides, I'm already feeling vulnerable as the new person in the group."

Some of the energy seeps out of Reggie and he slumps forward, sighing. "You're right."

Don pipes up. "What if we all shared something at the next supper club?"

"Are you going to explain some elaborate math equations to us?" Skepticism laces Reggie's words.

Don shoots him a scathing look. "No. I practice close-up magic in my free time. I could do a few tricks." He raises an eyebrow at Reggie, daring him to make another snarky comment.

Reggie just nods. "That sounds neat. I could share all of my wine knowledge."

There's a collective groan, and Don rolls his eyes. "We've all already heard plenty about your wine knowledge, Reggie."

"Well, fine." Reggie crosses his arms.

"I could perform a monologue or something," Nora says.

I'm intrigued by the idea of seeing Nora perform in person. "I like the idea of everyone sharing something. I'd feel much more comfortable not being the only one. Kind of like a talent show."

"Ooooh!" Reggie claps his hands together. "Can we have a prize for the best performer?"

The group laughs. "You can be in charge of that," Louise says. "I'll just provide the food if that's okay with you all."

"Louise, you've been feeding and hosting us for months now. Why don't I host and cook for the event? I redecorated the living room and am dying to show it off."

She considers for a moment. "Are you sure?"

"Yes."

"Well, can I at least bring dessert?"

"You're just trying to get out of performing."

Louise's smile is playful. "You're right. Will it work?"

"I'm fine with it." Reggie winks. "Less competition for me to win the amazing prize I come up with!"

25

I'M PACING AROUND Julie's guest bedroom with my phone clutched in my hand, trying to build up the courage to ask Rachel out again. I feel bad for scaring her at the park. Should I call her? Text her? I'm not sure which method she prefers. I'll text in case she's somewhere she can't talk, like work. One decision down.

Now, how should I start the conversation? Jump right in or start with small talk? Why am I overthinking this? *Because I like her.* I smile at the thought. *Come on, Tom, you can do this. Just say hi.*

Wait. Is it too early to text? My phone reads seven-thirty a.m. She's probably up getting ready for work, right? If I don't do this now, I'll lose my nerve.

I stop pacing, click on Rachel's name, and pull up our text string. I type 'Hi' and hit send.

Oh, Tom, that was dumb. Hi? That's it? She won't respond to that. She had a late night, your text woke her, and now she's mad at you. She will never respond to anything you send again. My thoughts are spiraling out of control. "Get a grip."

I growl and toss the phone onto the bed and turn toward the door. The phone pings. My head whips around and I dive onto the bed, knocking the phone to the floor. I scramble to pick it up.

Rachel: Good morning, Tom. Are you in the U.S. or

somewhere amazing like Bali?

She includes an emoji of a beach umbrella on an island. I grin.

Tom: I'm still here in chilly Asheville, though Bali would be nice. I didn't wake you, did I?
Rachel: No. I'm just about to leave for work.
Tom: Oh, good.

My body tingles as I anticipate her next text. After a minute without a response, I realize she's waiting for me to explain why I'm texting. I suck in a deep breath for courage and send another message.

Tom: Are you free on Thursday evening? I thought we could do something festive together.

I watch three ellipses dance in the text bubble and hold my breath.

Rachel: I'm busy on Thursday.

My body deflates. Maybe she isn't into me like I thought. I search my brain for a dignified response. My phone pings again and I brace myself for the "I just want to be friends" text.

Rachel: But I'm free on Saturday evening if that works for you.

My heart does an aerial in my chest. Saturday! I'm free on Saturday.

Tom: Saturday is great. I'll pick you up at your place around seven?

Rachel: That works.
Tom: Excellent. Wear warm clothes.
Rachel: Where are we going?
Tom: It's a surprise, but we'll be outside.
Rachel: Okay. See you on Saturday.

I let out a whoop and punch the air. Another date! I have planning to do. A knock at my door ends my reverie. I open it to find Julie looking concerned.

"Is everything okay in here?"

I'm grinning like a fool but can't help it. "Yeah. Why?"

"I heard an odd noise. Did you hurt yourself?"

I chuckle. "No. I'm fine. I have a date on Saturday."

Julie smiles. "Way to go, Tom! The woman from the chocolate shop?"

"Yes."

"Cool. I'm heading into work. Are you riding with me?"

I nod, unable to contain my smile. Today is going to be a great day. "Give me five minutes."

26

Rachel

ONE MORE LOOK around the room verifies everything's set for book club. We're discussing *The Count of Monte Cristo,* which I found riveting. It's our longest read yet and I wonder if everyone finished it. Next month, it'd be fun to do something lighter and Christmas-themed. I'm racking my brain for a classic we haven't read that fits the bill, but I've got nothing.

My body needs somewhere to put my energy, so I straighten up the cups and plates at the refreshment table. Disappointment stabbed me when I didn't see Tom at the chocolate shop today, but we'll see each other in two days. I wonder where we're going. Tom showed consideration by telling me to dress warmly for the date, which I appreciate. It is a date, right? He didn't say date when he asked me, though it seemed implied. Maybe I'm helping him pick out a live Christmas tree. No, it's too early for that.

Regardless of what we're doing, I kind of hope it's a date. I keep an eye out for him when I'm around town, but haven't seen him since we had dinner. I can't deny I'm into him, but I'm not sure how he feels about me. Until I understand Tom's intentions, I'll keep my feelings under wraps. Maybe he just needs a friend, though I hope that's not the case. Voices drift in through the door. I push thoughts of Tom away and prepare for the Book Babes.

"Okay, ladies. We need to decide on our book for next month. Perhaps something Christmassy?"

Susan smiles. "That sounds like a great idea."

Lori nods. "I like it too. It'll help get me in the mood."

"Are there any classic Christmas books besides *A Christmas Carol*?"

Anna wrinkles her nose. "I'm sure we've all read that one."

"We read *Little Women* last year," Deb says. "I can't think of any others."

Fearing this scenario, I'm prepared with an alternate suggestion. "What if we choose another contemporary read? I believe Debbie Macomber has a lot of books that take place at Christmas."

"Debbie Macomber?" Anna says. "Isn't she known for writing romance novels?"

"Is she?" Even to my own ears, the innocent tone is unconvincing.

"Rachel," Lori says, "do you want to read a romance novel?"

Oh no, she's using her mom voice. They're onto me. "Well, Christmas involves love and family, right? It might be nice to read something light-hearted and fun, especially after the behemoth we just tackled."

Lori hits me with her best stern look designed to make its recipients squirm. "There's something you're not telling us."

I want to deny it, but my flaming cheeks are spilling the beans.

Lori purses her lips. I crack under her knowing gaze. "Fine. I went on a date with someone."

I'm bombarded with questions like a suspect in an interrogation room. "Where'd you meet him?" "What does he do?" "Where'd you go?" "Did you kiss him?" "Is he cute?"

I hold up my hands to halt the onslaught and wait for everyone to quiet down. "Can we get back to books if I share some details?"

Anna bats a hand in front of her. "We're fine with reading whatever you want to read. Give us the good stuff!"

Everyone else nods. I roll my eyes and sigh dramatically, but my lips twitch as I hold back a smile. I raise my fingers as I answer each question in order. "I saw him around town a few times before officially meeting him at a park with his dog. He's a photographer. We had dinner at Gli Amanti. No, we haven't kissed. He's very cute."

"You know we just want you to be happy," Lori says.

"I know, but things didn't end great with Thayer, so I'm not quite ready to jump back into the relationship pool."

"It's just dating," Deb says. "Don't worry about where it's going. You're still young. Just have fun."

"Not *that* young."

She ignores my statement. "You've got plenty of time. Look for someone who loves you and supports you, no matter what."

That's good advice. "Thanks. And on that note, let's read *Starry Night* by Debbie Macomber for next month. It's about a reporter who tracks down a secluded author in the wilds of Alaska at Christmastime."

"Maybe life will imitate art," Susan says, "except it's a handsome photographer winning over an up-and-coming author."

I shake my head, but I'm smiling. "You ladies are too much."

27

Rachel

I STUDY MY reflection in the bathroom mirror. It took three different hair styles to settle on keeping it down and loose since I plan to have my knit cap on most of the time. I smooth down my sweater, hoping I have enough layers for whatever is happening tonight. I've got on a pair of fleece-lined black jeans, knee-high socks, faux-fur-lined boots, and a thick, emerald green sweater over a tank top. It's not supposed to get down to freezing tonight, but I'm often colder than the average person and know I'll need my gloves, scarf, and hat to keep my teeth from chattering.

My fingers drum on my leg, desperate for occupation as I count down the minutes until it's time for my date with Tom. I walk into my bedroom and glance at the clock on the nightstand. Six fifty-five. Five more minutes. What if Tom's late again? My heart sinks. What if he's a chronically late person? I'm an early bird so our relationship would be doomed.

I don't want to think about potential impediments to our relationship, so I focus on potential options for our outing tonight. Dinner? If so, I probably shouldn't have eaten a sandwich. Though what restaurant forces you to eat outside in the cold? More Frisbee lessons? A vision of his abdominals flashes in my brain, and I grin. I wouldn't mind seeing those again, but it's already getting dark, so that's improbable.

My mind and body are buzzing with a mixture of anxiety and excitement. I'm intrigued by whatever surprise Tom has for the evening. I hope it's an enjoyable experience. *Anywhere I am with Tom will be enjoyable.* The thought sobers me right up. Oh no, am I falling for him? It's too soon, right?

The door buzzer sounds, startling me. I rush to the door and press the button. "Hello?"

"Hey, it's Tom."

He's here! I check the time on the microwave. Two minutes early. That's a good sign. "Okay, I'll be right down."

I throw on my coat, hat, and scarf, stuffing my gloves into a pocket. I check myself in the hall mirror before opening the door and rushing to the lobby. When my foot hits the last step, I settle myself, brushing my hands down the front of my coat. I force myself to stroll across the lobby floor. I find Tom standing just outside the door. He smiles at me, revealing his dimple, and my insides turn to jelly. Uh oh. This isn't good.

"You look warm," he says. "Are you ready?"

"I guess so."

"Great!"

Tom turns toward the curb and gestures to an idling silver SUV. He opens the passenger door and I climb in. I hadn't considered that our adventure might require driving. After buckling my seat belt, I remove my scarf and hat. I'm pleased to find the car interior clutter-free. In fact, it looks recently vacuumed. I give Tom another tick in the plus column to go next to the one he got for being early.

Tom grins at me from the driver's side. "I'm excited! Are you?"

I feel more nervous than anything. Now that we're in a confined space, I can tell he's wearing cologne and I like whatever it is. I want to lean closer for a deep sniff but restrain myself. "Kind of."

Tom's shoulders slump. "Only kind of?"

"Well, I don't know where we're going?"

Tom straightens up again. "Oh right! I thought you might enjoy a surprise. I hope this is fun. We'll find out soon."

"You haven't done this before?"

"Nope, but I'm told it's a very festive time. We can judge my source's reliability together."

He puts the car in gear and pulls away from the curb. I watch the road, trying to cipher out where we're going. We drive several miles in silence. When I glance over at him, I notice his troubled expression. Is something wrong? Maybe he's regretting asking me out on a date. I turn toward the side window, my heart in my stomach.

Tom clears his throat. "How was your week?"

I relax a small amount. "It was good."

There's another long stretch of silence. Should I try to keep the conversation going? What can I ask that will get him talking? It hits me how little I know about him. I need to change that. Tom speaks again. "My sister said she saw you in her store buying a bunch of truffles on Thursday. Did you have your book club this week?"

"Yes. Your sister recognized me?"

"She noticed us talking last time I was working, and I said we were friends."

And there it is. We're friends. Disappointment smothers me like a wet blanket. "Ah."

"What book did you discuss?"

"*The Count of Monte Cristo.*"

"I read that in high school. I'm glad it's a page turner because there are a *lot* of pages."

I'm surprised he's read it, though I'm sure there are plenty of things that would surprise me if I knew them. People are fascinating.

"All of that deceitfulness and revenge makes for an exciting story," he continues.

Succinct and true. Perhaps it was a memorable read for him. "I suppose that's an accurate synopsis."

"Can I tell you a secret?"

His voice is soft, which causes me to lean in. "Sure."

"I'm a sucker for a happy ending."

His words and the meaningful look he shoots me cause warring emotions to erupt inside. I'm disappointed that he didn't reveal anything personal, but there's also a spark of hope that perhaps he's talking about us. *Get it together, Rachel. You're reading too much into this.* "Is that so? What other books have you read with happy endings?"

I'm still leaning toward Tom and his cologne overwhelms my olfactory receptor. I smell cedar and something else. He turns his head, and I realize my nose is inches from his neck. I pull away quickly and shoot my gaze out the front window. I grab a lock of hair and twirl it through my fingers. Heat creeps up my throat.

"Let's see," Tom says. *"King John's Jewels* had a happy ending. The guy found treasure and love. Sounds like a win-win to me."

What's he talking about? Oh yeah, I asked him about books. "That's true. What else?"

"*Elevation* by Stephen King."

My head jerks back, my gaze swinging to his face to see if he's joking. "How can anything by Stephen King have a happy ending? He writes horror books."

"Have you read it?"

My nose wrinkles. "No. I'm not a big fan of that genre."

"There are macabre moments, but the theme is seeing the good in life rather than hatred and division. The main character grows in kindness and compassion, which is a good ending to me."

"Seeing as how I haven't read it, I can't counter your argument, but I suppose self-improvement is a happy ending. Okay, I'll give it to you."

Tom chuckles. "Thank you for the magnanimous spirit, your majesty."

I scowl and open my mouth to respond, but snap it shut when he winks. He was trying to rile me up on purpose!

"What about you? What books do you like to read?"

I rub my hands together. Now we're on comfortable ground. "All kinds! Except for horror, as you now know. Non-fiction is great because I learn new things. Action and adventure give me a taste of different parts of the world. Sometimes I enjoy historical fiction to understand what life was like in different eras. And, of course, contemporary fiction."

"What's next on your to-read list?"

"The Book Babes are reading *Starry Night* by Debbie Macomber."

"Who are the Book Babes?"

"That's the name of my book club."

"Did you choose the name?"

"No. We started out as the Classic Chicks after one member said it was what she called the group in her head because we only read classic books. This year we've started reading more contemporary fiction, so we wanted a new name. Book Babes was the popular vote."

"Interesting. So what's the book about?"

"I haven't gotten very far into it, but the premise is a journalist searching for a reclusive author to interview for her magazine. She tracks him down to his secluded cabin in the wilds of Alaska."

"That doesn't sound very Christmassy."

"It takes place in December."

"Does anything romantic happen in this secluded cabin?"

I'm glad it's dark inside the car so Tom can't see my pink cheeks. "I haven't read much, but the odds are good. The author's famous for those types of books."

I wait for an embarrassing follow up question and am surprised by what Tom says next.

"We're here."

He pulls up to a gatehouse and shows his phone to the

attendant. I smile at the holiday lights adorning the structure. We drive along a winding road until a bend opens up to the parking lot. Christmas lights assault my eyes from every direction. There's a large building outlined in white lights to the left. There are colored lights on bushes, lights in trees, and lights lining the sidewalk as far as I can see.

I'm still gawking when Tom parks the car. He turns my way, flashing a broad smile. "Ready for some Christmas fun?"

He pulls a knit cap out of his pocket and tugs it on. Before I can answer, he's out of the car. I scramble to get my scarf, hat, and gloves on. I reach for the door handle, but it pulls away from me. Tom's standing at the open door with his hand out. My heart thumps at this act of chivalry. Another tick in the plus column. I place my gloved hand in his, swing my legs to the side, and stand up. He lets go as soon as I'm out and shuts my door for me. I'm disappointed that the contact was so brief. Is he not a hand holder? I've found my first minus.

A slight pressure at the small of my back nudges me forward. The layers prevent me from feeling the touch of Tom's hand, but warmth still shoots up my back to my neck. I'd prefer holding hands, but this'll do for now. He guides me through the parking lot and into a building toward a woman in a red sweater covered in jingle bells. Her white curly hair and half-moon spectacles conjure thoughts of Mrs. Claus in my mind.

She smiles and hands me a map of the grounds. "Enjoy the lights. Santa is taking pictures until ten over at the Education Center. There are stands along the way selling coffee, hot cocoa, and snacks."

"Thank you." I shoot a playful smile at Tom. "Are we going to see Santa while we're here?"

"If you want to." He points to a staircase. "That way to the gardens."

"I thought you said you haven't been here."

"I haven't. That sign says 'To Gardens' and there's an arrow pointing up the stairs."

My cheeks flush. "Oh. Yeah, I see."

He nudges my shoulder, and I catch another whiff of his cologne. I wonder if I could get it as a candle. Maybe I'll ask him what it is later. "Let's go see the lights."

We walk up the stairs and through a set of doors. I open the map and study it. I point to my right. "That's the Heritage Garden. Next is the Quilt Garden and then the Stream Garden. We can follow that path to the Education Center."

"You've got the map, so you're the navigator," he says. "Let's see it all."

"Okay."

Seizing the moment, I grab his hand and pull him along. Our first sight is a small wooden house covered in lights. It makes me think of Santa's workshop. Lighted, color-changing balls dot the grass in the middle of the oval path. Every bush and tree around me is electric with rainbows of color.

"That's pretty amazing." Tom says, a note of awe in his voice.

I tear my gaze from the lights and focus on him. I notice a ring of amber around his brown eyes and a few gold flecks toward the pupil. I avert my gaze when I realize I'm staring. *Keep it together, Rachel.* "Can you imagine the time required to put lights on everything here? It's breathtaking. When I get a house, I want my display to rival this place."

"If I spent this much time decorating my yard, I'd have to leave it up all year just to feel it was worth it."

The smile he directs toward me warms me from head to toe. My gaze lingers on his lips. The thought of them pressed against mine jolts me. I let go of his hand and step back. I have a personal rule against kissing in public. It's awkward watching other people make out. That my mind considered kissing Tom here in the garden with witnesses concerns me. I take another step away from Tom, turn, and start walking. "Come on," I say with a glance over my shoulder, "let's go see what the Quilt Garden's all about."

28

Tom

IT TAKES A few seconds for my feet to move. I'm not sure what just happened, but Rachel dropped my hand like a hot poker. I was quite enjoying the physical connection with her and I thought she was as well. I'd love to know what she's thinking right now. She's stopped in front of a large raised area of square stones interspersed with flowerbeds containing three different plants arranged in clusters. Lights are threaded among the plants, casting a strange hue over them.

There's a staircase to the right of us. Choosing boldness, I grab Rachel's hand, threading our fingers together, and tug her toward the stairs. They lead up to an overhead viewing area and now I see why this is called the Quilt Garden. The layout of the plants and stones look just like a bedspread my grandmother used to have at her house. The lights in the flowerbeds make four-petaled, color-changing flowers. Rachel gasps beside me. I follow her gaze to see what has her attention. Beyond the quilt garden, a giant metal Christmas tree covered in color-changing lights flashes intricate designs and patterns. Two tall, thin trees with impressive red and white lights flank the artificial tree. I turn to Rachel. "Do you want to continue to the next garden?"

She tears her gaze from the tree to meet my eyes. "Can we get closer to the big tree?"

The unfiltered joy in her expression delights me. "Of course. You're in charge, remember?"

"How do we get there from here? There's a wall between us."

I scan the area for a quick route to the giant tree and then turn back to Rachel. "Follow me."

I squeeze her hand with mine and guide her down a second set of stairs, past the quilt bed, and around the wall. I stop in front of the giant Christmas tree and fix my eyes on Rachel's face. Her head tilts back as she takes in the full stature of the tree. Her smile grows until her entire face is as bright as the lights around us. Her smile's infectious and soon my own cheeks stretch as far as they can go.

Inspecting the tree for myself, I must admit it's pretty amazing. My eyes move from the tree to our surroundings. Colorful plastic chairs and couches line the patio around the tree. Patrons occupy some of them, but a few are free. I tap Rachel's gloved hand with my fingers and then lead her over to a bright pink couch.

"This is magnificent, Tom." Her voice has a breathy quality to it that makes my heart swell. This date is a hit. I'll have to thank Julie for the suggestion.

"I agree."

The adoring look in her eyes when she looks at me takes my breath away. "Can I tell you a secret?"

My heart stutters. What's she going to say? That she likes me? That she wants to kiss me? I'd like to kiss her. *Stay cool, Tom.* "Of course."

She leans in toward me and my body mirrors hers, jumpy with anticipation. Is this it? Are we going to kiss? My gaze drops to her mouth. She stops an inch from my face and whispers. "I'm a sucker for Christmas trees."

Oh. That's it? I clear my throat for time to get myself together. She seems to be flirting with me, so there's hope yet. "Oh, yeah?" Do I sound flirty? I'm trying to.

"Yeah. They're just so wonderful to look at and remind me of happy childhood memories."

"What's your ideal Christmas tree?"

Rachel leans back against the chair and taps her lips with her gloved finger. I can't help watching her finger and wishing it were my lips against hers instead. *There's still plenty of time. Don't rush it. It'll happen.*

"It has multicolored lights, a big star on top like this one, and a big red ribbon wrapped around the tree."

"Ornaments in Christmas colors like red, green, and white?"

"No. That would be pretty, but I prefer ornaments that tell a story. When I was a kid, my aunt sent me an ornament that reflected an interest I had each year."

It hasn't slipped my notice that Rachel's just shared something personal with me. I want to know more. "What were some ornaments she gave you?"

"I have a little ballerina from when I took dance, a baby in a bassinet from the year I was born, a nutcracker ornament from our trip to the ballet, and a palmetto tree from a week in Charleston during high school. Each one has a special memory for me and I love it."

"It sounds like your aunt is quite involved in your life."

"She is. If I ever have kids, I'm going to give them ornaments that represent milestones in their lives. I'm already doing it for my nieces. They're still too young to understand, but maybe they'll appreciate it when they're older."

"That sounds like a great idea."

Rachel rubs her legs with her hands. Is she cold? "Should we walk around some more? Maybe grab something hot to drink?"

"Yes, let's continue the tour." She looks at the map, then stands up and points. "This way to the Stream Garden."

In addition to trees wrapped in white lights, the garden boasts a few lighted creatures, including a heron and a frog. At the end of the garden, waterfalls of lights cascade from tree branches and perform a light show to music playing over hidden speakers.

"Where to, Miss Navigator?"

Rachel looks over my shoulder. "I think that building over there is the Education Center. Shall we go see if Santa's in?"

I stifle a groan. I'm willing to play along only because it means spending more time with her. "Sure."

29

Rachel

THERE'S A LARGE crowd inside the building. Some people are holding cups with wisps of steam escaping from the plastic lid. Others are standing in a roped off line. My eyes scan the line leading up to a big gold chair upholstered in red velvet fabric. I turn to Tom. "I see Santa's chair, but I don't see Santa."

"Let's move closer," he says.

It's warm in here, so I remove my hat and gloves and stuff them in a coat pocket. Near the front of the line, there's a red and white-clad figure bent down next to a wheelchair. Santa's listening to a small boy who's speaking and waving his arms in all directions. I smile and give Tom my most hopeful expression. I know what I'm about to ask sounds dumb. "Can we take a picture with him? He seems so sweet."

Tom's eyes track the long line of people. "Are you sure you want to wait in line?"

"I do. Tell you what, I'll grab us two cups of coffee to warm us up while we wait."

He shrugs. "Okay."

"Great! How do you like your coffee?"

"Black is fine."

I stick out my tongue in disgust. "Yuck."

Tom laughs. "I won't make you drink mine." He studies me

for a second. "You're two sugars and a splash of milk, right?"

"How did you know that?"

"Just a lucky guess."

I push his shoulder to be playful. "Okay, Mr. Lucky. You get in line and I'll be back soon with some caffeine."

When I return, there are a dozen people in front of us. This may take a while. Good thing I came prepared. "I brought us something sweet," I say, pulling a small bag out of my pocket.

Tom's eyebrows shoot up. "Are those churros?"

"Not South American authentic, I'm sure, but when has sugar and cinnamon ever tasted bad?"

Tom takes one. My hands are full, so I stick the bag back into my pocket so I can grab a churro of my own.

"How is it?" I say.

He swallows his bite. "Tasty, but not as good as the ones in Arequipa."

"You've been to Peru?"

"I have."

"You're a genuine world traveler."

"I've been to every continent except Antarctica." He leans in closer and I breathe in his woody scent. I have to stop myself from sticking my nose against his neck for another sniff. "Not great conditions for surfing."

There's an envious pang in my gut. "I'd love to travel."

"Where do you want to go?"

I sigh. "Everywhere."

"Where have you been so far?"

"Nowhere. I don't even have a passport."

He looks directly into my eyes and I have to force myself to not look away. "If you could go anywhere, where would you go?"

I don't have to think about it. "Hawaii. It has everything—jungles, volcanoes, beaches, sun."

"Don't forget chocolate," Tom says, nudging my arm and winking.

I nudge him back. "I haven't forgotten."

My gaze settle on Tom's lips, and I notice a few grains of sugar and cinnamon dotting his lower lip. A vivid daydream of me leaning forward and removing them with my tongue flashes through my head and my face warms. I force my eyes up to his face and realize that he's watching me. Did he see me staring at his mouth? I sure hope not.

"You know," he says, "you don't need a passport to travel to Hawaii."

"I know. But it's not easily accessible from here. Plus, I don't even want to know how much it would cost. I hear everything is so expensive."

"Prices are higher, but plane tickets are reasonable if you hit a sale or can be flexible with dates."

"What do you consider reasonable?"

He shrugs. "Six or seven hundred dollars round-trip."

My mouth drops open. Is my Hawaii dream within reach? "That's cheaper than my rent," I say without thinking.

Tom laughs. "That's one way to see it."

My mind mulls over the possibility of Hawaii becoming a reality. A hand on my arm makes me jump. I look up at Tom. "I'm sorry. Did you say something?"

"It's our turn," he says, nodding over my shoulder.

I spin around. "Oh, sorry. Guess I got lost in thought."

As I move forward, the strangeness of visiting Santa as a grown-up hits me. It doesn't seem appropriate to sit on his lap, so I stop in front of the chair. Tom steps up next to me. "Hi Santa," I say, a little embarrassed now that I'm here.

"Well, hello there," Santa says, his voice cheerful and booming. "How can I help you two young people this evening?" His eyes sparkle with good humor.

His kindness makes me feel at ease and gives me courage. "We would like to take our picture with you, please."

"I'm delighted," Santa says. He leans forward. "But first,

what's your Christmas wish?"

I giggle, my nerves making me feel awkward, and look at Tom. "Go ahead," I say.

Tom shakes his head. "This was your idea. I think you should go first."

What would I like for Christmas? *A kiss from Tom,* my mind screams. I glance sideways at Tom and then back at Mr. Claus. "Santa, can I whisper it in your ear?"

"Of course you can, my dear."

I lean over, balancing myself on the arm of the big chair, and whisper my wish. I straighten back up, the discomfort of vulnerability washing over me. Santa gives me a wink. "I'll see what I can do."

He turns to Tom. "What would you like for Christmas, young man?"

Tom smiles and bends down. He holds up a hand to block his mouth as he whispers something to Santa. Whatever his wish is, it takes longer to tell Santa than mine. Santa's eyes dart toward me and away again.

Santa motions for Tom to come close and then lifts his own white-gloved hand and whispers something into Tom's ear. I watch Tom's face for hints. His eyes round and then a wicked grin spreads across his face. It feels like a circus has taken up residence in my stomach with all the swooping and twisting it's doing. I'm not sure I want to know what they're plotting.

Tom straightens back up. "Thanks, Santa."

I narrow my gaze and tilt my head, trying to show my suspicion, but he just shrugs and looks away.

"Alright," Santa says, "everyone get close and say 'Christmas cookies.'"

Santa's helper snaps a photo and then hands Tom a small card, which he pockets. "You can see your pictures back at the Exhibit Center."

"Thanks." He turns to me. "What now?"

I'm not ready to let it go. "What did Santa say to you?"

"He told me about a toy train exhibit. He called it a mini Polar Express."

I scoff. "I don't believe that's what he said."

"Believe it because it's the truth."

"What did you tell him you wanted for Christmas?"

"First, tell me what you wished for."

Nope. Not going to happen. Tom wins this round, though there's still plenty of game left. "Let's go find the trains Santa told you about."

"Sure. May I see the map, please?"

"Be my guest."

Tom's fingers brush mine as he takes it and something zings up my arm. The way his eyes widen makes me think he feels it, too. Now I really want to know what he told Santa.

30

Tom

A SMALL SHOCK runs up my arm when our hands touch. I shake my head clear and look down at the map in my hand, Santa's instructions running through my mind. I find the railroad, and trace a line back to our current location. I hope Santa's right and the trains aren't running tonight, which will give me some privacy with Rachel. Maybe without a crowd, I can act on the tension I feel humming between us. *Oh, please, let this work out.* I close the map and hand it back to Rachel. "Okay, follow me."

I reach for her hand and lead her outside, then down several sets of stairs to a large lawn. It's dark down here and seems like the perfect place to tell her how I feel, but then I hear the whistle of a toy train and my hope plunges to the bottom of the Mariana Trench. Rachel's head snaps up, and she looks around. Ahead of us are oversized lighted ornaments and candy canes lining a path leading to a well-lit area next to a small shed decorated like a gingerbread house. She takes the lead, pulling me toward the trains. I follow along, drowning in disappointment.

I perk up a little when we reach the miniature winter wonderland. Two trains chug around mountains, through towns, and over a rushing river, passing one another at the train station on separate tracks. Each storefront in the town has a wreath or garland and there's a large lighted fir tree in the town square. It's a neat display, but it's not what I had in mind. I'll have to keep my eyes open for another opportunity.

"Santa was right," Rachel says. "This is pretty cute. Did you wish for toy trains?"

"Not exactly. Where to next?"

"I believe the greenhouse has some bonsai trees inside. If they're lighted, I bet they'll look like miniature Christmas trees."

Rachel looks at me, her eyes filled with excitement and wonder. I chuckle.

"What?" she says, her smile turning down at the corners.

"You remind me of Buddy the Elf. He loves Christmas trees too."

"Better than being a Scrooge."

"Touché. Let's go see them."

Rachel leads us up the stairs and past the giant tree. We walk through a light-strewn tunnel and into the greenhouse. Bonsai trees strung with tiny lights adorn several tables in the room, along with a large fir tree decorated with live plants.

"The bonsai trees look like little homes for fairies," Rachel says.

I smile. "Yeah, they do."

"Which tree is your favorite?"

I grab her hand and pull her over to a gnarly tree with white bark, small green leaves, and tiny white lights strewn throughout the branches. "This one."

"Why?"

"It's so bright and white. It makes me think of hope and new beginnings."

"Huh." She studies the tree before shrugging her shoulders. "I gotta be honest, Tom. I don't see it."

I give her hand a squeeze which draws her gaze to mine. "Well, I do," I say, hoping she catches my underlying meaning.

Her eyes widen and her mouth forms an "O" but no sound escapes. I step toward her and reach for her other hand, threading our fingers together.

"Which bonsai is your favorite?" My voice is low and intimate.

"I was going to pick the blue one with tiny dots because it reminds me of the night sky, but yours has merit."

My pulse quickens, and one side of my mouth quirks up in a half smile. "Oh, really?"

"Yes, really."

My gaze drops to Rachel's mouth. Her teeth are nibbling on her bottom lip. I swallow hard when the urge to kiss her flares inside my chest. I discreetly survey our surroundings. We're alone in the greenhouse so now's the time. I clear my throat, preparing to say something, but all thoughts fly out of my head when my gaze meets hers again. If eyes are windows to the soul, there's a woman in hers with a flirty smile beckoning me closer. My desire is a magnet pulling me toward Rachel. I lean forward, my eyes scanning from her lips up to her mesmerizing eyes. Her lids droop and I know this is it. *It's happening!* I can't believe it. I move a step closer. Our noses are millimeters apart. I tilt my head to the right, my heart hammering in my chest. I shut my eyes, moving closer still.

31

A LOUD CREAK startles me. My eyes shoot open and I jump back away from Tom, my heart pounding in my chest. My head whips around toward the sound and my stomach drops. *Oh no. Not him. Anyone but him.*

"Hi, Brett." My voice drips with venom. Inside my head, I scream in frustration.

"Rachel! I thought that looked like you." One look at the grin on Brett's face tells me he interrupted us on purpose.

"Yes, it's me."

Brett sticks his hand out to Tom. "Hi, I'm Brett."

"Tom."

Tom gives me a questioning look. "Brett and I work together at the bookstore," I say. "In fact, I believe he helped you find a book once."

"Oh yeah, that's right," Brett says. "Good to see you again."

"What are you doing here?" I ask.

"I came with some friends. They're in the gift shop, but I wanted to check out the tiny trees." He looks around. "And they're adorable. What about you guys?"

I was just about to be kissed. "Same. This place is pretty impressive. I'm surprised you never told me about it, knowing how gaga I get over Christmas lights."

I give Brett my most murderous-looking eyes. Maybe he'll get the hint and leave.

"I just heard about this event today. I was planning on telling you about it at work on Monday, but it seems you've already discovered the allure."

He's obviously alluding to Tom. I narrow my eyes, wishing I could harm him with a look. I hope Tom isn't catching Brett's jabs.

Brett smirks and shakes his head. "I better head back to my friends. See you at work, Rachel." His wink informs me we'll be talking about this on Monday.

The door closes and we're alone again. I sigh, my shoulders slumping. The moment's ruined. "What now?"

"Is there anything we've missed? Anything else you'd like to see or do?" Tom says.

Besides have your lips pressed against mine? Instead of saying that out loud, I pull the map out of my pocket and look it over. "No, I think I'm good."

I glimpse the giant tree out the window and walk closer for one last look. I wish I could absorb its beauty into my soul. The tree does its work and a few moments later, I'm smiling again. I look to my right. Tom's standing next to me, but he's not looking at the tree. My insides squeeze under his gaze. "What is it?"

"Your face is radiant when you look at the lights."

"I know it's silly that this makes me so happy."

"It's not silly at all. It's wonderful when you can find joy somewhere." Tom's gaze seems distant.

"What are you thinking about?"

"Surfing."

I'm shocked he's broached this subject, but play it cool. "How so?"

"Being on a board relaxes me. *Was* relaxing for me. Focusing on the swells and not my problems. Waiting for a wave to call me and that magical feeling of getting barreled. There's nothing better."

His face lights up while he's talking, but clouds over when he finishes. My heart aches for him.

"Now all I have are memories," he says.

"How long ago was the accident?"

"About three years ago. I had surgery to repair my leg and then six months of physical therapy. While I can walk without a limp, my finesse with a surfboard is nonexistent. I just can't get a good feel with my foot anymore due to nerve damage."

Tom's posture is one of defeat and I feel helpless in the face of his sorrow. I wrap my arms around his waist and squeeze, wanting to offer comfort. He puts his arms around my waist and pulls me snug against his side. My head drops onto his shoulder, my forehead resting against his neck. I close my eyes and breathe in his woodsy scent. Everything feels right in this moment. I feel pressure at my temple, followed by a light scratch of facial hair as Tom leans his cheek against my head. I wish we could stay this way forever.

32

THE FEEL OF Rachel in my arms is a balm for my soul. It was uncomfortable sharing the pain of my past, but Rachel's kindness and now the opportunity to hold her close were well worth it. I'd love to cuddle in the greenhouse all night. Maybe just another minute?

I breathe in and catch a whiff of coconut. It reminds me of tropical islands, palm trees, warm sunshine, and the soothing sound of waves crashing on the beach. I sure wouldn't mind trading this cold weather for the shores of Oahu. The sun, sand, and waves along the North Shore are like heaven for me. I won the surfing World Championship there three years ago.

I was in top form and just hitting my stride. It's what frustrates me the most about the accident. I'd still have many good wave-riding years ahead of me if only that distracted driver hadn't run the red light and smashed into the car I was driving. Wishing and what-ifing won't change anything. I must accept my life as it is, not as it used to be.

It's a crisp night in November and I'm enjoying Christmas lights with a beautiful woman. A woman whose arms are circling my waist. I could get used to this reality. I wish her co-worker hadn't interrupted us, though. I sigh.

"Is everything okay?"

Rachel's breath tickles my throat. The sensation relaxes me. "Yes, I'm fine."

Her arms loosen around me and I stifle a groan when she lifts her head off of my shoulder and takes a step away from me. "This has been lovely, Tom, but we should probably go."

"Alright. Let's go find the car."

She reaches for my hand and slides her fingers between mine. We walk side-by-side back into the main building.

"Uh, Tom?"

Her tone puts me on alert. "What's wrong?"

"Can we find the restroom first?"

"Of course."

While waiting in the lobby, a small booth with frames and photos with Santa catches my eye. I dig into my pocket and pull out the card they gave me at the Education Center. Might as well check out the picture.

The attendant smiles when I hand her the card. The photo takes my breath away. Rachel looks gorgeous, as always. Her eyes shine out of the picture at me. Well worth the awkwardness of seeing Santa as adults. It's our first picture together. Maybe I should get one. "How much is a picture?"

"Do you want a five by seven, an eight by ten, or an ornament?"

"There's an ornament?"

The attendant holds up a piece of white porcelain that's round with red and green triangles on the top and bottom that look like little Santa hats. There's a photo pocket in the middle. She turns it over to reveal a photo of the large metal tree surrounded by the words "North Carolina Arboretum." I smile. That's perfect. "Definitely the ornament."

When Rachel returns from the restroom, I'm standing at a large map of the Arboretum. "Sorry that took so long. There's always a line for the women's restroom. You look happy. What'd I miss?"

I realize I'm bouncing on the balls of my feet and grinning like a fool. I force my body to still and try to dim the wattage of my smile. "Nothing. I'm just in a good mood. Shall we go?"

I hold out my hand, and my heart leaps when she takes it without hesitation. I'm still amped up about the surprise gift I have for Rachel and swing our arms as we walk toward the car. When should I give it to her? I'm sure the perfect time will reveal itself.

"Are you humming 'Here Comes Santa Claus'?" Rachel's words break into my thoughts.

Oops. I feel a little silly about my giddiness. *Get it together, Tom, or you're going to ruin the surprise.* "Yeah, I guess I am. Sorry. The lights seem to have put me in a festive mood."

"No need to apologize. I enjoy seeing you happy."

Her words fill my heart. This may be my best date ever.

33

Rachel

"WHEN'S YOUR NEXT trip?" I ask when we're in the car headed to my apartment.

"I'm going to California on Wednesday to spend Thanksgiving with my parents. Then I'll head back to Oahu for work."

Something about what he says sends an alert to my brain. What about it is bothering me? It'll come to me soon. "It's nice you can spend the holiday with your parents. Will your sister be there too?"

"No, she has to stay and manage the store. Asheville gets a lot of visitors over the holiday weekend and she wants to make sure she has enough inventory to capitalize on the extra crowd. She has Friendsgiving with people in town. My brother will be in California, though."

"Where does he live?"

"New York City. I hear he's bringing his girlfriend with him, but I'll believe it when I see it. He's canceled on the last couple of holidays. What are you doing for Thanksgiving? I'm sure Julie would include you in her celebration."

"I appreciate the offer, but that would feel awkward since I don't know your sister. Anyway, I'll be in Greenville per usual. My brother and his family live there and host most of our holidays. My parents come up from Atlanta and my sister comes over from Charleston. It's a fun time."

"I remember you saying your siblings are both older, but who's the oldest?"

"My brother."

Tom smiles. "Mine too. My brother is five years older than me and my sister is two. What about yours?"

"My brother is also five years older, but my sister is only nine minutes older."

His brow furrows. "Did you say nine *minutes?*"

I grin. This is always a fun conversation. "Yes, we're twins."

Tom's mouth gapes open. "You're a twin? Are you identical?"

"We are."

"What's she like?"

"Abbie's athletic. She played three sports in high school and went to college on a basketball scholarship. She's now an athletic trainer at the College of Charleston."

"Impressive."

"Yes, I'm very proud of her. She's doing what she loves."

Tom glances over at me from the driver's seat and gives me a look. I give it right back. "What?"

"It sounds like your sister's following her dreams. Why aren't you?"

I look away and sigh. "Abbie's good at what she loves. I'm just a wanna-be author."

"Why don't you think your writing is good? You seem to love doing it. Did you receive poor grades in English?"

"I had excellent grades in school and was part of my college's newspaper staff for a couple of years. I don't know if my writing is good enough for a sophisticated audience. College students are pretty easy to please as long as it's funny or disparages their sports rivals."

"I think you're not giving yourself enough credit. When I read your story, I'll find out for myself. How's it coming, by the way?"

I gasp, realizing what my brain was trying to tell me earlier. "Friday! I hadn't realized that our deadline was the day after Thanksgiving. Neither of us will be here. How am I supposed to give it to you?"

Tom smiles. "Email it to me."

I slap my forehead. "Oh yeah, duh. Email. A logical option. I'm so dense."

"I just think you don't want me to read it."

"Maybe. At least I'll get to see one of your pictures in return. That almost makes my humiliation worth it."

Tom takes my hand. "Why are you being so hard on yourself?"

I stiffen. *Might as well tell him.* I release my breath, focusing on our intertwined fingers. "A guy I was dating said my work is sophomoric."

"And you believed him?"

"He's an English professor and author, so, yeah."

I venture a look at his face. His eyebrows are pinched together, and he's frowning. "Maybe your writing was better than his, and he was jealous."

I laugh at the ridiculous suggestion. "I doubt it. He was most likely being honest, so rejection wouldn't crush me later. Anyway, don't get your hopes up that you'll be reading some sort of masterpiece. My goal is that it's entertaining."

"I'm very much looking forward to your story, despite what others may have said. I feel honored to read it."

The tightness in my chest loosens. I squeeze his hand in appreciation. He's so kind to me. I'm enjoying spending time with him. Too soon, we pull up to the curb of my building. Tom puts the car in park and unbuckles his seatbelt. I stop him from opening his door with a hand to his chest. "I can make it from here just fine."

"Are you sure?"

"I'm sure. Thanks for such a lovely evening. This was

wonderful."

"I had a good time, too."

Tom's gaze darts down to my lips. The heat in his eyes ignites a small flicker inside my gut. Brett's not here to ruin it now. I lean toward him, my heart thumping, and he meets me over the center console. My eyelids flutter closed. His breath is a warm puff on my skin. I crack one eye open wondering why our lips haven't touched yet. The scene from *Hitch* when Alex is teaching Albert about the 90/10 rule pops into my head and a small chuckle escapes. Tom's eyes fly open just as I decide to go for it. I reach up, lightly grasp the back of his neck, and pull him to me. Our lips connect and my heart explodes like fireworks. Heat spreads from my lips down to my toes, lighting up every nerve ending on the way down. After a few seconds, the pressure against my lips eases and I groan in protest. I remove my hand from Tom's neck and look away. When I risk a glance over at Tom, he's grinning like he just won first prize in a contest. He places a hand on my cheek, caressing my skin with his fingers. "Wow," he says.

I laugh, some of my nervousness easing. "Wow is right."

Was that a fluke or do we really have such fiery chemistry? I'd better do some more research. Turning my upper body back toward Tom, I bite the corner of my lip for courage and close the distance between us again. When our lips meet for the second time, my whole body sighs. Tom deepens the kiss and my body tingles with pleasure.

I can't remember ever experiencing a kiss like this. Maybe I haven't been doing it right. Or not with the right person, at least. That first kiss was definitely not a fluke. I get lost in the sensations ricocheting around in my body while our mouths communicate without words.

A horn blast makes me jump and my head bangs against the roof of the SUV. One hand goes to my heart to calm its rapid beat while the other cradles my sore head. Did Tom lean on the steering wheel? He looks through the back glass of the car and groans. I turn around. A man in a big truck is gesturing none too kindly at us to move. Tom chuckles. "I guess our time in the loading zone is up."

"I guess so."

He grins at me, and I smile back. I don't want to leave the car. Without conscious thought, I lean toward Tom again. Before I get very far, there's a sharp knock on the driver's side window. I look over Tom's shoulder. It's the man from the truck and he's scowling and pointing toward the "Loading & Unloading Only" sign on my side of the car. "Alright, alright," Tom says, throwing up his hands.

I open the door and step out onto the sidewalk. "Good night, Tom. This was fun. We should do it again sometime."

He grins. "Most definitely."

34

Rachel

I'M STANDING IN a snow-covered yard next to a cabin. Huge mountains loom in the distance. My breath escapes in white puffs of air, but I don't feel cold because Tom's standing behind me with his arms looped around my waist. His stubble prickles against my ear when he leans forward. Instead of whispering sweet nothings, he coughs. My brow furrows. That's not what's supposed to happen next. I blink my eyes and shake my head. Refocusing my attention, my gaze fall on Brett, who's standing in front of me with a smirk on his face. Ugh, I wish I was in Alaska with Tom.

"What are *you* thinking about?" he says.

I know he can't read my mind, but it feels like he sees right through me. "Oh, nothing. Just pondering something I read earlier." I pick up the book that's open on the counter in front of me for emphasis. That's right, I was reading my book club pick. That explains the snowy setting.

Brett quirks an eyebrow. "Yeah, sure. I bet you're thinking about that guy I saw you with the other night."

"Why do you say that?"

"I doubt anything in a book would make you smile like that."

Color rises to my cheeks. How is he able to read me so well? "How am I smiling?"

"Like you've won the lottery."

No use denying it anymore. Brett won't drop it until he's satisfied. "Fine, you caught me."

"I knew it. What's his name again?"

"Tom Haynes."

Brett tilts his head and frowns. "I know that name from somewhere. What does he do?"

"He's a photographer."

He shakes his head. "Nope, that's not it."

I shrug. "I don't know what to tell you."

He turns and wanders away from the register, muttering to himself. Maybe it'll keep him busy for a while and he'll forget to tease me about Saturday night.

📖

"He's a surfer!" The declaration startles me and I knock over some books I'm shelving in the children's section.

"Brett, you scared me," I say, clutching my chest.

He has the decency to look contrite. "Sorry about that. I didn't recognize him before because he used to have longer hair, but that's him."

"Have you met him before?"

"No, but I used to follow his career. People thought he would be the greatest of all time."

This is news to me. "The greatest of all time?"

Brett nods his head and looks at me like I'm an alien. "Yeah. He won the championship right before his career ended."

"How did you figure out who he was?"

"The internet. Haven't you Googled him?"

"No. I don't look people up online. That's kind of weird."

Brett tuts. "He's probably checked you out."

"Well, he won't find anything. I'm not famous or anything."

"Does this mean you haven't seen his surfing videos?"

"I didn't know there were videos."

159

He pulls his phone out and starts typing. "You've got to see him on a board."

"You know you aren't supposed to have your phone out while you're working."

"I'm on break. Besides, this is important." Brett turns his screen toward me. "This one's awesome."

A huge wave fills the screen. A surfer, looking as small as an ant compared to the water below him, drops from the top of the wave and slices across it, his hand dragging along the wall of water. The curl of the wave closes over top of him. The wave appears to crush the man, but then he shoots out into open sky. I exhale, surprised to find I'd been holding my breath.

I turn to face Brett. "That was Tom?"

"Yep."

"That wave was huge!"

"That's the Bonzai Pipeline in Oahu. It's known for its colossal waves." He tilted his head and peered at her. "You really didn't know?"

I shrug. Guess there's more to Tom than I thought. "When he told me he used to surf, that's not what I imagined. And he won the championship?"

"Yeah. Fun fact, they announce the winner after this competition in Hawaii each December."

Hawaii. The word rings loud in my brain and memories flit through my mind. *Tom went to Hawaii a month ago. He came into the store and bought a book for sightseeing.* I lock eyes with Brett. "The book!"

My feet carry me toward the back of the store. Brett rushes to catch up. "What book?"

I don't answer, but continue walking until I reach the travel section. I run a finger across the titles until I find it. *Water Sports in Hawaii.* I pull it out and turn to the table of contents. I flip to the surfing section and thumb through it until a photo freezes me. There's a large picture of a man partially hidden by a wave. His right profile faces the camera, his chin-length brown hair plastered to his cheek. He's grinning like he's having the time of his life. The dimple in his cheek is unmistakable.

Brett gasps. "That's him! How did you know about this book?"

"When I helped him find some travel books, he looked through this book before choosing another one. I thought he'd acted a little funny, but forgot about it until just now. I guess he didn't want me to know about his past."

Why would Tom want to keep me in the dark? Is he ashamed of something? Why doesn't want to talk about that part of his life with me?

"Well, it's cool you're seeing someone famous. Think you could get me an autograph?" Brett waggles his eyebrows at me and I laugh, despite my inner turmoil. "I'm just kidding. Kind of."

"Is he truly famous? I mean, do many people follow surfing?"

"He starred in ads for surfboards and some surfing brands. He's famous in the surfing world, but not mainstream popular."

"Oh." I take one more look at the photo and then put the book back on the shelf. "We should get back to work."

On our way back up front, Brett nudges me with his shoulder. "For what it's worth, I'm happy for you. Tom seems like a nice guy."

Right now, I'm not so sure. Is Tom hiding something? I need to know why he's so dodgy about his past.

📖

My computer bounces up and down in my lap, thanks to my jiggling right foot. My story deadline is today and I'm trying to summon the courage to send it to Tom. I've worked hard on it, but the thought of him reading it causes bile to rise in my throat. I swallow it back down. *Get it together, Rachel. It's just a story. All of your hopes and dreams wrapped up in a few thousand words. Nothing to fret about.*

Great. Thanks for that, brain. I let my finger hover over the Enter key that will shoot my email through the internet and into Tom's inbox. Or however that works.

"What are you doing in here?"

My body jolts in surprise, and my finger stabs the key. With a whoosh, the email rushes off through cyberspace. *Well, at least that's done.* "Abbie, you startled me."

"You look like you were thinking pretty hard about something."

"I was hesitating about a decision, but you helped me, so thank you."

"What were you doing?"

"Trying to force myself to email someone."

"What's so hard about that?"

"I attached one of my stories to it."

Abbie sits down next to me, her interest piqued. "Oh really? Who did you send it to?"

"A friend."

Abbie smirks. "Someone convinced you to share your work? Who is it? I'd like to thank her."

I could let her think it's a female friend, but I hate lying to my sister. Besides, I'm kind of dying to talk to her about it. She *is* my sister, after all. "Him."

Abbie's eyebrows shoot up. "*Him*, huh?"

"Yes."

"Could this 'him' be *more* than a friend, sister dear?"

"Maybe." I'm avoiding her eyes.

"Mm-hmm. Have you kissed him?"

I stay quiet, but the smile spreading across my face gives me away. I have a terrible poker face.

"You have! Who is he and why am I only now hearing about him?"

"His name is Tom. We've gone on a couple of dates, but that's it. It's not serious or anything."

"Are you going to see him again?"

I sure hope so, but I'm not ready to tell Abbie that yet. "We'll have to see. He travels a lot with his job. He's a sports photographer."

"Have you seen any of his pictures?"

"I haven't, but he's supposed to send me one today."

"Can I see it?"

"Sure. How's Charleston? Are *you* seeing anyone?"

Abbie laughs. "Nice transition. Charleston's good. Work is going well, though I've been keeping an eye out for openings at bigger schools. I'd like to work for a more prestigious program."

"I hope a position opens up somewhere you're interested."

"Thanks, sis."

"I noticed you didn't answer the question about your romantic life."

She gives me a pointed look. "That's because I don't have one. Are you going to let me read the story you sent Tom?"

"Only if you promise to tell me how awesome it is."

Abbie grins. "You know it!"

35

Tom

THE OCEAN AIR fills my lungs and I smile at the briny smell. The rhythmic pounding of waves on the shore is a familiar lullaby. Families are building sandcastles, playing bocce ball, and jumping waves. Some people are in the water with surfboards. Gorgeous days like today are when I miss living on the coast. The sun on my face and the light breeze rustling my hair and clothing are heaven. My phone vibrates in my pocket and I pull it out. I have a new email.

I open my inbox and see it's from Price, R. The subject is a grimacing emoji face. I chuckle and open it up.

Hi Tom, Happy day after Thanksgiving! Hope you're enjoying your time with family. Here's my story as promised. I look forward to your photo. Sincerely, Rachel

Oh right, the photo. I've already looked through the folder of my best images and settled on three. One shows the curl of an immense wave. The water's a brilliant blue with foamy white streaks. It feels like it will crash over the viewer at any moment. The second picture is a vibrant orange sunset with the silhouette of a surfer on top of a wave. The contrast of the surfer and the sky is striking. The last picture is of a surfer being hoisted into the air. His face is triumphant, a fist raised in celebration.

I click over to my drafts folder and open the one addressed to

Rachel. After adding a brief message, I send it. Back in my inbox, I click on Rachel's email, scrolling down to the attachment. *Criminals in Costa Rica.* The title intrigues me. I check the time: two-thirty. With nowhere to be until seven, I open the document and read the first sentence.

I lower the phone from in front of my face and look out at the ocean. My back feels tight from staying in one position so long and I twist my torso to relieve the discomfort. My mind replays the story I just read. The action was fast-paced; the characters were likable. I felt genuine concern that the hero would not reach the stranded couple in time. I'd laughed out loud when the drone appeared. It was engaging, suspenseful, humorous, and had a happy, satisfying ending. I couldn't ask for anything more.

I check the time, shocked to see it's four-thirty. I've been reading for two hours? It hasn't seemed that long. I search for the word count. Thirty thousand. Seems like a lot of words for a short story.

I shake my head, amused. How can I convey how much I loved it in an email? I should just call her. What time is it out east? Seven-thirty. Not too late. If she doesn't answer, I'll leave a message. A notification pops up on my screen informing me that I only have ten percent battery life left. Guess I should charge it first. Wouldn't want it to die mid-conversation. I stand up from the ground, brush the sand off the seat of my pants, stretch to loosen my tight muscles, and head for the parking lot.

36

Rachel

I'M SPRAWLED ON the couch in a slight stupor, my belly uncomfortably full after a dinner of delicious leftovers. My sister's scrolling through her phone on the other end of the couch while my brother and father watch football from twin recliners. My mom and sister-in-law are putting the girls to bed in the playroom. I pull my phone out from the pocket of my yoga pants when I feel it vibrate. Tom's name appears on the screen and I dash down the hall to the room I'm sharing with my sister. Closing the door, I drop onto the bed, and answer the call. I suck in a deep, steadying breath to calm my racing heart. "Hello?"

"Hi, Rachel. It's Tom."

"Hi, Tom. How's California?"

"It's great. Sunny and warm, with a light breeze."

"You're making me jealous. Here it's cold and windy with a high of 48."

He laughs. "Brrr. Sorry."

I smile. I adore his laugh. It sounds so carefree. "To what do I owe the pleasure of a phone call?"

"I just finished your story."

My throat feels dry and my pulse pounds in my temple. "You read it already?"

"I did, though I'm surprised to learn your idea of a short story is thirty thousand words.”

I close my eyes and grimace. “You thought it was too long.”

“No, it wasn’t too long. It was the perfect length to create a suspenseful, engaging, and coherent story.”

“Does that mean you thought it was okay?”

“It was much more than okay. It was fantastic!”

A smile spreads across my face. He liked it! Wait. Calm down. He could just be saying these things to spare my feelings. I tamp down my elation. “What did you like about it?”

“I liked that the hero was more like an everyman, not some super muscle-y, professional wrestler type, but still fit, intelligent, and sharp. The suspense and situations were believable. I was concerned about how the missionary couple was going to escape. The drone was a genius move.”

I’m glowing from his praise. “I had a little inspiration for that.”

“I thought so. It made me laugh out loud. I only have one question.”

“What’s that?” I hope my voice doesn’t betray the jittery feeling in my stomach.

“Will the hero have a love interest in the next story?”

“There isn’t a next story, Tom.”

“Well, there should be. I want to know what other adventures Jackson Tyler goes on.”

“Thanks, Tom. That’s very sweet of you.”

“I’m serious, Rachel. That was a great story. You should think about submitting it somewhere.”

His words sober me. “That seems a little extreme.”

“You’re a very talented writer and you want to be published. I think it’s possible, but you have to show your writing to someone in the business.”

My smile dims, and my fingers find a loose string on the comforter. “Why are you pushing this, Tom?”

“Because you should pursue your dream. Doing something

you love is the best feeling in the world. I want you to experience that like I have."

His comment reminds me of what Brett said about his career. "Speaking of doing what you loved, why didn't you tell me you were a world champion surfer? That's an outstanding accomplishment, Tom."

There's a beat of silence. "You know about that, huh?"

"Yeah, I do. I saw a video of you on a gigantic wave. You should be proud, not hiding your accomplishments."

"I *am* proud of my surfing career. I just don't enjoy explaining the reason behind my sudden retirement."

His words make my heart lurch. "The accident. Oh, Tom, you're right. I'm so sorry."

A sigh comes through the phone. "It's okay. I know you aren't trying to be hurtful. It was a terrible time in my life."

"Did you have a lot of support to help you through?"

"My parents were great. So was my buddy Jeff. He helped me accept the fact that surfing was no longer an option for me. He was a sturdy support through the whole Bethany thing."

"Who's Bethany?"

Another beat of silence. "Bethany was my fiancée."

I gasp. "You were engaged? What happened?"

Horror grips me at my lack of sensitivity, and I rush to backtrack. "I mean, if you want to tell me. I don't want to pry."

"No, I'll tell you. I should have told you already. Bethany and I met at a surfing competition four years ago. She approached me, said she'd been watching me all week, and was glad that I'd won. She asked if she could take me out to dinner to celebrate. I thought she was cute, so I agreed. We hit it off, and she gave me her number. She worked with one of the sponsor companies, so I saw her at other competitions."

He pauses and I remain quiet until he continues. "We hung out a few more times before becoming a couple. At the end of the following year, I won the surfing title and proposed. We planned to get married after the next season was over. The car accident happened four months later. I learned in July that the damage to my foot meant the end of my surfing career. Bethany told me she didn't want to marry me anymore and broke it off. She started dating another surfer on the circuit soon after."

I cycle through a range of feelings while listening to Tom's story—jealousy, compassion, sorrow. I settle on anger. "*What?!* She broke up with you while you were recovering from a major trauma and immediately started dating someone else?"

"You got it."

"What is *wrong* with her? That is *not* right. Why would she *do* that?"

Tom chuckles, but there's not humor behind it. "I had those same thoughts. My guess? She didn't love me. She just loved what my success could provide for her."

My heart aches for Tom. "You think she only wanted you for your fame?"

"I wasn't exactly famous, but yeah. My buddy Jeff says she's now engaged to last year's world champion."

No wonder he doesn't like to talk about that part of his life. "Oh, Tom. I'm so sorry. What she did was horrible. You don't deserve that. You're a wonderful person and anyone who can't see that isn't worth your time or attention."

"Thanks, Rachel. You're very sweet."

I don't know what else to say after Tom's confession. Thankfully, he does. "So, did you look at the photos I sent you?"

"My nieces have monopolized my time today. There was a break when nap time rolled around, but by then I'd forgotten to expect an email from you. I can look now."

"Sure."

"I'm putting you on speaker so I can grab my computer. I want a bigger screen to view the photo." I turn on my laptop. "Okay, I see your email. Tom, you sent me *three* images."

"I thought you might appreciate a few examples of my work."

I grin at his thoughtfulness. "You thought right. Alright, I'm opening the first one. Oh, Tom, it's beautiful."

"Which one are you looking at?"

"The big blue wave."

"That's one of my favorites."

"The color's so brilliant and the wave looks so powerful. I can almost hear the rush of the water and feel the spray on my face. It's so dynamic."

"I like your description. You created quite a picture with your words."

"Well, I *am* a writer."

"That you are, and a good one, too. Open the next image."

It's a small blessing Tom can't see me blush from his compliment. "Okay, so this one–" The photo fills the screen and I'm stunned.

"Rachel, are you there?"

"I'm here, Tom, sorry. The sunset took my breath away. The color contrasts are amazing. I don't know what else to say about it. I'm speechless."

Tom chuckles. "That sounds like a compliment."

"You are correct. You do an amazing job capturing the gloriousness of nature."

"Thanks. Ready to see the last one?"

"Most definitely." I click it open. "Oh, he looks so happy! And those guys holding him up look just as excited. It's an atmosphere of joy and triumph. I feel happy just looking at it. And a little jealous."

"Jealous? Why's that?"

"It makes me want my own group of supporters in my corner, cheering me on and celebrating my successes. Victory feels even better when it's experienced with others. Don't you agree?"

"I do. But you have your book club. They support you, don't they?"

"Well, yeah, but I don't know. Receiving the support of

people in your field is unparalleled. They understand everything you go through to achieve success, which gives their praise more weight."

"I get what you're saying and it's true. When I watch surfers, I know just how difficult their tricks are and appreciate their success as an insider."

My body floods with warmth at his understanding. "Exactly."

"I hope you find that."

My throat feels tight, and it takes me a minute to speak. "Thank you. Anyway, back to your pictures. You did a great job capturing emotion in your photos. You have quite a gift, Tom."

"Thanks. Your word pictures were quite colorful."

"Just putting voice to what I see. You know, you could sell these if you wanted. Hang them in a gallery or something."

"Nah."

I don't like his quick dismissal of my words. It reminds me too much of me, and I'm beginning to believe I've been selling myself short for years. I don't want Tom doing the same. "For real. These pictures belong in a museum. They could win photo contests or–"

"Rachel. Stop."

There's a bite to his voice and I freeze up. What just happened? "Did I say something wrong? I didn't mean to offend you."

There's a hiss over the phone like a breath being released slowly. "I like my life as it is. I don't need more money or fame. Just leave it be."

"Tom, that's not what I meant. I think your work is incredible."

Awkward silence stretches between us. I'm searching for a safer subject when Tom speaks. "I should let you get back to your family. I'll let you know when I'm back in town. We can get dinner and catch up."

We hang up and I'm a ball of confusion. I replay the

conversation in my head. *That was weird.* Our conversation took a nosedive when I suggested he share his work. I guess it was the wrong thing to say. How was I to know? He's the one pushing me to share my work with others. Why would he resist the same advice? It doesn't make sense and seems hypocritical. Anger seeps into my muddled emotions. I huff out a breath, frustrated. I need someone to help me figure out how our call got so off course. I get up from the bed to go find Abbie.

37

Tom

THAT DIDN'T GO as I'd hoped. Rachel's effusive comments about my photos made it seem like she understood just what I was trying to say, but I didn't care for the push to commercialize my work. Yes, photography is my job and I have entered contests here and there, but I prefer to be anonymous at competitions these days. The new guys don't recognize me and my old competitors don't bring up the past. I'm through with pursuing fame. I've already been down that road and don't care to travel it again. All it does is lead to heartbreak. I start the car and drive back toward my parents' house, still turning the conversation over in my mind.

It surprises me she knows about my championship year. Did she look me up? It's easy to find the information, but why would she research me? Is this a sign that she's just like my ex? She suggested I try to sell my pictures in a gallery which is something Bethany did, but she also sounded furious about my ex's behavior. Maybe her concern is a ploy to keep me from realizing the truth. It doesn't help that my feelings for Rachel are growing. I file the conversation away, reminding myself to keep my eyes open for additional signs that she might be using me before I get in too deep.

Speaking of being in too deep, Rachel's story was fantastic. It's hard to believe she can't see her talent. I'd love to help her regain confidence in her writing ability. Maybe my brother can give me some advice.

I pull into the driveway and head inside my parents' house. In the kitchen, mom and Charlie's girlfriend, Serena, are chatting together at the table. I pass through to the living room where dad and Charlie are watching a football game. Well, Charlie is at least. Soft snores from the recliner confirm my dad's asleep. Charlie's on the couch looking at his phone. It seems like a good time to talk to him. I sit down next to Charlie, keeping my voice low so I don't wake my father.

"Hey Charlie, can I ask you something?"

"Sure."

"Is your company looking for new authors?"

He puts down his phone and turns to face me. "We're always interested in new talent. Are you considering writing about your surfing career? Someone from our nonfiction department would be interested in that."

I shake my head. "No, thanks. A friend let me read her work. It's fantastic and I think a professional should look at it."

"A friend, huh?" Charlie gives me a teasing smile. "What does she write?"

I try and fail to keep a straight face. "Is action and adventure a genre?"

"It's under the fiction umbrella. How long is the story?"

"Thirty thousand words."

Charlie nods. "That's a novella, not a novel. Are you sure it's not just the woman you like?"

I narrow my eyes. "I see what you're getting at but it really was a great story. I read the whole thing on the beach this afternoon."

"You read it in one sitting? That sounds promising." Charlie taps his chin with his index finger. "Our publishing house rarely accepts unsolicited manuscripts. However, I know an agent who's been very successful in representing fiction authors with action stories. I'll send you her information and you can pass it along to your friend."

"Thanks, bro. By the way, I really like Serena."

Charlie grins. "Me too."

Charlie texts me the agent's online submissions form. I read the list of requirements. It seems straightforward enough. Will Rachel do it, though? I'm not sure. What if I were to submit the story on her behalf? I dismiss that thought and compose an email to send Rachel the contact info.

Rachel, My brother works in publishing and gave me contact info for an agent that represents action stories. I've attached a link to her website. I think you should send her your story. What's the worst that could happen? -Tom

38

DECEMBER

Rachel

IT'S A STRUGGLE to concentrate at work today. Tonight's the supper club talent show, and my stomach is in knots. Tom's rave review gave me an initial boost of confidence, but it's since worn off. Especially since he also seems to think submitting my story to an agent is risk-free. Um, hello, there's always the genuine possibility of rejection. I told this to Tom via email and I think he understood. He seems to be over whatever upset him when we'd talked, but I haven't brought it up for fear of another negative reaction. I hate relational tension.

I asked his opinion on which part of my story to share and he suggested I start at the beginning and, quote, "leave them begging for more." I didn't have a better idea, so that's what's happening. The first few pages are sitting on my kitchen counter at home. A new worry surfaces. *Maybe I should have practiced reading it out loud.* Too late now because I need to run by Little Shop of Sugar to pick up a few truffles. Louise is bringing dessert, but this is a special occasion and special occasions demand truffles.

I'm surprised to find the shop void of customers when I enter. I check the sign to make sure it's not closed for the day. The bells jingle merrily. A woman in a chocolate-smeared apron and chef's hat enters from another room. She smiles and I see an immediate resemblance to Tom. "Hello. How can I help you?"

"You must be Julie." She nods. "I don't think we've officially met. I'm Rachel."

"You're Tom's friend, right?"

"Yes."

"Nice to meet you. Tom's not here, he's in…"

"Hawaii," we say at the same time.

Julie laughs. "Of course you know where he is."

I cringe when I feel the telltale heat on my face. "We've been emailing."

"Are you here for book club treats?"

"No, that's every third Thursday. Tonight is supper club."

"You have a lot of clubs."

"Just those two, and tonight's a special evening, so I thought I'd bring a special treat. Your truffles make everything a celebration."

Julie beams. "Thanks for the compliment. What can I get for you?"

"Blackouts, of course, because they're my favorite. I'd also like some milk chocolates. Do you have any seasonal treats?"

"We have sugar cookie caramels, pecan pie caramels, and a coconut and macadamia truffle."

I stick out my tongue. "Ugh. Not a coconut fan. A couple of each of the other two and a couple of dark chocolate pistachios caramels. Those are my second favorite."

"You have good taste, but don't knock the coconut ones without trying them. It's just a coconut liqueur. There isn't any actual coconut in it. I know texture's an issue for some people."

"Alright, add one of those and I'll try it. I pre-judged your Ancient Treasures truffle because it has cayenne pepper, but Tom convinced me to try it and it was pretty good."

"I'm glad to hear that Tom is a persuasive chocolate salesperson. I'll pass on my appreciation. Do you need anything else?"

"That's it."

Julie rings me up and hands me the bag. "It was nice to meet you, Rachel. Hope to see you again soon."

"Nice to meet you, too. I'll report back on the coconut truffle. Does it have a name?"

"Not officially, but I'm considering calling it Coco-Nutty."

I groan. "Coco-Nutty. Really?"

Julie shrugs. "I like the name. Can you think of anything better?"

"Not off the top of my head, but I'll think on it."

Back in my car, I arrange the chocolates in a decorative tin, setting the coconut one to the side. I eye it for a minute, feeling a bit of déjà vu, before picking it up and taking a bite. I close my eyes and chew. There's a hint of coconut and a pleasant crunch with the nuts. The flavors go well together.

I don't know why I'm surprised; Julie's truffles are always amazing. This one reminds me of being at the beach, maybe on a tropical island. At least what I imagine it's like. I know who can tell me for sure. Setting down the half-eaten chocolate, I grab my phone and send Tom a text.

Rachel: Do you equate coconut and macadamia nuts with being on a tropical island?

Realizing it's almost one p.m. in Oahu and Tom is probably working, I set down my phone and finish arranging the truffles. I pick up the Coco-Nutty truffle and pop the rest in my mouth before placing the lid on the tin. *Beach Nut! That's what it should be called.* I grin, pleased with myself. Next time I see Julie, I'll share my name idea. My phone pings with a text alert. My heart flips when I see it's Tom.

Tom: It might remind me of a Hawaiian beach, but I don't like coconut. Weird texture.

Rachel: I think so too! But your sister bullied me into trying her newest creation with coconut liqueur and I thought it was pretty good.

Dots pop up on Tom's side of the screen. I'm giddy waiting for his response.

Tom: Julie bullied you?

Rachel: No, I'm kidding. She was very nice.

Tom: Okay good. When's your supper club?

Rachel: I'm heading over soon. Are you working?

Tom: I have a break. Let me know what the group thinks of your story.

Rachel: I'm a little nervous.

Tom: Your story's great and your friends will think so too.

Rachel: Thanks for the vote of confidence.

Tom: Anytime. You're a talented writer and a wonderful person.

His praise buoys me all the way over to Reggie's house.

39

Rachel

NORA OPENS THE door when I knock. She looks as stylish and fabulous as ever. "Hi, Nora. I brought some special goodies since it's a unique night for supper club."

She leans in and I give her a quick hug and an air kiss. It still feels silly to me, but when in Rome, right? "It is indeed. Are you ready to share your story?"

"I have to admit I'm a little nervous, but Tom read it and seemed to enjoy it, so that's given me a bit of confidence."

"That's wonderful, Rachel."

In the kitchen, Louise is at the stove. "I brought some chocolate from Little Shop of Sugar for the evening. I know you were in charge of dessert, but I couldn't help myself."

Louise turns, oven mitts on her hands. "Well, that's perfect. Reggie called me earlier with a food emergency, so I didn't have time to make the cake I'd planned. You've talked so much about that place, I'm eager to try one."

I give Louise a warm hug, inhaling a rich aroma that makes my mouth water. "I'm sorry you're not getting the night off, but it smells fantastic in here. What are you making?"

"Beef bourguignon."

My eyebrows shoot up at the French-sounding name. "Sounds like a lot of work."

"It's just a fancy way of saying beef stew."

"I'm sure it'll be delicious, like all of your meals. Can I help with anything?"

"No, dear, I've got it. Go on into the living room. We're still waiting for Don to arrive."

I greet Reggie, and he hands me a glass of something red. "What's this?"

"It's called Antica Terra. It's a Pinot Noir from Willamette Valley in Oregon."

I take a sip. "This is amazing."

Reggie leans toward me and whispers. "It should be for a hundred dollars a bottle."

I choke on my second sip. "What? Reggie!"

"We're celebrating our talents tonight." He laughs at my concerned expression. "It's fine, Rachel. I already had it in my collection."

"Well, I guess the bottle's already open. We might as well enjoy it, right?"

"That's the spirit."

"I like your place, by the way. This room looks amazing."

"Thanks. Most of the decor came from my trips to Tuscany."

Voices raised in greeting float in from the kitchen. "It sounds like Don's here," Reggie says. "He said he was bringing a colleague."

My nerves jump to high alert. *I'll be performing in front of a stranger. Great.* Well, at least I probably won't see them again.

Don walks into the living room, a big smile on his face. "Hello, everyone. I brought a friend with me this evening. I thought he and Louise could be our judges."

A slim man in khakis, an oxford blue collared shirt, and penny loafers enters the room. My eyes slide up to his face and I freeze, my stomach twisting. I'm quite familiar with his curly blond hair, square jaw, bright blue eyes, and black-rimmed glasses.

I can't tear my eyes away and notice the way his eyes widen

when he recognizes Nora. His gaze grazes over Reggie. I tense, waiting for the moment he spots me, but his eyes flick over me without recognition. That's odd. He walks toward the buffet for a drink but pauses mid-stride, turning back in my direction. *Ah, now it's clicked.* We lock eyes. There's a hint of panic amidst the surprise in his expression, but he recovers quickly. "Hi, I'm Thayer St. Clair," he says to the room. "I work with Don at Warren Wilson."

Reggie shakes Thayer's hand. "Welcome to supper club, Thayer. Glad to have you."

I sit down heavily on the couch. *Oh, no. No, no, no. Thayer's here.* Panic rises in my chest. This is awful. I haven't seen him since before he broke up with me and now I have to bare my soul in front of him. *He's going to eviscerate me. What am I going to do?* My breathing's shallow and I feel a little light-headed. My face burns with humiliation.

I beeline to the bathroom, sliding silently behind the group congregated in the living room. Grateful to find it behind the first door I try, I close the bathroom door and lock it. I set my glass down on the sink, afraid my shaking hands will lose their grip. *Come on, deep breaths. It's not a big deal. The night is supposed to be fun. You're with friends. You can do this.* I stare at my reflection in the mirror, willing myself to believe the things I'm saying. I jump at a knock on the door and barely catch my glass before it tips over into the sink.

"Rachel, are you okay?"

"I'm fine, Nora," I say through the door.

"When you're finished in there, can we talk for a moment?"

I sigh. I was hoping she'd go away so I could get myself together, but I could use a friendly face. I open the door and try to sound like I'm not freaking out. "Hi, what's up?" I wince at the noticeably high pitch of my voice.

"That's what I want to ask you. Is something wrong, Rachel? Your face went white and then quite red. Are you having an allergic reaction to the wine?"

"I'm definitely reacting, all right, but it's not to the wine."

"Tell me what happened. Maybe I can help."

I peek behind Nora to see if anyone is nearby. I pull her in and lock the door. Nora's forehead creases. I'm touched that she's concerned for me. "Thayer's my ex."

"Oh my." Her face softens into a look of concern. "When did things end?"

"About five months ago."

"Was it a nasty breakup?"

"He broke up with me through a text, so it wasn't great."

Nora scowls. "That's not very gentlemanly."

Her reaction gives me a little validation. "No, it's not. I haven't seen him since we broke up, and now I have to read my story in front of him. It's going to be a disaster!"

"Why do you say that?"

"He doesn't like my writing. He's going to say something bad about it."

"Why do you care what he thinks?"

"I know I shouldn't. But he's a published author, so…"

"Are his books best sellers?"

"No, he writes history books. Mostly about wars America's fought in."

"Those sound like very boring books."

I giggle. "They kind of are. I tried to read his first two when we were dating and couldn't get past the section detailing what weapons they used for each war. Although, being a book lover, I read the library one, and it had a few interesting parts."

"If his books aren't your cup of tea, then why does his opinion matter?"

Her question gives me pause. Why does his opinion matter? Especially since we're not together anymore. I don't need to impress him. "You know, that's very true. I never thought about it that way. So what if he dislikes my work? I don't care for the snoozefests he writes."

Nora smiles and pats my arm. "That's the spirit. We should

join the others. My stomach's growling over the smells coming from the kitchen."

"Mine too. Thank you, Nora. I needed this. Now I don't feel so alone."

"I'm on your side, Rachel. Don't think about Thayer. Just read to me tonight."

"Okay, I'll try."

Reggie claps his hands together. "Okay, everyone, it's time for the main event. I made an order of performances for the evening. Nora, Don, Rachel, me. Sound good?" Everyone nods. "I also made a scorecard for the judge. I didn't know we'd also have a guest judge, so you two will have to share. We'll average the scores."

Louise and Thayer nod their agreement.

"Excellent," Reggie says. "Then let's adjourn to the living room for an evening of wonderful talents."

"Wait just a minute," Don says. "First, show us the prize. I want to know what I'm going to win."

"Oh right! I can't believe I didn't remember to mention that. I'll be right back."

Reggie disappears down a hall and returns with a small green gift bag, which he plops onto the table. "The winner will receive…drum roll, please?" Don taps his index fingers on the edge of the table.

He pulls out a silver plastic crown adorned with large fake blue jewels and plunks it on his head. A white sash comes next, which he brandishes across his chest. It reads *Best Person* in sparkly, blue letters.

Don groans. The rest of us laugh. "That's fantastic," Nora says.

"I know. I will wear this to every supper club from now on,"

Reggie says.

"You wish. I have just the place for it on my mantel."

Thayer turns to Nora, excitement in his voice. "I bet your mantel already has several golden statues adorning it. Am I right?"

"A lady never tells."

"And a gentleman never asks! That's such a brilliant line. You were so great in that movie. In all your movies, actually. I think *The Big Show* is my favorite."

"Thank you." Nora turns away from Thayer and gives Reggie a pointed look. "Shall we get started?"

"Of course."

"Maybe you should give the prize to the judges for safekeeping," Don says.

"You're right." He removes the crown and sash. "I'll get them back soon, anyway."

"Don't count on it," Don says. "My sleight of hand will blow the judges away."

"I love your confidence, Don."

The group moves to the living room. Nora walks to a small table set up in the center of the room and stands behind it, facing the couches where we're all seated.

"I chose something a little different from what you might expect," she says. "Tonight I will make origami animals."

Nora picks up a purple square of paper and turns it into a butterfly. She makes a turtle, two fish, and a dragon with the remaining papers. It's impressive, but I don't know that it's sash-worthy. Not that I think my story has much of a chance, either.

Louise claps. "That was fantastic, Nora. Well done."

Nora takes her seat and Don stands up. "I guess it's my turn."

Grabbing a box from next to his seat, he removes a black tuxedo jacket with tails and puts it on over his white-collared shirt. He attaches a black bow tie to the neck of his shirt before reaching under his jacket and extracting a flat, black disc. He thumps the middle of it with his finger and it pops out into a top hat.

"Bravo," Nora says.

"I will need an assistant for my first trick. Thayer, will you do me the honor?"

Thayer gets up and stands next to Don. "What do you need me to do?"

Don removes his top hat, reaches his hand in, and withdraws a deck of cards. He opens the box and gives the cards to Thayer. "Please look at these cards and confirm that it's just an ordinary deck."

Thayer fans them out in front of himself. "They look normal to me."

"Thank you." Don extends his hand, and Thayer places the deck in it. "I will now run my thumb along the cards to make a cut. Tell me when to stop."

"Okay."

Don moves his thumb along the edge of the deck. "Stop," Thayer says.

Don holds up the top half of the deck, showing the card to everyone except himself. A nine of hearts. He hands it to Thayer. "Hold it so I can't see what it is."

He reaches into his pocket and produces a black permanent marker. "I want you to write your initials large in the middle of the card and show it to the group, but not me." He pauses while Thayer complies. "Now, take the deck and stick the card somewhere in it. I'll turn my back so I can't see."

Thayer slides his card in and straightens the deck. "I'm done," he says.

I'm on the edge of my seat. How is Don going to find Thayer's card?

Don turns back around and takes the deck from Thayer. He shuffles it a few times and then walks over to Louise, crouching down in front of her. "Louise, please tap the top of the deck five times while concentrating on the card with Thayer's initials?"

"Of course." She furrows her brow and then lightly taps the

deck five times.

Don clears his throat and tugs at his bow tie. "Great. Uh, could you tap it again, but with a little more oomph?"

Louise's lips curve down at the corners. "Is this better?" she says, tapping more firmly.

Don smiles. "That's perfect. Thanks, Louise."

He returns to Thayer in the middle of the room. "Louise has now summoned your card to the top of the deck. Will you take the top card, please?"

Thayer picks up the top card with exaggerated slowness, drawing out our anticipation of the revelation. His shoulders sag when he looks at it. He turns it toward us. The seven of spades. "Sorry," he says, looking at Don. "That's not my card."

"What? Maybe it's the next one."

The king of clubs.

Don frowns. He picks up the next card and looks at it. No initials. He flips the deck over onto the coffee table and spreads it out so that all the cards are visible. "Which one of these is your card, Thayer?"

Thayer slides them around on the table. "My card isn't here."

Don scratches his head. "Where could it have gone?" His face brightens, and he points into the air. "Aha! I know what happened."

He looks at Louise. "I shouldn't have asked you to tap the deck twice. The card stayed with you because your summons was so strong."

"I don't have it," Louise says.

"Do you have any pockets in your clothing?"

Louise inspects her outfit. "Just one here in my sweater."

She sticks her hand inside, and her eyes widen. She removes her hand along with the nine of hearts card with "TSC" written in the middle. We gasp in surprise before bursting into applause.

Don smiles. "Thank you, folks. That's my show for this evening."

"How did you do that?" Thayer says.

Don winks. "A magician never tells, either."

I startle at a tap on my shoulder. Reggie smiles at me. "You're up."

I try to swallow down my nerves. "Right."

I walk around the table, removing my story from my back pocket and unfolding it. Nora gives me a discreet thumbs-up when I look to her for courage. It's show time.

"Wow, Don. That's going to be a tough act to follow. Okay, so this story is called *Criminals in Costa Rica.*"

I flatten the papers against my chest to straighten out the creases, take a steadying breath, and begin. I find a rhythm which eases my anxiety. I'm surprised to feel something akin to joy while I'm reading. It almost feels like this is what I'm meant to be doing.

I finish the last page, take the papers away from my face, and focus on the table in front of me while I give myself a minute to prepare for whatever response I'm going to receive. Will they look bored or disappointed? Or worse, pitying? Time to find out. I find Nora first and she's smiling, which is encouraging. I look next at Louise, but her head is down. Reggie looks shocked. Was my story that bad? Now I'm worried. Don's focus is on his wineglass as he swirls the liquid around. These reactions are not at all comforting.

I might as well go for broke. Thayer looks pained. He's embarrassed for me, isn't he? I shouldn't have agreed to this. I take swift steps back to my seat and grab my wine glass, hoping I look unaffected.

"Is that it?" Reggie says, breaking the awkward silence.

I look at him, a little confused. "What?"

"Is that how the story ends? Because I'm worried about that missionary couple. Are they going to find a way out? Surely the poachers don't kill them and continue to decimate the jaguar population? Please tell me, there's more!"

I smile and my shoulders relax a smidge. Maybe his reaction wasn't from my terrible writing. "No, that's not how it ends. This is just the first part."

Reggie exhales. "Oh, thank goodness. Will you tell us how it ends? Better yet, send me the rest of the story so I can find out for myself."

My heart lifts a little. "Does this mean you liked it?"

"Liked it? I loved it. It has suspense, intrigue, danger, love. What's not to like about it?"

"Thanks, Reggie."

"Yes, very well done, Rachel," Nora says. "Please send me the rest of the story as well."

"Yes, of course. I can email it when I get back home. Does everyone want a copy?"

Louise and Don nod. Thayer's focused on his phone, his attention somewhere else. Of course. *Maybe Nora's right and my style isn't his thing.*

"And now," Reggie says, using an announcer's voice. "The moment you've all been waiting for."

He grabs a music stand and a case from a hall closet. Setting the case on the coffee table, he removes several pieces of metal and fits them together. He sets music on the stand, adjusts the flute on his lips, and begins.

I don't recognize the song, but it's beautiful. I close my eyes to focus on the music. Reggie finishes the piece, moves sheets around, then plays a song that's familiar to me. Where have I heard that before? When I figure it out, I have to stifle the laugh that wants to burst out of me. Reggie catches my eye and winks.

He takes a small bow afterward, seeming to enjoy the applause of his audience.

"That was lovely, Reggie," Louise says. "When did you learn to play the flute?"

"Middle school band."

Reggie puts his stuff away before sitting down next to me. I nudge him and whisper, "Did you just play 'The Best Song Ever?'"

"I did. Think it'll help me win?"

I shrug. "I don't know. There were some pretty amazing acts this evening."

"Quite right." He clears his throat to get everyone's attention again. "Now that everyone's performed, it's time for our illustrious and impartial judges to retire to the kitchen and deliberate. The crown and sash are on the kitchen table, so when you've chosen your champion, please present the prizes to the winner."

Thayer stands up and extends his arm to Louise. They disappear into the kitchen.

"You were all so fantastic," I say. "I'm glad I'm not a judge."

"Your story was very engaging," Don says.

"I enjoyed the variety of performances," Nora says. "We have quite a talented group."

Reggie refills our glasses while we wait. I remember my special treat and walk to the kitchen. I rap my knuckles on a cabinet and peek my head around the corner. "Knock, knock. Sorry to interrupt. Just came to grab the chocolates."

Louise smiles. Thayer narrows his eyes, frowning. I choose to ignore his glare, grab the tin, and return to the living room.

"What do we have here?" Reggie asks.

"I picked up a few treats from my favorite shop. I wanted to make this evening extra special."

I remove the lid and give a quick tutorial of the truffle flavors.

Louise and Thayer return to the living room with the crown and sash. "It was stiff competition," Louise says. "You were all so wonderful, but there can only be one winner. Tonight's champion is…"

"Don!" Thayer says.

Thayer sets the crown on his head and places the sash over his shoulder. Louise claps and we join in.

"Congratulations," I say.

Don nods at me, a big smile on his face. "Thanks, you guys."

"Oooh, chocolate," Thayer says. He grabs one and pops the whole thing in his mouth. His eyes light with pleasure. I'd forgotten that he, too, is a chocoholic. He used to steal from my stash when we were together. I don't miss that. "Mmm, this is excellent."

"Are these the ones from that shop you like, Rachel?" Louise says.

I nod and point to a Blackout. "This one's my favorite."

Louise picks it up and takes a bite. Her eyes close and her lips curl up as she chews. "Delicious."

"So glad you like it."

"Speaking of things you like, Rachel, give us an update on Tom," Reggie says.

My eyes dart over to Thayer. He's looking at me with a note of interest. I break eye contact and search for a friendlier face. I find Nora, wondering if my mortification is clear from my expression. Am I really being forced to talk about my new interest in front of my ex? Nora tilts her head and shrugs her shoulders. There goes my hope of a rescue from this awkward situation.

"He's in Hawaii for work. He said he liked the story when I sent it to him. That's about it."

Reggie isn't satisfied with my answer. "Have you gone on another date with him?"

My discomfort increases. I need a distraction. Where's a sinkhole when you need it?

"Let's give her a break, Reg." Nora says. "She shared her story and brought these delicious chocolates. We don't also have to grill her about her personal life."

My knight in shining armor! Thank you, Nora.

"Fine." Reggie sighs and turns to Thayer. "What about you? Are you seeing anyone?"

"Reggie!"

"What? I need my gossip from somewhere, Nora."

He looks over at Thayer. "Tell us about yourself. What do you do? Do you have a girlfriend? Interesting stuff like that."

Thayer's eyes dart to me and away again. Does he look a little uncomfortable? I feel a twinge of joy. "I'm an English professor at

Warren Wilson. I also write books."

Reggie's eyes light up. "What kind? Mysteries? Adventure? Horror?"

"No, I write history books about war."

Reggie's nose scrunches up in disgust. "That sounds boring. No offense."

My lips twitch, but I keep my expression neutral. *Thank you, Reggie!*

"None taken," Thayer says, though I can tell he's a little annoyed.

"Girlfriend?"

"I've been seeing someone for a few months, but it's not serious."

My brain kicks into high gear at his statement. A few months? Did he already have someone else lined up when he dumped me? But he said he needed to concentrate on his new book project. Guess he lied and it really was me. I know I shouldn't care, but it still stings to hear he's moved on so fast. I know I'm supposed to feel better off without him, but, like Meg Ryan says in *When Harry Met Sally*, "Why didn't he want to marry me?" Okay, so I didn't exactly want to marry him, but you get the picture.

I've endured enough Thayer for one night. It's time for me to go. I hug Louise and whisper in her ear that I'm leaving.

"So glad you came tonight. And thank you for bringing the chocolates. I see why you rave about them."

I smile. "Please enjoy whatever doesn't get eaten by this crew."

"That's very kind of you. I'll return your tin."

"Rachel's leaving," Louise says to the rest of the group.

I hug Nora and Reggie and wave to Don and Thayer, who are chatting in the corner. Thayer ignores me. Oh well. I need to move on. Thayer certainly has. I grab my coat from the closet and leave, knowing I'll process this evening the entire drive home.

40

Tom

I'M DYING TO find out how Rachel's dinner group went last night. I was hoping she'd text me, but no luck. Does that mean it didn't go well? She's likely at work, but I can at least get the ball rolling.

Tom: How'd it go last night?

I return my phone to my pocket and begin setting up my equipment. I love being back in Oahu, my favorite place on earth. It's a little bittersweet with all the memories of surfing attached to it, but it also reminds me of good friends and feelings of joy. Especially when the days are as perfect as today—bright, warm sun and minimal clouds. The lack of wind means a sweaty day for me, but excellent conditions for surfing.

My pocket vibrates, and I smile when I see Rachel's name.

Rachel: The talent show was fun. The group seemed to like the story. They want me to send them the ending. Well, everyone except Thayer, of course.

I'm thrilled for the positive response, but wonder what's up with this Thayer guy. It seems like a jerk move not to encourage a friend.

    Tom: Who's Thayer?
    Rachel: My ex. The author.

I'm deluged with a surge of anger and a strong desire to protect Rachel from the creep. *Calm down, Tom.* How do I respond without sounding jealous?

    Tom: Yikes. How was that?
    Rachel: I panicked when I first saw him, but Nora helped me calm down and then I just did my best to ignore him. He ended up being one of the talent show judges.
    Tom: Who won the competition?
    Rachel: Don. He and Thayer are colleagues.

I scowl at my phone. How convenient.

    Tom: How did it feel reading your work in front of everyone?

I want to ask specifically about Thayer, but that seems too intrusive for a conversation over text.

    Rachel: I was nervous, of course, but got more comfortable the longer I read.
    Tom: That's great! I'm proud of you.
    Rachel: Thanks.
    Tom: Have you thought any more about sending it to an agent?

I wait for a response that doesn't come. There aren't even any ellipses pulsing on the screen. Did I push too hard? No, I'm just being encouraging. When three dots appear a few minutes later, I exhale in relief.

Rachel: I just don't think I'm ready yet.

I don't want to force her to do something that she doesn't want to do, but it's frustrating because I recognize her talent and believe her dream is attainable. I'll just have to keep encouraging her and hope she sees what I do.

Tom: I understand. I'm so glad it went well yesterday.

Rachel: Thanks. I have to get back to work. I appreciate you checking in.

📷

With the Pipe Masters in full swing. I spend my days taking pictures and the evenings editing and sending the best ones to the league's website and various sponsors. Jeff's on course to win the title and I think he'll do it. He's slaying the competition right now.

My mind often drifts to Rachel. I'm enjoying whatever's developing between us. The thought of returning to Asheville and spending more time with her excites me. Maybe I'll get an apartment in Asheville and stop imposing on Julie. Though if Rachel's writing career takes off, she could travel with me. The diverse locales could give her ideas for future stories.

Whoa, now. I'm not even ready for something serious again. Especially because I don't know what Rachel's angle is yet. I doubt she's interested in my career like Bethany was. I'm not a famous surfer anymore. Sure, my pictures were featured in a few magazines and I've won a few awards, but I doubt she knows about that. Unless it's something else she's researched about me. The thought sobers me. Maybe I should ask her what she knows about me. A tap on my shoulder interrupts my train of thought.

"Hey, Tom. Long time no see."

The voice freezes me in place. Did I conjure her with my thoughts? I turn around, dread pooling in my gut. "Bethany. Hi. What are you doing here?"

"Johnny's competing, duh." She giggles and pushes my shoulder like we're still friends.

I stiffen but try to keep my voice even and free of emotion. "Of course. How's he doing?" I know how he's doing, but it seemed like the polite thing to say.

"He's second, just behind Jeff."

Seeing Bethany is a shock to my system, though it's a miracle I haven't seen her before now. She most likely follows Johnny around to all of his competitions. *Just like she used to follow me.* I shake my head to get rid of the bitter thought.

"Did you hear we're getting married in January?" she says, thrusting her hand toward me. There's a diamond the size of a clam on her finger. Is she trying to make me jealous? I plaster on a smile.

"Uh, that's great."

"It is. So how are you?"

"I'm good."

"I saw you won a National Geographic award. Congratulations."

"Thanks." My tone is less than cordial, but I can't help it. I haven't seen her since our breakup and now she's flaunting her engagement? Why did she approach me, anyway?

"How did you use the prize money?"

Ah, there it is. Of course she'd ask about my winnings. All she cares about is fame and fortune. "That's none of your business."

She holds her hands up in front of her. "Just trying to make conversation. You don't have to be rude."

My last shred of restraint snaps. "*You* didn't have to dump me when my career ended. I sure hope Johnny stays healthy."

Bethany takes a step back like she's been slapped. Her smile morphs into a hurt frown. "Oh wow. *That's* your story? Good to know. If you need to blame me to feel better about everything, go ahead, but don't pretend to me you're innocent."

The initial remorse I felt from her surprised reaction dissipates. "What are you talking about?"

"The accident changed you, Tom."

That's the understatement of the year. "Yeah, I know. I couldn't ever surf again and you moved on to someone who could still win championships."

"You think I was only with you for what you could give me? That's messed up. It wasn't like that at all."

Feelings of abandonment and rejection swim to the surface of my heart. "It sure looked like that to me."

"You were depressed after the accident, remember? You were in pain and the physical therapy left you exhausted each day. I tried to make you feel better by bringing you photo albums from all the places you've been. Your surfing buddies sent you cards and emails after I contacted them. My efforts only seemed to make things worse. I couldn't do anything right. You said things that hurt me."

Her eyes fill with tears. Was I mean to her after the accident? My memory from that time is hazy, so it's not impossible.

"I became afraid to even visit you," she continues, "unsure of what mood you'd be in. I lost my fun, sweet Tommy. In his place was an angry, depressed, and unpredictable man. I didn't know if you'd ever be yourself again. When you refused to see me for more than a week, I decided that was it. I couldn't take any more. So, yeah, I broke up with you and tried to move on, but you can't honestly say I didn't try my hardest. I was there for you until you pushed me away too many times."

I feel the sting of sympathy, but then my eyes catch on her ring and I shove those feelings away. "If you cared so much about me, why did you date Johnny right after our breakup?"

Bethany scowls and sticks her hands on her hips. "I don't need to justify myself, but we were friends for a long time. He asked me about you and offered suggestions on how to help. He helped me throw that party for you when you got out of the hospital, remember? Anyway, he was there when I was trying to heal from our breakup. And, yeah, it turned romantic. He provided the emotional support you couldn't give me."

Some of what Bethany says feels true. I don't recall ignoring her like that, but my period of depression left gaps in my memory. "I kind of remember some of that. I didn't mean to hurt you."

"Forget it. It's in the past." She sighs. "I'm going to go. I'd say it was good to see you, but…"

"No, I get it. For what it's worth, I'm sorry."

"Yeah, sure. Bye Tom."

I watch her leave, my mind reeling. My narrative about that terrible time differs quite a bit from hers. Maybe I've blocked out my destructive behavior. I should reconsider pinning all the blame on Bethany, especially if what she says is true. My phone buzzes in my pocket, and I retrieve it.

Rachel: Hi Tom! Just thinking about you and wondering what you were doing right now.

My smile is automatic.

Tom: Hi Rachel! I'm on the beach at the competition. I was just thinking about you too. How's work?

Rachel: Busy like usual around the holidays. How many more days of competition?

Tom: We're in the quarterfinals and my buddy Jeff is in the lead.

Rachel: That's awesome! Tell him good luck from me. Hope to meet him someday.

Warmth spreads through my body. I like that she's interested in meeting Jeff. It seems like a sign that she's considering a future with me. Should I tell her about seeing Bethany? Another text comes through while I'm debating.

Rachel: My break's up. Gotta get back to work. I miss you!!!!!

The excessive use of exclamation points makes me smile. I really like this woman.

Tom: I miss you too.

I'll tell her about my encounter with Bethany the next time we talk. It's not that big a deal I talked with my ex-fiancée.

📷

I lean back in the booth at Nani's and groan, rubbing my stomach for emphasis. "I think I ate too much."

Jeff laughs. "Everyone eats too much here. That's the point."

"Maybe I'd eat less if I knew when I'd be back."

"Dude, you know you'll be back here next month for the Sunset Open."

I grin, caught. "Yeah, you're right. I'm just making excuses for why I can't help myself."

"I understand, bro. The food is delicious. Speaking of which, are you finished?"

I slide my plate across the table. "You're still hungry? How can that be?"

"I'm like a bottomless pit during competition. You know that. You used to be just like me."

"Very true. I guess standing on a beach with a camera all day doesn't burn quite as many calories."

"Speaking of which," Jeff says, speaking with his mouth full, "who was that I saw you talking to today?"

"When?"

"During the competition. She was tan, blond, and wearing a blue dress."

I sigh. Of course, Jeff caught our interaction. "That was Bethany."

"*Your* Bethany? No way."

"Not my Bethany anymore and yes way."

"Why'd she come talk to you?"

"I don't know. But she said something that's gotten me thinking."

"What's that?"

"After my accident, was I hostile toward you?"

Jeff furrows his brow. "What do you mean?"

"Bethany said I was angry and cut off communication with her at times, but I don't remember. I might have blocked that out."

"Well…"

"Please, just tell me the truth."

"You were low for a while, man. I know you weren't yourself, but it was hard to be around you sometimes."

I hunch forward. "All this time, I've been blaming her for everything."

Jeff shrugs. "She seems to be fine, and so are you. It doesn't help to dwell on things you can't change."

"I guess you're right." I shake my head. "Enough about that. Let's talk about *your* fabulous life. You're dating an incredible woman and practically the tour champion. You just need to reach the semi-finals and you're golden."

"Yep. I'm feeling good, but I don't want to jinx myself. It depends on the wave conditions too."

"You're being too modest. You can ride like nobody else, even in the worst conditions."

"Thanks, man. It's because I've had such tubular competition over the years."

My mind flashes through memories of us surfing together. "Seriously, though, it's been awesome watching you this year.

You're slaying the competition. When you win, are you going to pop the question to Lisa?"

"When I win. I like your confidence in me. And no, I'm not."

"Oh. Is everything okay between you two?"

"Yeah, things are fine. They've never been better, in fact."

"Then what's the hold-up? I thought that was your plan."

Jeff glances around the room before leaning in toward me, motioning me closer. He whispers. "Because we're already engaged."

I jerk back, surprised. "What?"

"Yeah, man. It happened last week."

I'm thrilled for my friend, but I feel a twinge of envy. I should be married right now, but I'm still very single. "Congrats! I'm happy for you and Lisa."

"Thanks. I'm pretty stoked. Anything new with you and Rachel?"

"We've been on a couple of dates."

"That's cool."

"It is."

Jeff sighs and rolls his eyes.

"What?"

"Come on, man. Tell me more. I know she works at a bookstore. What else? Details, bro!"

What should I share? I know he's trustworthy. I blurt out what's been on my mind most. "Her dream is to be an author."

"What kind?"

"I'm not one hundred percent sure, but she showed me an adventure story she'd written that was good. It could definitely be up on shelves with those already published."

"That's some high praise."

"The only problem is that she's hesitant about sharing her work."

"Do you know why?"

I release a long breath. "She says she isn't ready. She recently dated some jerk author who told her she wasn't any good."

"Hmm. I'm sorry to hear that, but there's nothing you can do besides be supportive and let her move forward on her own time."

"I know. It's just frustrating. Although…"

Jeff narrows his eyes. "I know that look, man. Whatever you're thinking, it's probably not a good idea."

"Charlie gave me info for an agent who represents her style of books. I have Rachel's story in my email…"

"No," Jeff says sternly. "You know you can't do that. It's a breach of trust."

"But I really want her to succeed. If the agent likes her story, it could be the push she needs."

"What if the agent doesn't? How would Rachel handle receiving a rejection she didn't expect?"

His words make me pause, but I dismiss them quickly. "I really don't think that'd happen."

"I don't know, man. She should make the first move. It's her dream, not yours. Going behind her back is a bad idea."

"Those are good points." He's not going to endorse my idea, so it's time to change the subject. "Have you and Lisa picked a date?"

"Yeah, we're getting married in February in Huntington Beach."

"Man, that's quick."

"Not really. We've been together for three years. February's before the season begins so we can honeymoon before I have to travel again."

"I guess that makes sense. Do you know where you want to honeymoon? Some place tropical?"

"Nah, man. Islands remind me too much of work. We're looking at places not on the circuit."

"That's cool. Well, congratulations again."

"Thanks. By the way, will you be my best man?"

The earnest look he gives me makes my throat catch. I clear it before I respond. "I'd be honored."

41

Rachel

LOUISE STEPS OUT of her apartment just as I reach my own. "Good evening, Louise."

"Hello, Rachel. Happy Friday."

"I'm so thankful it's the weekend. I have a half-day tomorrow and then can rest. Work's been so busy."

Louise pats my shoulder. "Sounds like you're worn out. Would you like to come in for some tea?"

"That's so sweet of you, but I'm not a tea drinker. I just want to get into my pajamas and relax in bed with a good book."

"That sounds nice, too. Are you reading anything good?"

"Just this month's selection for book group. It's *Starry Night* by Debbie Macomber."

"I adore Debbie's books. I haven't read that one. If you like it let me know."

"You can borrow it when I'm finished."

Louise nods her assent. "I'm happy to see you this evening because I've wanted to tell you how much I enjoyed your story. Thank you for sending the second half out to the group. It was very suspenseful. I rarely read those types of books, but I couldn't stop reading yours."

"Thanks for the compliment."

"Have you thought about publishing it?"

"I have, but I'm afraid of being rejected. I'm not ready for that."

"I think it's quite good and so does everyone else in supper club. Speaking of which, are you coming to dinner on Monday?"

The thought of seeing Thayer again makes me hesitate. "I'm not sure. I'll have to check my work schedule tomorrow. We have extended hours for the holidays, so I may work late. I'll let you know tomorrow evening if I can come."

"Okay, dear. I hope you'll be able to make it."

"I've enjoyed coming. Your friends are delightful."

"They're your friends now, too, you know."

I smile, hug Louise, and go into my apartment. I wish I could hole up in here all weekend, but work calls. It'd be nice to have fewer hours, but even if I do somehow become a published author, I know many authors still have other jobs to cover the sporadic income they receive from their books. Maybe I should query an agent to see if I have what it takes, but where do I find people interested in short stories? I guess that's what the internet is for. I add research on short story publishers to my mental list of tomorrow afternoon's agenda.

When I get home from work the next day, I dash to my bedroom and change into black yoga pants, my favorite gray hoodie, and some fuzzy socks with polar bears on them. Settling onto the couch with my laptop, I turn the television to the Food Network, ready to relax in front of a marathon of holiday bake-off competitions.

I type my query into the search bar. *Where do you submit a short story for publishing?* I'm not expecting to find many results, but it turns out there are quite a few journals and publications accepting manuscripts in the fifteen to fifty thousand word range. I click through several links and read through the submission requirements, saving the most pertinent options in a document. I'm not quite ready to pull the trigger, but I'm getting there. And a lot of this progress is thanks to Tom.

Why did I ever listen to Thayer? He seems to be the only one who doesn't think I can write. Maybe he *was* jealous, though I can't see why. He writes in a different genre and has even received an award for one of his books.

Was he trying to control me? Did filling me with insecurity and self-doubt make him feel manly? It wasn't a healthy relationship if that's true. I sigh. Why did I give a man so much power over my self-confidence? I've always been independent and self-possessed. Well, until I met Chris. Memories from that time surface and I stuff them back down. Today isn't the day to visit that part of my past.

Tom isn't asking me to be different, though. He's encouraging me to flourish and be my best. Thinking about him yields an involuntary smile. What's he up to right now? It's still early in Hawaii, so sleeping is my guess. I'll send him a text to read when he wakes up.

Rachel: Hey Tom. Just thinking about you and wondering what you're up to. When are you coming back to Asheville?

I hope that doesn't sound like I'm desperate to see him, though, I kind of am. He brightens my day and is fun to spend time with. And he's a good kisser. I drop my phone on the cushion beside me and continue my internet search. The agent Tom emailed about represents many of the best-selling authors in the action market. I feel incompetent compared to that list. She'd never want a nobody like me. *But they were nobodies at one point, too.* I obviously still have work to do in the self-confidence department.

I close my laptop and pick up the television remote, flipping through channels until I see *Little Saint Nick*. It's guaranteed to put me in a more festive mood. Now that I'm friends with Nora, I'm quite proud of her for making such wonderful films. *Yet another person to draw inspiration from.*

My phone buzzes. I pause the movie and pick it up.

Tom: Hey Rach! Great to hear from you. I'm taking pictures on the beach. Not sure when I'll be back. I'm visiting my parents for Christmas.

I may not see him until January?! That's depressing. I'm surprised at how strongly I feel about such a long absence from Tom. We've only been on two dates, so I can't be that into Tom, but my emotions seem to say otherwise. I'm not sure how to respond to his text. *Just be honest.*

Rachel: I hope you're having fun. I miss seeing you.

I hold my breath. What will he say? My eyes bore holes through the screen while I wait for a response.

Tom: I miss seeing you too.

I hug the phone to my chest, leap off the couch, and twirl around the room. When I realize what I'm doing, I stop. I'm undeniably smitten. My phone buzzes again. This time it's Louise.

Louise: Can you come to supper club on Monday?

Oh yeah, supper club. Work won't interfere, but I don't want to see Thayer. My lips twist while I think. I'll just say I can't make it without giving away why. I nod, satisfied with my decision, and send the reply. *Now I just have to avoid my apartment until supper club's over.*

📖

I leave work and head toward the Haywood Street Market. It's an indoor mall of shops, a bar, and a large food court area. I love it because I can get dumplings, gyros, pizza, and hard cider all in one place. Not that I'm planning to order all of that tonight. I just like the variety it offers.

Tonight is a gyro and cider night, for sure. I purchase my food and sit down at one of the community tables and study the surrounding people. The next time Abbie's in town, I'll have to bring her here.

When I tire of crowd watching, I pull a book out of my bag and read while I eat. I take the last bite of my sandwich and hear my name from somewhere nearby. Assuming it's directed at someone else, I ignore it until there's a tap on my shoulder.

I turn around in my seat and come face-to-face with Thayer and a pretty redhead. I try to school my face into a disinterested look. "Thayer, hi."

"I thought that was you. What're you doing here?"

"Eating dinner. Aren't you doing the same?"

"Yes, we are." He turns to the woman beside him. "Savannah, this is Rachel. Rachel, Savannah."

I nod at her. Savannah is taller than Thayer. She looks young. Like college student young. "How do you know each other?"

Savannah smiles at Thayer. "We met at Warren Wilson College."

I can't help myself. "Are you a professor too?"

"No, I'm a student. I took Thayer's English literature class last semester."

I swing my gaze to Thayer and see that his cheeks are pink. At least he has the decency to be a little embarrassed that he's dating someone fifteen years his junior. I'd thought our eight-year difference had been a lot. Maybe, the younger the woman, the more control he feels. I hope for the woman's sake that he's as smitten as she is and will love and support her, even if that wasn't my experience. It's not her fault he was a jerk to me.

"How are you and Thayer connected?" Savannah says.

"We're just old friends," Thayer blurts, giving me a pleading look.

I'm tempted to correct him, but don't want more drama tonight. "Yes. Old friends. Are you two a couple?"

Savannah wraps her arm around Thayer's waist. "We are. We've been dating for five months."

Right around the time Thayer sent me the break-up text. I notice Thayer grimace, which confirms we both know what the math adds up to.

The air is thick with awkward tension. Thayer clears his throat. "Are you here with Tony?"

I know he used the wrong name on purpose but don't bother to correct him. "Nope, I'm here alone, enjoying dinner and a book. I just finished my dinner, so I guess I'll head home."

I toss the book into my bag, chug the rest of my cider, and pick up my tray. "Enjoy your evening. It was nice to meet you, Savannah."

Without a backward glance, I discard my trash and push through the doors to the outside. My phone tells me it's only seven-thirty, still too early to head back. I pause, remembering that the only reason I declined the dinner party was to avoid Thayer. *And look how that turned out.* I'm not as fazed by that experience as I expected. Thayer and I are over and he's seeing someone new. Who cares? Maybe I can finally let go of everything involving Thayer, including his opinion of my writing.

I walk along Patton Avenue toward Pack Square, enjoying the window displays. The city is getting into the holiday spirit and I love it. Tiny smock dresses in one of the window displays catch my eye and am surprised by a pang of longing to have a reason to buy baby clothes. I could get one for each of my nieces for Christmas, though they'd prefer toys. Maybe someday I'll have a daughter and can buy her cute dresses. I need a partner first.

My mind turns to Tom. Does he want kids? His current lifestyle doesn't seem conducive to family life. He travels so much, he'd never see his family and I don't have a job that would allow me to travel with him. I realize how far my thoughts have wandered and shake my head to bring myself back to reality. I barely know Tom. We've kissed once and I'm already thinking about life as his wife? *Slow your horses, woman.*

I hug my arms to my chest, aware that my coat is not protecting me from the cold. I turn and hurry toward my apartment. Should I text Tom and tell him about my run-in with Thayer? I want to talk about it, and it's a good excuse to connect with him. I rummage through my bag for my phone and type while I walk.

Rachel: Hi.

My phone pings almost immediately.

Tom: Hi.

I'm relieved for his fast response. My fingers fly over the keypad.

Rachel: I just had an unusual encounter and need to share it with someone.
Tom: Unusual, huh? You've got my attention.
Rachel: I was out to dinner and ran into Thayer and his new girlfriend.
Tom: How was that?
Rachel: Awkward. She's a student who took his class last semester. They've been dating since right about the time Thayer broke up with me via text.

I add three surprise-eyed emojis.

Tom: Wow. That sounds very awkward. I'm sorry you had to deal with him. I hope he wasn't negative to you.

While working on my response, my phone dings again.

Tom: He broke up with you in a TEXT????
Rachel: Yes, he did.
Tom: What did he say?
Rachel: Basically, 'It's not you, it's me.'
Tom: He said that tonight?

I'm confused. I reread the text string and find the mix up.

Rachel: Oh, no. He wasn't negative tonight, other than pretend like he didn't know your name.
Tom: You've told him about me?
Rachel: He was at the last supper club and the group asked about you.

What does he think about being discussed by my friends? My guess is either flattered or creeped out.

Rachel: I hope you don't think it's weird that I've mentioned you to some friends.
Tom: No, that's not weird. I've talked about you to Jeff and my siblings.

What has he said about me? I'm afraid to ask. Does he see me as someone with long-term potential? I kind of hope so.

Tom: Are you working for the rest of this week?
Rachel: I am. Saturday too. It's the busy season for retail.
Tom: Gotcha. I have to go. Nice chatting with you Rachel.

My heart sinks when our conversation ends. I can no longer deny my feelings for Tom. We just finished messaging and my mind's already trying to figure out when we can do it again. At least we connected for a bit. I don't like the time difference. I also hate that I don't know when I'll get to see him again.

42

Tom

I HATE THAT Rachel had an unpleasant encounter with her ex, but am pleased she texted me about it. Perhaps it means she sees me as someone important in her life. I certainly enjoy sharing my days and activities with her.

I'd like to heed Jeff's advice to let Rachel carve her own career path, but am still frustrated at her lack of faith in herself. I want to help change that. Now that she's had two run-ins with someone who torpedoed her confidence, I really want her to have a win. I bet she'd gain the courage to submit it if someone in the business praised her work.

What if I have Charlie look over her story and give a professional opinion? It'd just be between me and him. If he thinks it's bad, no harm done. I won't tell her and will pull back on my encouragement. If he likes it, then I can casually mention it to Rachel. It's a brilliant idea! A win-win for sure. I compose an email to my brother, attach the story, and hit send. Now, we'll wait and see.

I check my email later in the day and am surprised to see he's already responded.

I read the story and liked it a lot. You were right—it's good. I sent it over to Pam in the fiction department to get her thoughts. I'll let you know when I hear from her. All the best, Charlie

My happiness sinks like a lead balloon with the knowledge that another person in the company is reading Rachel's story. That wasn't supposed to happen. It sounds like good news, but it doesn't quite feel right. Probably the fact that the story is now more public than I intended.

Should I tell Rachel about what I've done? She'll most likely be upset with me for not getting her permission first. If it's rejected as well, she'll be devastated. It's probably better to wait and see what Charlie's colleague says about the story. She'll send Charlie her feedback and he'll pass it along to me. Rachel won't have to know anything unless it's good news.

📷

When I open the door to Julie's apartment, she's snuggled under a blanket on the couch watching a Christmas movie. "Tom! What are you doing here? I wasn't expecting to see you until we're all in California for Christmas."

I shrug, dropping my bag on the floor. "I thought I'd make a quick stop back here for a couple of days. You know, experience the winter weather so I don't get spoiled by the sun and sand."

Julie tilts her head and narrows her eyes, studying me for a moment. "You're back to see a certain someone, aren't you?"

I grin. "Maybe."

"Wow, Tom. Coming all the way back here just to see Rachel. That's quite a gesture. Some might even call it romantic."

"I have tons of frequent flyer miles. Might as well use them, right?"

Julie comes over and hugs me. "Well, I'm happy to see you. By the way, if you have some free time, I could use extra hands at the shop. It's crazy right now."

"Sure, I can help."

"Thanks, Tom. I can always count on you. Now, tell me your

plans for while you're here."

Julie pulls me over to the couch and we sink down into the soft cushions.

"I want to ask Rachel out, but that's as far as I've gotten. I only have three days, so I'd like to make them count. Do you have any suggestions?"

Julie grins. "I thought you'd never ask."

From my spot on the sidewalk in front of Page Turner Books, Rachel is visible at the register. She gives each customer a smile while ringing up their purchases. Energy zips through my body, propelling me toward the front door.

I tug my hat down lower over my face and enter the store. The line to check out is a dozen people deep, so I decide to kill some time and let the crowd thin out. I walk toward the back of the store, trying to remember where the adventure books are located.

"Can I help you?"

I recognize the clerk from the other times I've been in the store. I look at his name. "Hi, Brett."

Brett's eyes widen, and then he grins at me. "Ooooh, hiiii. I didn't recognize you."

I put my finger to my lip. "Shhhh. I'm hoping to surprise Rachel."

He lowers his voice. "Oh, okay. Can I help you with that?"

"Yes. Will you tell me where I can find the adventure books? This store is a maze."

"Yeah, sure. Follow me."

Brett leads me down one aisle before making a few turns that lead us to the doorway that enters the cave-like room I remember. "Thanks."

"No problem." Brett looks at me expectantly.

I give him a questioning look. "I think I'm good now."

Brett shifts his weight from one foot to the other. "I'm a big fan. I didn't recognize you before with your short hair, but I followed your career. You were so awesome."

"Thanks."

"Well, I'll leave you to it," Brett says. "Let me know if you need anything else."

"Appreciate it."

Brett turns to leave, but then spins around again. "And I'm very sorry for interrupting you two at the Arboretum. Rachel's like a sister to me and it's hard to pass up an opportunity to give her a hard time."

I give him a friendly smile. "No worries. I have an older sister, so I know what you mean."

Scanning the shelves for the Lost Treasures series, I find the next three in the series and grab them off the shelf to read over Christmas. *Rachel could have her own book on this shelf if only she'd put herself out there.* I'll think more about that later. Right now it's time to surprise Rachel and ask her out again. I smile with anticipation.

There are only two people in the checkout line when I return to the front of the store. I pull a chocolate bar out of my coat pocket and set it on top of the stack of books I'm carrying. The person in front of me grabs their bag and leaves. I set my stack on the counter, watching Rachel from under the brim of my hat. She turns toward me and gives me a quick smile before reaching down to grab the books. She freezes and gasps. Her eyes dart up to me.

"Tom!" She lunges over the counter and squeezes me around the neck before drawing back, embarrassment evident by the shy look on her face. My cheeks strain from the width of my smile.

"Sorry about shouting your name," she says. "What are you doing here? I didn't expect to see you until next year."

My whole body tingles with pleasure at Rachel's enthusiastic reaction. "I had a few free days, so I thought I'd stop in and experience the winter weather I've been hearing so much about."

"I'm so happy to see you. I'd love to keep chatting, but it's quite busy in here." She nods at the line of people that has accumulated behind me.

I nod. "I don't want to keep you from your job. I came by because I wanted to see if you were free for dinner this evening."

"I have to work until seven-thirty, but I'm free after that."

"That sounds great. Shall I pick you up here?"

Rachel looks down at her outfit of black leggings, boots, and a plaid shirt dress. "As long as I can eat in this, that's fine."

"That's perfect." *You're perfect.*

We smile at each other until someone in line coughs, breaking the spell. I chuckle. "I guess you should ring me up so the line can proceed."

"Oh, right." She picks up the chocolate bar and sets it behind the counter. "Thanks for the chocolate, by the way. You didn't have to."

"I know. I wanted to do something special for you."

"Well, I appreciate it. Just seeing you is the best gift."

"I'll keep that in mind for the future." I give her a wink, then tap my credit card to the reader. Rachel puts the books in a bag and hands it to me. "Here you go. I guess I'll see you this evening."

"Looking forward to it."

I step back outside into the brisk air. *Well, that went well. Now to figure out where we're going for dinner.*

43

Rachel

TOM'S WAITING NEAR the curb with a bouquet of red and white roses when I exit the store. "For me?"

Tom extends them toward me. "For you."

I bury my nose in the bouquet and inhale. They smell amazing. I lean over and give Tom a hug and a peck on the cheek. When I pull back, he's smiling so big that his dimple is quite prominent. Without thinking, I press my finger to it, letting my hand rest along the side of his face. "I love your dimple," I say. Tom quirks an eyebrow. I blush and remove my hand from his cheek.

He takes my hand and threads our fingers together. "Are you hungry?"

"Quite. I only had a salad for lunch."

"Then let's go."

We walk to the end of the block and cross the street. My feet slow. "Tom, are we going to Haywood City Market?"

"That was my plan. It seemed like the best option for a last-minute dinner date. Do you not like it?"

"Oh, I like it very much."

Tom stops walking and looks at me. "Is there a problem?"

"Not exactly. I ate there the other night."

"If you're worried about a repeat meal, I'm pretty sure there are multiple options."

"There are, and many are quite delicious. The Market is where I ran into Thayer and his new girlfriend."

Tom's face softens with empathy. "And you're concerned you might see him again."

"Yes. Is that silly?"

He lets go of my hand and pulls me into a hug. "No, it's not silly. Do you want to go somewhere else?"

I'm enjoying being in his arms more than I probably should. It feels so right it's almost scary. The thought that I could stay like this forever concerns me. Is it too soon to have such strong feelings? I realize Tom's waiting for a response, but I've been lost in my own thoughts that it takes a minute to remember the question.

"No, it'll be fine. The last time I tried to avoid Thayer, I ended up running into him. Might as well eat somewhere I like. Besides, you're with me this time, so I won't be alone."

"No, you won't."

Tom kisses my forehead and my heart swoops. My stomach lets out a loud gurgle. Tom chuckles and releases me. "Let's get some food in you."

I push my plate away and stifle a yawn.

"I'm sure you've been working hard this week," Tom says. "Can I walk you back to your apartment?"

"I can hang out a little longer."

As soon as the words leave my mouth, a second yawn escapes. "I guess I'm more tired than I'd like to admit."

"Let's get you home. Do you work until seven-thirty tomorrow?"

"I only work until four."

"Great. Would you like to do something after work?"

He wants to see me again tomorrow? Yesss! I try to keep my inner freak-out under wraps. "I'd like that very much."

"Would you be interested in going ice skating?"

"Sure, but you're aware the closest one's in Greenville, right?"

"How far away is that?"

"About an hour."

"I'm game if you are, unless you'll be too tired?"

"No, I'll be fine. Let's do it."

We reach my apartment building and stop at the steps out front. We stare at each other until I lose my nerve and look away. "Thank you again for the flowers, Tom. They're beautiful and quite Christmassy."

"You're welcome, my lady."

He leans forward, takes my hand, and kisses the back of it. I laugh. He's so fun to be with.

Another yawn escapes my mouth. "Sorry," I say.

"No worries. Get some rest and we'll have more fun tomorrow."

"Yes, sir." I salute him, turn on my heels, and march inside the building.

When I make my escape from work the next day, I find Tom leaning against his SUV. Despite a rough night of sleep, I've been a ball of energy all day. Tom's visit feels the same as Christmas did when I was a kid—lots of excitement and an overactive imagination that won't shut off at night. I've been wondering all night if he flew back just to see me. Maybe I'll ask him later.

Tom opens the car door and ushers me inside. "My lady."

Feeling playful, I curtsy in front of him before climbing into the passenger seat. "Good sir."

I'm wearing jeans, a sweater, and wool socks for our adventure. Tom is also in jeans and a sweater. He looks quite handsome. He shuts my door and walks around to the other side of the vehicle. "You look nice," he says.

"Thanks. So do you."

"Ready for an adventure?"

"With you? Always."

His dimple flashes at me before he turns his focus to the road. We pass a few minutes in small talk until Tom gives me a sideways glance and clears his throat. My heart thumps hard, nervous about whatever he's about to say.

"You haven't said anything good about your ex-boyfriend, and I've been trying to figure out why you dated him."

So it's a dating history discussion. Does this mean that Tom's interested in us becoming more serious? I hate talking about past relationships, but there's never a perfect time. Might as well get it over with.

"Things didn't end well, but he was very different when we met. In hindsight, I wonder why I kept dating him once he became negative and dismissive of my writing."

Tom remains silent. I decide to start at the beginning. "He was very sweet and spontaneous, sending me flowers and surprising me with little gifts. He sent funny texts when he knew I was having a bad day. Things were nothing but sunshine until I showed him my story. I expected some constructive criticism, but he said my writing was too bad to critique."

I chance a glance at Tom. His face is stony, and his grip on the steering wheel is turning his knuckles white. I take a deep breath. "After he rejected a second story I gave him, I avoided talking about my writing, but things were never the same between us. He'd occasionally make disparaging comments about my 'author fantasy,' as he called it. You know the rest of the story."

"I can't believe you let him kill your dream."

I study Tom's profile. I like his straight nose, dark hair, and gold-flecked brown eyes. My stomach does a little flip. He seems agitated by my story, so I place my hand on his arm.

"Why would someone who likes me lie to me?"

"Because he was jealous of your ability? Perhaps his ego couldn't handle the competition."

I raise one eyebrow, skeptical, and shrug. "I guess I'll never know."

Silence permeates the car. I stare out the front windshield until Tom speaks again. "Can I ask you another question?"

"Sure."

"When we were at the park, did my Ms. Independent comment remind you of your relationship with Thayer?"

I guess we're getting it all out on the table today. I take a deep breath to try to calm myself. "No, that was from another relationship."

"Do you feel comfortable talking about it?"

"It's difficult, but I'd rather do it all now and be done. Are you sure you want to hear it?"

"I'm sure." Tom reaches across the center console and grabs my hand, giving it a light squeeze.

"I met Chris in my sociology elective at college. He was very charming and attentive. He'd wait for me outside of class so that he could sit beside me and asked if we could study for tests together, but we usually ended up just talking. Then he asked me out on a date. He sent me flowers and sweet texts. We were madly in love by semester's end. At least, that's what I thought."

The memories weigh me down, and I have to collect myself before continuing. "A few months later, things changed. He'd ask me where I was going and tell me to check in via texts throughout the day. Sometimes he'd show up unannounced to wherever I said I would be. When I had plans with friends, he'd pressure me to cancel them and hang out with him instead. He often made me feel guilty by saying that I was too independent and didn't need or love him. I ended up quitting the school paper to spend more time with him. My friends stopped asking to hang out after I canceled on them so much. Chris and I were together all the time, unless I was in class. One day he started making comments about how needy I was, that it was no wonder all my friends had stopped hanging out with me. Nothing I did made him happy—I was always too much or not enough."

Tom scowls. "That guy is a jerk who didn't appreciate you at all. I'm sorry he did those things to you. That sounds like a terrible experience." He squeezes my hand, and the gesture reassures me.

"It was, but I thought if I could just become the perfect balance, then Chris would become the kind, caring guy I'd met in class again."

"So what happened?"

"After a few more months of walking on eggshells, he said it wasn't working for him anymore and he dumped me. I went to his apartment to fix whatever had gone wrong and caught him making out with another girl in his truck."

"Ouch."

I give him a wry smile. "Tell me about it."

"What did you do?"

"Nothing. I was so emotionally beaten down by then that I felt I deserved what he'd done."

"You didn't. He was abusive."

"Yeah. My sister convinced me to go to therapy when I finally confided in her. The counselor helped me see the truth of the situation and work through some of the baggage I'd accumulated, but it still affects me sometimes."

"I'm so sorry that you experienced that, but I'm glad you found some support. Those were all lies, you know. You're not too much. You're wonderful, just as you are."

"Thanks, Tom. Though not everything about my experience with Chris was bad."

"What do you mean?"

"I moved up here to put him and that past behind me. If I hadn't done that, I would never have met you."

Tom smiles. "That sure would have been a shame."

The ugly parts of my life are out in the open now, and I feel lighter. Especially considering Tom's kindness and understanding. I smile, my heart grateful. He brings my hand up to his lips and kisses it. I lean over and rest my head on Tom's shoulder. I close my eyes, contentment washing over me and relaxing my body.

44

Tom

THE TEMPTATION TO sit and watch Rachel sleep in the seat beside me is strong, but I've been looking forward to skating with her most of the day. It's a prime opportunity to hold hands. I rub my hand up and down Rachel's arm to wake her. "Rachel, we're here."

Her eyes flutter open. She lifts her head and looks around. "Did I fall asleep?"

"You did."

"Oh, I'm sorry. That's embarrassing."

"No worries. Your snoring was quite cute."

"I was snoring?"

I laugh at the horrified look on her face. "No, I'm just teasing."

"Geez, Tom."

"Is everything okay?"

"Yes, everything's fine. I didn't sleep well last night. I may have been a little excited about seeing you today."

It feels good to hear her that. I'm choosing to believe that falling asleep in my car is a sign that she feels comfortable with me, not that I'm a boring conversationalist. I exit the car and walk around to open Rachel's door.

"Thank you," Rachel says, sliding out of the seat.

"Do you want to skate or eat?"

"Let's skate first."

We rent skates and take to the ice. Our start is a little shaky, but my muscle memory returns and soon I'm skating backward in front of Rachel.

"Show off," she says, but she's smiling.

I reach for her hands and we skate a few laps around the rink, then I turn back around so we can skate side-by-side. I'm enjoying being outdoors and doing something active with Rachel. I want a partner who is adventurous and open to new activities.

Rachel looks so beautiful this afternoon with cheeks rosy from the cold weather. She's wearing a white knit hat with a puffball on top that makes me grin every time I look at it. Her eyes seem even brighter than usual. I could stare into those blue-green pools for days.

My stomach rumbles. I wonder if Rachel's hungry as well. "Would you like to keep skating or get some food?"

She flashes me a smile. "I could eat. Like just about always."

"Let's return the skates and check out the food trucks."

Rachel chooses a barbecue sandwich with chips. I order a hamburger with fries. We find an empty picnic table and sit, eating in amiable silence while our eyes alternating between staring at each other and people watching. I'm mid-bite when Rachel emits a strangled gasp, her eyes locked on the crowd.

"What is it?" I turn to look for the source of her alarm, my body pulsing with adrenaline. "Is Thayer here?"

Rachel blinks her eyes, relaxes her shoulders, and chuckles. "No, nothing as terrible as that. Everything's fine."

"Are you sure?"

"I'm fine. I just spotted my brother and his family in line at one of the food trucks."

I turn back around before realizing I have no idea what they look like. "Do you want to invite them to join us? I'll hold the table."

"Are you sure? It'll be chaotic if my nieces join us."

"It'll be fine."

"Don't say I didn't warn you."

Rachel walks over to a man with reddish-brown hair, a woman with long dark hair, and two little girls. A sudden longing twinges my heart. I hope to have a family myself one day. That could be possible with Rachel. I enjoy being with her and can see us enjoying many adventures together. She must like children, because she's currently got both of her nieces in tight hugs.

She stands up, hugs the adults, and gestures toward me. I raise a hand and wave. Rachel returns to the table with one of the girls in a stroller. She picks the toddler up out of the stroller and sets her on her lap. "They're going to get their food and then join us." She looks down at the girl, a smile on her lips. "This is Lucy, one of my nieces. She's two."

"Hi, Lucy. I'm Tom." I look at Rachel. "I don't have a lot of experience with kids. What do I need to know?"

"If you can have fun, then you'll be a kid magnet. They just want someone to play with. Though here's your warning, Natalie is a talker. She'll bend your ear for as long as you let her."

"Good to know."

Rachel's brother sits down beside her, setting food on the table. His wife sits near me and helps the other child sit between us.

"Tom, this is my brother, Paul, and his wife, Jackie," Rachel says. "That's Natalie next to you. Guys, this is my friend, Tom."

"Nice to meet you, Tom," Paul says.

"Same," I say. "You have a beautiful family."

"Thank you. How long have you known my baby sister?"

I smile. Of course, there's an interrogation. "We met a few months ago at the bookstore where she works."

"Oh. Are you an author?" Paul glances at Rachel, raising an eyebrow.

Rachel scowls. "No, he's not an author. He's a photographer."

Paul returns his gaze to me. "Did Rach tell you she wants to be an author?"

"She did. I think she can do it. Her work is superb."

His eyebrows fly up to his hairline. "You've read some of her work?"

"I kind of forced her to share it with me. She also shared it with her supper club."

Paul looks over at Rachel. "Is that so? Well, good for you, Rach." He turns back to me. "I've been telling her for years that she has talent, but she doesn't believe her big brother."

Rachel rolls her eyes. "Anyway," she says, done with the conversation. "Natalie, how's kindergarten?"

"It's great, Aunt Rachel! I have two new best friends named Gabby and Ava. We have a pet goldfish named Goldie. And I can already count to one hundred. Do you want to hear?"

Before anyone can respond, she launches into it. "1, 2, 3…"

We listen to her work her way toward one hundred. I use the opportunity to study the faces at the table. The other adults are smiling and watching Natalie. Lucy is paying no attention to her big sister. Her focus is on eating all the chips from Rachel's plate. After what feels like an eternity, Natalie finishes up. "…98, 99, 100!"

"Bravo," Paul says.

"I'm impressed," says Rachel. "That's a long way to count."

Natalie beams with pride. She's obviously enjoying the attention. Lucy squirms on Rachel's lap, probably because she's eaten all the chips.

"I can't put you down, Lucy. It's too crowded here," Rachel says.

"I'm done eating," I say, looking to Jackie for permission. "I can take her to watch the skaters while the rest of you finish."

"She's sometimes shy with strangers. If she's okay with it, then I am," Jackie says.

"What do you say, Lucy? Want to go watch people ice skate?"

She studies me, her face inscrutable, before reaching her arms out toward me. I rise from the table and take her from Rachel.

"I want to go, too," Natalie says.

"You're not finished with your food," Paul says.

"Yes, I am. I'm full."

"The more the merrier," I say.

Natalie squeals and climbs down from the picnic table. I shift Lucy to one arm and hold my other hand out to Natalie. "Come join us when you're done," I say, my eyes on Rachel.

"We will," she says.

When we reach the rink, I push a bench up to the railing so that Natalie can stand on it. I set Lucy up on the edge of the rink, wrap an arm around her to keep her steady, and support Natalie's back with my other arm.

Natalie launches into a play-by-play of what she's seeing.

"There's a boy with a blue hat and a girl with pink skates. That girl is turning in circles in the middle of the rink. Look at the lights on that building. I've never skated before, but I bet I'd be great. Oh no, that boy fell down…"

I smile while the girl chatters on. Lucy seems content observing everything. It feels nice pretending to be a parent for a bit, especially because of the affectionate look I received from Rachel when I took the girls. I could get used to this.

A hand wraps around my shoulder, and Rachel gives me a side hug. Paul and Jackie appear on my other side behind Natalie. Jackie holds her arms out toward me. "I can take Lucy now. We need to head home and get these girls into bed."

Paul puts Natalie on his shoulders while Jackie straps Lucy into the stroller. "It was nice to meet you, Tom."

"So nice to meet you. Your girls are delightful."

Rachel hugs Jackie and then gives high fives to both of her nieces. "So great to run into you today. See you at Christmas!"

"Shall we head back as well?" I say.

"I suppose so."

The drive starts out quiet. Rachel's staring out the window

and I'm curious about what she's thinking. I don't have to wait long.

"I'm quite impressed that the girls warmed up to you," Rachel says, turning to face me. "Lucy's usually a tough nut to crack."

I shrug. "Guess I got lucky. They're a nice family."

Rachel nods. "Paul's a great dad and husband and Jackie is amazing as well. I hope I'm a good a wife and mom like her." She sighs.

"What's the sigh for?"

"Oh, just daydreaming about having a family of my own."

"You want kids?"

"I do. Maybe two or three. What about you?"

"Same."

She smiles. "Good."

"Good, huh?"

I lift an eyebrow in her direction and she turns away, but not before I see color splash across her cheeks.

"Anyway, this has been a fun evening," she says.

"I thought so, too."

"Thanks for coming up with the activity. I'm feeling more in the Christmas spirit after that. In fact, I think I may put my tree up tomorrow. Would you like to come over for dinner and help decorate it?"

"That sounds fun. What time?"

"How about six-thirty?"

"Six-thirty it is. What's for dinner?"

"I don't know yet."

"A surprise, I like it. Is there anything I can bring?"

"Dessert?"

"I can do that."

Conversation flows between us for the rest of the drive. Rain starts falling about ten minutes out and is coming down in sheets when I pull up to her apartment. "I'm sorry I don't have an umbrella in the car," I say.

"That's okay. I can make a run for it," Rachel says.

She unfastens her seatbelt. "Thanks again for a fun evening."

"I enjoyed meeting your family."

"Yeah, they're great. So, I'll see you tomorrow?"

"I'll be there with bells on."

Rachel opens the car door and dashes to her apartment building. Safely under the building's awning, she waves before unlocking the front door and disappearing inside. The date went well. The weather hampered my plans of walking her to her door, but tomorrow evening I'll be in her apartment. I can hardly wait.

45

Rachel

THE CHEESE IS bubbling on top of the lasagna when I peer inside the oven. Almost ready. I put the finishing touches on the salad and stick it in the fridge. After a manic afternoon cleaning the apartment, pulling Christmas boxes out of the storage closet, and preparing dinner, I'm ready for the evening to finally begin.

There are fifteen minutes before Tom's expected arrival, plenty of time to get dressed. I pull on my favorite Christmas sweater which is red and green with a cat in a Santa hat and the words *Meowy Christmas* scrawled across the top. I look through the Christmas-themed accessories in my jewelry box. Jingle bell earrings seem appropriate for my date with Tom. Satisfied with a check of my reflection in the mirror, I return to the kitchen to start the garlic bread. The doorbell sounds and I rush to push the button. "Hello?"

"Hi, it's Tom."

"Come on up, apartment 3C." I buzz him in the front and crack open my front door. I bounce on my toes to release some of my restless energy. Tom will soon be in my apartment! The oven timer goes off and I remove the lasagna to cool.

"Knock knock. It's Tom."

He's here! A wall blocks my view of the front door. "Come in. I'm in the kitchen."

Tom comes around the corner carrying a white paper bag with Little Shop of Sugar's logo on it in one hand and a bouquet of white lilies and roses in the other.

"Flowers *and* chocolate? You sure know the way to a girl's heart."

Tom grins and hands me the flowers. "I hate to break it to you, but the chocolate is our dessert."

"Let me put these in some water. They're exquisite." I kiss his cheek. "Thank you, Tom."

"You're very welcome."

I rummage through my cabinets for a vase. The aroma of garlic reminds me that dinner isn't quite ready yet. "Would you mind checking the bread in the oven for me?"

"Sure. It's lightly browned."

"Please take it out and turn off the oven."

I fill the vase with water and add the flowers. The dinner table has a white tablecloth with a border of Christmas trees and is topped with two place settings, minus the plates that are stacked in the kitchen. The flowers look perfect in the center.

Tom's eyes are on me when I turn back toward the kitchen. Anxiety floods my system. Maybe hosting Tom isn't the best idea. His presence in my home makes me feel a little overwhelmed. I'd love to replace it with the comfort we've found the past couple of days.

Tom smirks. Can he tell I'm nervous? "What?" There's an edge to my voice.

"Are you wearing jingle bells?"

I touch my ear. "Yes."

"I love it," he says. "However, I thought *I* was supposed to be the one with bells on."

My shoulders relax. This feels more normal. I make a show of looking him up and down. "Well, where are they?"

Tom pulls a bracelet dotted with small bells out of his pocket and shakes it to make them jingle.

My head tips back when I release a belly laugh. Tom's laughter joins mine. When our amusement dies down, my stomach gurgles. "I guess it's time to eat. I thought we'd make our plates here and then carry them to the table. Is that okay with you?"

"That's fine."

"I'll fix us drinks while you make your plate. Would you like water or wine?"

"I'll have whatever you're having."

"Wine it is." Maybe it'll help me relax some more.

When we're both seated, Tom looks at me expectantly. I look around the table. "Did I forget something?"

"No. I just wanted to make a toast before we eat." He raises his glass and clears his throat. "To you, for opening up your home to me and making a delicious meal. You are kind, caring, fun, and considerate, and I'm very glad we met."

He leans forward and clinks his glass to mine. He doesn't comment on my flaming cheeks. I'm not used to such effusive compliments. "Thank you. That was very nice, but you shouldn't comment on the food until you've tried it."

"Is there something I need to know? It looks and smells amazing."

"No. I'm just teasing. The lasagna is my grandmother's recipe. I make it all the time."

"If it's a family recipe, it must be good."

He cuts a piece of lasagna and puts it in his mouth. His eyes widen. He opens his mouth and pants like a woman in labor.

"What is it, Tom?" I stand quickly, the chair legs squeaking across the floor.

He shakes his head and motions for me to sit back down, which I do. He chews, swallows, and takes a big swig of wine.

"Are you okay?"

"I'm fine. I didn't think the lasagna would be so hot."

I wince. There goes our perfect night. "I'm so sorry, Tom."

He smiles. "It's okay, Rachel. I did it to myself. I really am fine. Tell me about your day while it cools."

"It was busy. The new book by Kaitlyn Beckett flew off the shelves. We ran out of copies before lunch. And a children's book about Santa's dog is also popular right now."

Tom gives me a skeptical look. "Santa has a dog?"

"He does in this story. The dog, whose name is Snowflake, hides away in the sleigh on Christmas Eve and causes shenanigans. It's quite cute, actually."

"I'm sure it's lovely. Tell me how your family celebrates Christmas. Do you buy gifts for every family member?"

"I do. There are only five adults and two kids, so it's not excessive. I buy books for everyone. I have a discount from working at the store, so it's not too hard on my budget."

"You get a discount, huh? Can you share it with family and friends?"

"I can." I quirk an eyebrow. "Tom, are you just dating me for my book discount?"

"That and to make sure you'll continue to keep my sister's store in business." He winks.

I lean back in my chair and sigh. "That place is heaven. I love that every time I open the door, I'm blasted with the mouth-watering smell of chocolate. If she could bottle her air, I'm sure it'd be a best seller."

"You really are a chocoholic."

"Guilty. Let's finish this food so we can get to the good stuff."

"Pardon me, but this lasagna seems like the good stuff to me. It's delicious, Rachel."

"Thanks. What did you do today?"

He sets down his fork and puts his forearms on the table, leaning closer to me. "Let's see. I took Sadie to the park, helped Julie at the store, and checked into my flight for tomorrow."

My smile vanishes. "Oh, right. You're headed to sunny California and then back to Hawaii. Two beachy paradises."

Tom holds my gaze. "I think it's paradise right here."

I look away, both pleased and embarrassed by his insinuation. I pop the last bite of bread into my mouth and look back at Tom, but he's focused on his plate, scooping up the last of his lasagna with his fork. When we're finished, I carry our plates into the kitchen, my head still spinning from his comment. I like what he's saying, but struggle to believe his sincerity. My other relationships began with lots of flirting and sweet words and look what happened. I know Tom isn't Thayer or Chris, but I still have a hard time trusting men's words and intentions.

Tom follows me into the kitchen with our wine glasses. "Can I refresh your glass for you?"

"Yes, thank you. I'll put the food away and then we can work on the tree."

"I didn't see a tree when I came in."

"That's because it's still in the box. It's artificial."

"Ah. I'll take our glasses into the living room and see if I can locate it."

When the kitchen's cleaned up, I pull out a snowman-shaped plate to put the chocolates on. The bag also contains a small, wrapped package. Did Tom get me a Christmas gift? I squeeze it to my chest before setting it on the counter.

The other item in the bag is a familiar gold box, which I open. There are four chocolates—two Blackouts and two dark chocolate pistachio caramels. My favorites! How thoughtful. I transfer them to the plate and carry them into the living room, setting them down on the coffee table next to the wine. I find a Christmas playlist on my phone and turn up the volume.

Tom puts the top piece on the tree. He stands back, his hands on his hips. "It looks a little scraggly."

"We have to fluff it."

When I'm satisfied with how the tree looks, I move it over to the wall near an outlet. We string lights on the branches, a mixture of colored and white. "The more lights, the merrier," I say.

"If you don't mind me asking, why are you putting up a tree this late, especially since you won't even be here for Christmas?"

"That's a fair question. It just doesn't feel like Christmas to me until my tree is up. My sister usually helps me, but she's been too busy with the basketball team to visit this year, and I just haven't gotten around to it yet. I'll probably keep it up until at least mid-January so I can enjoy it longer."

"I'm glad I could be part of your ritual this year. I haven't decorated a tree in years. It's probably because I don't have my own home."

"You don't?"

He shakes his head. "My sister lets me crash at her place when I'm here in exchange for helping at her store and walking her dog."

"Sadie isn't your dog?"

"Unfortunately, no. My lifestyle doesn't allow for pets, but I love borrowing Sadie when I'm here."

"That's understandable. You travel so much."

"I do. I love it, but I'm beginning to see the benefits of settling down somewhere."

He looks at me and the emotions swimming in Tom's eyes overwhelm me. I turn away and assess the lights on the tree, trying to wrangle my own feelings under control.

"The tree's looking great. Now for the fun part. The ornaments."

"Will you show me the ones your aunt gave you?"

I'm pleased that he remembers our conversation at the Arboretum. I take the lid off of a red plastic bin. "Of course. Hang up whichever ornaments you choose. I don't care where they go."

I point out the ones from my aunt as we decorate the tree. When the box is empty, I pick up the star and hold it out to Tom. "Would you do me the honor?"

"It would be my pleasure."

When the star's in place, Tom wraps an arm around my waist and hugs me to him while we look at the tree.

"It looks quite festive," I say. *Lame.*

"I think it's missing something," Tom says. He releases his grip and walks to the kitchen, returning with the small gift. "Open this."

I unwrap the package with care, not wanting to tear the red-and-white-striped paper. Inside is a small, white box. I remove the lid and gasp at its contents. Nestled in cotton is a white porcelain ornament containing a photo of us from the Arboretum. I take it out and cradle it in my hands. "Oh, Tom, this is beautiful."

"Turn it over," he says.

The reverse side reveals the lighted tree. My heart swells with affection. I launch myself at him, wrapping my arms around his neck. His hands bracket my waist.

"I take it you like the ornament," Tom says, his voice husky.

I pull back to look at Tom, my arms still around his neck. "It's beautiful. I love it."

He gives me his dimpled smile, and my cheeks stretch wide with my own grin. Tom's eyes flicker down to my lips and his smile fades. My eyes drift down to his mouth. When he captures his bottom lip with his teeth, my breath falters. My heart pounds in my chest. I look back up into his eyes which are now dark with desire.

His eyelids lower as he leans toward me. I'm a magnet unable to resist being drawn closer until there's no space between us. Our lips touch. Softly, at first, but then more insistently. My arms tighten around his neck. Heat shoots from my head to my toes. Our bodies are a perfect fit.

He removes his hands from my waist and cups my face, turning his head slightly so that our mouths fit perfectly together. One of my hands slides up into Tom's hair while the other wraps around his bicep.

Tom moves his hand from my face to behind his head and grabs my hand. My brow furrows, and I growl in protest when he breaks the kiss. He chuckles before removing my hand from his hair and bringing it in between us. "Something keeps bumping my neck," he says. "It's a little distracting."

I grin. I'd forgotten about the ornament in my hand. So glad I didn't drop it.

"Right. One sec," I say, pressing a finger to Tom's lips. He kisses it and I almost forget what I'm doing. I hurry over to the tree and place the ornament on a branch. I smile at our cheerful faces in the picture. Tom comes up behind me and encircles my waist with his hands, drawing me back against his firm chest. I shiver when his warm breath tickles my neck. He places a soft kiss just below my ear and I melt into him.

"It looks good," he says.

"Yes, it does." I turn around in his grasp and wrap my arms around his neck, kissing him lightly on the lips.

"So…" Tom says.

"So…" I echo.

"The tree's up."

"Yes, it is. Thanks for all of your help."

"My pleasure."

Tom's arms squeeze me a little tighter. "What should we do next?" he says.

I wouldn't mind kissing some more, but suggesting that seems a little overeager. What's something else that isn't as obvious, but still provides kissing opportunities? "Would you like to watch a Christmas movie?"

"Sure, that sounds fun."

Reluctantly stepping out of Tom's embrace, I grab his hand and lead him over to the couch. I position a blanket across our laps and turn on the television with the remote. I hold the snowman plate out to Tom. He smiles and picks up a chocolate. I take one as well, and queue up *Little Saint Nick*. All the lights are still on and it takes away from the romantic atmosphere I'm trying to set. I stand up and turn off the overhead lights, the Christmas tree's glow creating a more intimate setting. Satisfied, I sit back down and Tom readjusts the blanket over our legs. He laces our fingers together. I give a contented sigh and rest my head on Tom's shoulder.

When the credits roll two hours later, Tom hands me the blanket and stands up. "I should go."

"Yes, I suppose so. Especially if you have a flight tomorrow."

Tom groans. "Don't remind me."

"At least you're going to see your family. That should be fun."

I trail Tom to the door, wanting to squeeze every second I can out of his visit. He puts his hand on the knob, but then turns back to face me. I'm focused on his delectable mouth, so when his teeth graze his bottom lip, it's too much to resist. I pounce on him, my lips eager to meet his again. He falls back against the door and wraps his arms around my waist to anchor us.

"You're not making it any easier to leave," he says, chuckling, when we come up for air.

My face flushes, but I ignore the flutter of embarrassment. "You started it."

"How did I start it?" His eyebrow rises in challenge.

"You bit your lip."

"I–"

"Stop talking," I say, pressing my mouth to his. Tom smiles against my lips. After a few minutes, Tom's hold on me slackens. He pushes himself off the door and I step back.

"I wish I didn't have to leave you."

My fingers trace the side of his face. "I'll miss you, you know."

"I will too. You know…"

Hope flares within me. "What?"

"I don't *have* to be in Hawaii until January. What if I flew back next week, and we spent New Year's Eve together?"

"I would love that! I'll make plans for us." It feels like Christmas came early. My heart leaps in my chest.

"That'd be great. Though I'd be happy doing anything with you, even just curling up on your couch to watch a movie."

"Me too," I say dreamily.

Tom grins. "Thanks for dinner."

"Thanks for the ornament."

"You're welcome." He gives me one last kiss and leaves.

I close the door behind him and lean against it. That was quite an evening. I cross the room and run a finger over the photo of me and Tom. *Oh, man. I'm so into him.*

46

Rachel

EXHAUSTED FROM THE long workday, I drop my bag and coat at my feet and plop down on the couch. The store closed early tonight, thank goodness, and I don't have to return until the twenty-eighth. Hallelujah. I have New Year's Eve off, so Tom and I are free to be together.

I haven't yet settled on an activity, but I've done some research during work breaks and talked to my co-workers. Several restaurants are hosting parties, but I don't want to dance with a bunch of strangers.

Brett mentioned that he's going to a lock-in at the Pinball Museum. It's providing food and all-you-can-play games until one a.m. with competitions and prizes for high scores. It'll also have a big screen to feature the New York City ball drop. That would be a unique experience. It'd be fun to play against Tom and see how our pinball skills match up.

I grab my laptop off of the coffee table, pull up the website, and register us for the event before clicking over to my email. There are a bunch of ads from stores touting their "lowest prices of the season." I roll my eyes and delete them all. I completed my Christmas shopping weeks ago. Yes, mostly books, but who doesn't like books?

There's an email from Paul, probably some last-minute details about Christmas. I'm excited about celebrating with my siblings and parents. My phone rings and I dig around in my bag until I find it. Abbie's face smiles at me from the screen. I'm supposed to see her at Paul's house later tonight, so it's concerning that she's calling me.

"Is everything okay?"

"Hello to you too, Rach. Yes, everything's fine. I figured something out and wanted to share it with you."

I release the breath I was holding. "Oh good. I was nervous there for a second. What's so important that it couldn't wait until I see you?"

"You know those photos you showed me over Thanksgiving? One of them looked familiar, and I just remembered where I saw it. When I was in New York this summer for a conference, I went to a gallery housing the Sony World Photography award winners. Tom's sunset photo was there."

"Tom won a photography competition?"

"He's won several. I'm texting you some links."

I put Abbie on speaker and click the first link she sends. It's a newspaper article from a year ago about Tom winning the Georges Award in the Natural World and Wildlife category. The end of the article lists several other awards he's won.

"Whoa," I say. "He's a *famous* photographer."

"I'm impressed that he got a cover for *Time* magazine."

I'm stunned. "He was on *Time?*"

"Not him. One of his pictures. It's the second link."

I open it and see a black-and-white photo of a surfer standing on a surfboard, an enormous wave curling over him. "Trevor Graves Makes History," the cover announces.

Pride fills my chest, but it's mixed with uneasiness. "That's a big deal. Why wouldn't Tom tell me?"

"I don't know. He's accomplished a lot in his career. Most guys would brag about their achievements."

More emotions swirl through me—surprise, anger, hurt,

sadness. "I know. It doesn't make sense. I don't like that he's kept all of this from me."

"To be fair, it was pretty easy to find on the internet. Haven't you Googled Tom?"

"No. Why do people keep asking me that? Is that a normal part of dating these days?"

"I do it. Better to find out the dirt before you're too invested."

I sigh. "I guess I'm just old-fashioned."

"I found nothing bad if that makes you feel better. Anyway, see you in a few hours."

We hang up, and I mull over the new information about Tom. I don't like that he's been so quiet about his success as a photographer, especially since he seemed so against sharing his work publicly when I suggested it. It sounds like he's already done that himself. It just doesn't add up. I need answers.

I pull my computer back into my lap and return to my email. There's a message from someone named Pamela Green. The name isn't familiar but the subject line makes my heart beat faster. *Re: Criminals in Costa Rica.* How would a stranger know the name of one of my stories? Maybe it's some weirdly specific spam. Curiosity wins out over caution, and I open it.

Ms. Price, I had the pleasure of reading your submission and found it to be engaging and well-paced with a satisfying ending. It fits well into the action and adventure market. However, Quill Books only publishes full-length novels. Do you have anything similar in the 80,000-100,000 word range? I'm interested to read more of your work. I like your style of writing and the creativity of your story. Thank you, Pam Green, Acquisitions Editor, Quill Books Publishing.

My mouth hangs open while I reread the email. Is this some kind of joke? It sounds legitimate. I'm familiar with the publisher. But how did my story ended up at a publishing house? Did someone from supper club forward the story to someone with connections? My eyes narrow. This seems like something Thayer would do to humiliate me. But the joke's on him, because she liked it. Unless, of course, this is an elaborate hoax on me.

I open a new browser window and type in the publisher's name. Better verify the authenticity of the editor before I do anything else. I click on the official website and type the name into the search bar. It brings up an alphabetical list of employees. I scroll down until I find Pamela Green and a photo. She looks friendly enough, and she is an acquisitions editor. I guess the email's legit.

My heart flutters and a surge of energy lights me up from the inside. An actual editor likes my story and wants to read more of my work! I have a story that fits the length requirement, but it needs editing. Am I ready to take this risk? Since Christmas is tomorrow, I can take a few days to think through everything. This is exciting!

I'm desperate to share the news with a certain someone. I check the time. Eight o'clock. That's five o'clock in California. What's Tom doing?

Rachel: Hey, are you busy?

While I wait for a response, I scroll farther down the page. Sherri Gunther. Dan Guzman. Charles Haynes. Maureen Jakes. Teresa Lyons.

I pause, then scroll back up to Charles Haynes. Same last name as Tom. I bring the screen closer to my face and scrutinize the picture. The hair is lighter brown and his eyes are green but his jaw and nose look similar. He also has a small dimple in his cheek. Alarm bells clang in my head. My stomach is suddenly queasy. Is Tom somehow involved in this? All the excitement I was feeling leaks out of me at the realization that Tom might have submitted my work without permission.

My phone pings.

Tom: I'm at the grocery store. I'll call you in twenty minutes.

While I wait for Tom to call, my body alternates between being too hot and freezing, and my heart tries to push its way out of my chest. I shake my hands trying to get rid of the tingling in them. My body is a raging ball of anxiety. How do I handle this? Do I feign ignorance and see if he confesses on his own? I don't want to believe that Tom would do something like this, but the clues point his direction.

If what I suspect is true, how do I feel? Betrayed is the word that shoots to the forefront of my mind. I've told him many times that I'm not ready to submit. He should have listened to me. It's *my* dream, not his. How *dare* he make decisions about my work without consulting me! My anger is begging for a release. All it needs is a target.

I look at my phone. Only five minutes have passed. I stand up from the couch and pace around the living room. My hands are shaking. I consider walking to the park so that I can move around a larger space than the living room, but a glance at the dark sky outside squelches that idea. Besides, there's a good chance the conversation won't be pleasant, and I'd rather not have an audience.

The Arboretum ornament catches my eye. I march over, yank it off of the tree, and shove it in a side table drawer. I don't want to see his face right now.

I resume pacing, feeling like a tiger at the zoo, while I try to figure out how to start the conversation. I don't want to do or say something I'll regret later.

My phone rings and I pause mid-stride. This is it. I feel like I'm going to throw up. I swallow and take a deep breath before picking up the phone and stabbing the talk button. "Hello."

The formalness of my greeting seems lost on him. "Hey, Rachel. What's up? Are you just home from work?"

I'm too amped up for small talk. Best to just jump right in. "I was checking my email before I drive to Greenville and saw a message from someone at Quill Books Publishing." I'm doing my best to keep the emotion out of my voice, but it still wobbles a little at the end.

There's a noticeable pause before Tom speaks again. "Oh, yeah? What did it say?"

"It said that she read and liked my story, but it's too short for them to publish. She wondered if I had any longer works I could send to her."

"That sounds like good news."

His cautious tone of his voice is troubling. I'd think his first question would be about what finally convinced me to submit my story. Him not asking is a definite red flag.

"I suppose. However, I'm confused about how she got my story to begin with because I didn't submit it anywhere." There's silence on the other end of the line. I decide to throw out some bait and give him a chance to set things straight. "I wonder if a member of my supper club has connections."

"Could be."

My shoulders sag. I guess I'd hoped he'd be straightforward with me. "I guess I'll call around and ask."

"You don't need to do that."

"Why not? I need to know who did this." My voice is rising in volume along with the pain in my heart, but I have to get the words out. He needs to know how I feel. "It's my work and my right to determine who reads it and when. Nobody should have taken that from me."

"Rachel, it was me." His words slam into my chest and steal my breath. "I'm sorry. I should have asked you."

Anger overtakes the hurt inside. "Yes, you should have. Why would you do this after we talked about my not being ready?"

"I was wrong and I'm sorry. I sent it to my brother because I thought positive feedback from someone in the industry might give you the confidence you needed to send it yourself. I didn't think he'd share it with anyone else."

Anger heats to fury, hot and destructive like lava. "Oh, so my lack of confidence is *your* problem now? Am I broken? Are you trying to fix me?"

"No, that's not it at all. Look, I'm–"

I'm too keyed up to hear any excuses now. "No, you look. I explicitly told you I wasn't ready, and you ignored my wishes. This is my life, not yours. You pursued your dreams, I get it. Good for you. I wanted to prepare myself for all outcomes before putting myself out there."

Tom sighs like he's trying to deal with an unreasonable toddler which only increases the tension I'm feeling. "It's impossible to prepare yourself for every outcome. Sometimes you just have to jump in. And you got positive feedback, which is great."

"That's not the point and you know it. You broke my trust, Tom." My voice cracks on his name.

"Rachel, I'm so, so sorry. You're right, I didn't listen to you and I should have. You have the talent to get published and it would be a shame not to let the world read your stories. But you're right; it wasn't my place to decide for you. I was wrong and I feel terrible for breaking your trust. I'm really not that kind of person. It was a giant lapse in judgment. How can I make this right?"

He sounds contrite, but that's just because I caught him. His reasons may seem noble, but the fact remains that he deliberately went against my expressed wishes and tried to control an important part of my life. I've experienced more than my fair share of controlling men. I can't bear that kind of relationship again. I've come too far to get hoodwinked by another master manipulator.

"Tom, you went behind my back, and tried to control my life. I told you about Chris. No one will *ever* treat me like that again."

"I know that, Rachel. I wasn't trying to control you, just help."

I scoff. "It's not the intention that matters, it's the action and how it made me feel. I trusted you. I thought you were different."

My voice breaks and my eyes fill with tears. My next words are a whisper. "I guess I was wrong."

Tom's voice is pleading. "I *am* different. I was stupid and made a huge mistake. I'm not like your other boyfriends. I adore you."

I can barely see through the unshed tears in my eyes. I'm not sure whether they're from anger or sadness, but they're on the verge of spilling down my face. "It's my dream, and it's up to me to make it happen. In my time. What you did was selfish and self-serving."

"What about you pressuring me to put my work in a gallery? I don't want my work to be commercial. That's not my dream."

He's attacking me now? Deflecting blame, so mature. "I only suggested it once. I didn't rent gallery space for you. I didn't submit it to a photo contest. Though I hear you're already quite familiar with that process."

The phone is silent for a few seconds. "What?"

I can't believe he's making me spell it out. "I know you've won awards for your work, Tom. You had a photo on the cover of *Time* magazine, for goodness' sake. Why didn't you tell me? I have to learn everything about you from other people. Why don't you trust me enough to let me in?"

"I do trust you. I'm sorry I didn't tell you about those things, but they're really not important to me. Photography is my passion. I don't do it for accolades. And I hoped my success or failure wouldn't matter to you."

If he hasn't figured out I don't care about that stuff by now, he probably never will. Still, I feel a need to defend myself. "Tom, I don't like you for your success. I like how I feel when I'm with you. Why do you think I care about money or fame?"

There's a whoosh over the phone, like a long breath being expelled. "I don't think you're like that. I've just been paranoid since the whole thing with Bethany. But I talked to her, and she helped me see things from her perspective. I guess I was wrong about her, too."

His words bring me up short. "You talked to your ex? When?"

"Uh, about a month ago. I saw her at a competition."

My feet pace a new circle around the room, hurt springing up anew. He really doesn't tell me anything. "A month ago? And I'm just now hearing about it?"

"I didn't think it was a big deal."

My hurt solidifies into rock-hard rage. "You're saying that talking to your ex-fiancée doesn't register on the list of things you should tell the person you're dating? No wonder I know nothing about you." My blood is pumping with adrenaline. I want to destroy something.

"Rachel, it's not like that."

"How are we supposed to have a real relationship if you don't share anything with me?"

"I share things with you."

"Really? You didn't share the fact that you'd sent my story to your brother or that he sent it to a co-worker. You didn't tell me that you were a champion surfer and won awards for your photographs. And you didn't tell me about an apparently insightful meeting with your ex. All of those should have been high on the list of things to tell me."

"You're right. I'm sorry."

"Saying you're sorry isn't enough. I don't know if I can trust you. I don't even *know* you."

"Rachel, you know me."

"I thought I did. I don't know what to think anymore." My body slumps with fatigue, the adrenaline receding. A wave of sadness washes over me.

His voice has a desperate edge to it now. "I can explain."

I can't deal with this anymore. "I need to go. I'm done."

"Rachel, wait—"

I end the call and drop onto the sofa. I curl my legs under me, pressing myself into the corner. *Oh, Tom, why did you do that? I thought you were different.* Hot tears fill my eyes. I surrender to my heartache and let the tears flow.

47

Tom

SHE'S DONE? I pull the phone away from my ear and stare at the screen, confirming that Rachel did indeed hang up on me. I suck in a breath and blow it out. Jeff was right. I should have minded my own business. Yes, the editor likes Rachel's story, but they aren't offering to publish it. The inappropriateness of my behavior slams into me, and I cringe. I see now how unrealistic I've been to think she'd get a publishing deal out of the story. I want to blame Charlie for passing the story along, but I'm the one who gave it to him.

I feel terrible for going behind Rachel's back. Not only have I jeopardized our relationship, but I've become another guy she doesn't think she can trust. Can she forgive me? Is her trust in me permanently broken? I really wish I'd listened to Jeff, but that wave has crested and now it's too late. What can I do now? Anxiety and remorse jostle together in my body. I'm considering going for a run, but then the alarm on my phone goes, off reminding me I need to pick up Julie from the airport. Maybe she'll know what I should do.

📷

Julie opens the car door and plops down in the passenger seat. She reaches across the center console to hug me. I attempt a smile but my face muscles won't cooperate.

"Wow. I'm happy to see you too, little brother."

"Hi, Jules. Sorry. I really am glad to see you. I need some advice."

"Uh oh. What happened? Are mom and dad bugging you?"

I signal and pull out into traffic. "No. They're fine. It's Rachel." I take a deep breath and plunge in, telling her the whole story. "I feel terrible and want to fix it. What can I do?"

I glance over and see her face scrunched in thought. I hope she can see some way out of the mess I've made. I give her time to think while silently praying that a solution exists. When we reach the house, I cut the engine and turn toward Julie. "Well, what do you think?"

She gives me a weak smile. "You need to give her some space. She's obviously hurt. Giving her time to sort through everything might help rebuild the trust you lost. It's what I'd want."

It's not what I want to hear, but maybe she's right. "How much time should I give her?"

"There's not really a set timeline for healing, especially from betrayal. The ball's in her court."

My shoulders slump. "What if she never forgives me? I'm worried that I won't get another chance to prove that I'm trustworthy. I really like her and just wanted to give her more confidence in her writing."

Julie puts her hand on my shoulder. "Most women don't want men to fix things for them. They often just want them to listen and be verbally supportive. I'm sorry this is happening to you. I hope she gives you another chance and it works out, but right now, the focus should be on her. Give her time and be ready with a sincere apology."

"How long do I wait before giving up hope that she'll give me a second chance?"

"How long are you willing to wait?"

Her words sting. I'm not great at patience, but Rachel's worth whatever it takes. "As long as I need to."

"Good answer."

48

Rachel

A SMALL BUBBLE of joy rises in my chest when my eyes catch the festive lights adorning the front of Paul's house. I'm certain it's pure chaos inside with two little kids preparing for Santa's arrival. I can't wait to be part of it. Hopefully, it'll keep my mind off of what happened with Tom. I force my personal heartache to the back of my mind, paste on a smile, and open the door.

"Hello everyone."

"Rachel!" My mom is the first one to reach me and pulls me into a hug.

"Looks like I'm not the last one here. Where's Abbie?"

"She should be here soon. She got a later start than she'd intended."

"You're just in time to help the girls set up the milk and cookies for Santa before they skedaddle to bed," Jackie says.

"And carrots for the reindeer," Natalie adds.

I lean down and scoop my niece up into a bouncy, twirly, giggly hug. "Oh goody! Let's find all the stuff."

"We have a special plate Natalie made in preschool last year," Jackie says, pointing at the kitchen counter.

The design shows Santa and one of his reindeer, both made from small handprints. "Wow, this is really neat. Great job, Natalie."

Natalie beams. "I can get the carrots."

Jackie opens the fridge and pulls out a container of cut vegetables. Natalie counts out eight carrot sticks and arranges them on top of the handprint reindeer. "We'll put the cookie on top of Santa so he'll know it's for him."

"Excellent idea, Natalie. Where are the cookies?"

Jackie grabs another container and leans down to Lucy, who has joined us in the kitchen. "Can you pick out a cookie for Santa?"

Lucy selects a sugar cookie star and hands it up to me to set on the plate. "Thank you, Lucy."

I grab a glass from the cabinet and pour milk into it. "Do we have everything?" I ask Natalie.

She nods and skips back to the living room. I follow with the glass and plate. Natalie pats a spot on the coffee table. "Put them here."

"Yes ma'am."

"Alright girls," Jackie says. "It's bedtime. Say goodnight to everyone."

"Good night Nat and Lucy," I say, kissing each girl before they move onto the rest of the adults. My heart swells with love for my nieces, but a sharp pang follows. A reminder of how far away I am from having my own family.

When I wake the next morning, the house is quiet. The girls must still be asleep. I go downstairs to start the coffee. When I enter the kitchen, Abbie's already on the job. "Merry Christmas, Abbie."

"Merry Christmas to you too, Rach. I must admit I was a bit surprised to hear you'd be joining us. I thought you'd want to spend the holiday with your new beau."

My lips curve down. "He's spending it with his family in California. Besides, that whole thing is over, I think."

Abbie's eyes widen in surprise. "Oh, no. What happened?"

I fill her in on my phone call with Tom. "I don't know what to do. Now that I've calmed down and had some time to process, I think his heart was in the right place, but the execution was quite flawed. I really like him, but he broke my trust. Plus, I still don't understand why he's been keeping things from me. I mean, I only found out he talked with his ex-fiancée by accident."

"He talked to someone he *almost married* and didn't tell you?"

See, my sister gets it. "Yup."

"Wow. I'm sorry, Rach."

"It was just a lot all at once and I feel like maybe I don't really know him, you know?"

Abbie nods. "I can understand that. Keeping so much from you and going behind your back are pretty sketchy. I wish I could help."

"I don't expect you to know what to do. It's nice to have someone to confide in."

"You know I'm always here for you."

I give her a grateful smile and bump her shoulder with mine. "I know."

"Putting aside the Tom issue for the moment, I think it's great that an editor seems interested."

"Yeah, that part is pretty exciting."

"Are you going to send her another story?"

I lift my shoulders and scrunch up my nose. The thought feels a little scary, but also gives me a spark of excitement. "I might as well, right? I may not get another shot like this."

"True. Maybe if it works out, you'll be able to cut Tom a little slack. Especially if he ends up being partially responsible for your big break."

I tilt my head, frowning a bit. "That's a big if, Abbie. I suppose someone believing in me is better than someone trying to sabotage me, but I just hate when people try to control me. I need some time to figure out whether it was just an honest mistake or if he's more like Chris than I want to admit. I will never be in another relationship like that."

"That's reasonable. It doesn't sound like malicious intent on Tom's part, but it's better to be safe than sorry. And it may benefit him to be in the doghouse for a bit and think about what he could lose."

She winks at me, and I can't help but grin. "You're so bad, Abbie."

After way too few days, I'm once again driving up I-26 toward Asheville. I didn't hear from Tom at all, not even on Christmas. Maybe he wasn't as invested in the relationship as I was if he can let go of me so easily.

My mind returns to that terrible conversation. I thought I'd found someone considerate who supported my author dream, but his version of support looked more like control. I suppose others might see it as generous of him to use his contacts on my behalf and get my foot in the publishing world. It just felt manipulative to me.

If I'm being honest, it's probable I'm projecting some latent anger and frustration on Tom. I never got to confront Chris or Thayer about the way they treated me. Perhaps I shouldn't allow my past relationships to affect my present so much. But setting aside all the publisher drama, I'm still quite bothered at how little Tom shared with me. Would I always find out important things from others? I can't be with someone who hides so much of himself. I told him about my Thayer encounters right away. I only want the same courtesy.

This quandary requires more time, but there's something I can do now. When I get home, I'll look at my manuscripts and choose one to polish and send to Pam. It's almost a new year. Time to let go of the past and seize a brighter future.

49

Tom

MY POCKET BUZZES and I yank the phone out, hoping with all my might that it's Rachel. I'm doing my best to give her the space she needs, but my fingers twitch with the desire to reach out to her via text nearly every second of the day. I've been rereading our emails and text string to feel close to her. I really miss her. I hope my mistake didn't kill our relationship. I'm almost tempted to go see her on New Year's Eve and beg for her forgiveness, but Julie would shoot down that idea. I glance at the screen and sigh. Not Rachel.

Jeff: Hey man. Save the date for February 14th and 15th! Rehearsal and dinner on the 14th, wedding and reception on the 15th in Oahu.

I blink, confused, and reread the text. Hawaii?

Tom: Congrats, man! I'll be there. Not California?

I look up from my phone to the waves crashing on the sand in front of me. I'd come to the shore earlier to think. It always gives me clarity, though all I've been doing for the past hour is berating myself over how epically I screwed up. The vibration of the phone in my hand draws me back to the present.

Jeff: We'll already be in HI for the Volcom Pipe Pro, so we figured we'd just stay and get married afterward.
Tom: Cool.
Jeff: Will Rachel be your plus one? I'm stoked to meet her!

I sigh and shake my head. I need to tell Jeff, but I can't do it over text.

"Whoa, you're calling me? You either have really good or really bad news?"

I wince. "Well, it's not great."

"What happened?"

I relay the story, including my conversation with Julie. "And now I'm in limbo. I hope she'll call, but Julie says there's nothing I can do in the meantime."

"Your sister's advice seems solid. I'm sorry, bro. I hope it works out for you, though."

"Me too. Anyway, I don't want to be a bummer when you're talking about getting married. I'm very excited for you. What do you need me to do?"

"Not much. We're keeping it pretty casual. Khaki shorts, a Hawaiian shirt, and flip-flops for the groomsmen. I'm sure you can handle that."

"You know it."

"Good. And we'll keep a seat next to you just in case. I'm rooting for you, Tom. You haven't been this into someone since..."

"I know. That's what makes me nervous."

"Dude, Rachel's not like Bethany. Let go of your hurt and make room for love. I know that involves risk, but the reward is more than worth it."

Could Rachel and I be together again by Jeff's wedding? I sure hope so.

50

Rachel

I'M SO TIRED my feet are like cement blocks I have to drag up the two sets of stairs to my apartment. It was a busy New Year's Eve at the bookstore. I'd offered to cover a co-worker's shift so I wouldn't be sitting at home moping about not being with Tom. Brett tried to convince me to join him at the arcade after work tonight, but I'm not in the mood. It'd just make me miss Tom more. My new plans are Chinese food and a movie. My key's in the lock when Louise comes into the hall dressed to the nines.

"Did you pick up dinner?" she asks.

That seems like an odd question, but I'm too tired to follow up. "Yes, on my way home from work."

"You worked today? I thought you had the day off."

Why would she think that? We haven't talked since before Christmas. "I covered someone's shift last minute."

"Huh. I thought I saw you here a couple of hours ago."

"It couldn't have been me. I was at work."

"Hmm. Guess I'm getting old. What are you doing tonight?"

I hold up the bag of takeout. "You're looking at it. What about yourself? You look gorgeous, so you must have plans."

"Thank you." Louise pats her coiffed hair. "The supper club gang is all meeting at Reggie's house to play games and watch the ball drop. Though you already know that because you got the invitation."

"That's right. I had plans, but they fell through. Obviously."

"Oh dear. I'm sorry."

Louise's genuine concern constricts my heart, and my eyes prick with tears. I blink rapidly to keep them from falling. "It's fine."

"Did something happen between you and Tom?"

I swallow the lump in my throat and nod.

"Oh, Rachel. I'm so sorry."

I wave my hands in front of my face to hold my tears in. "It happens. I'll be fine."

Louise pats my arm, concern clear on her face. "Would you like to come with me? The group would love to have you."

"That's kind of you, but I just want to lie around by myself in my pjs."

"Whatever you think is best. I guess I'm off then, but know you can call me if you need anything."

Louise wraps me in a firm embrace then heads down the stairs after tossing one last worried look my way. I step inside and close the door, taking a few deep breaths to regulate my emotions. Lights are on in the living room. I'm sure they were off when I left for work, but who knows? I've been a little scatterbrained lately. I set the food on the kitchen counter before removing my coat and hanging it in the closet. There's a face in front of mine when I close the door. "Boo!"

I jump and scream, smacking Abbie on the shoulder. "You scared me! What are you doing here?"

Abbie grins like the Cheshire Cat. "I wanted to surprise you. Looks like I succeeded. I thought you'd like some company to ring in the New Year." She sniffs the air. "Is that Chinese food I smell?"

"Yes. Lo mein and dumplings. Would you like to split it with me?"

"My favorites! Yours, too, I guess."

"Indeed." My eyes widen as everything clicks into place. "Hey Abs, did my next-door neighbor see you when you arrived? An older woman with short, white hair."

"Yeah. I waved, and she asked why I wasn't at work."

"Now my conversation with her makes sense."

Abbie smacks her forehead. "I didn't even consider her mistaking me for you. I forget that we're hard to tell apart sometimes. Sorry about that."

I laugh. "Don't worry about it. I'll explain everything to Louise the next time I see her. What do you want to do tonight? Please say 'hole up in the apartment.'"

"Yeah, that's fine. How about we eat the food you brought and watch *When Harry Met Sally*? It seems like a good New Year's Eve movie."

I smile. How can I say no to my favorite movie? "It sounds like the perfect evening."

"Where do you and your own Harry stand these days?"

"We're still in the place between Jess and Marie's wedding and New Year's Eve when Sally's not speaking to Harry."

She frowns, her eyes soft with sisterly concern. "Yikes."

"Tell me about it. Anyway, I'm starving. Can we talk about my disastrous love life after we eat and watch the movie?"

"No problem."

When the credits roll an hour and a half later, I flick off the TV and give a contented sigh. "I wish life was as easy as it looks in the movies."

"You mean to tell me Tom hasn't called or texted or left karaoke messages on your answering machine?"

I roll my eyes. "Nope. I thought he'd at least text me *Merry Christmas*, but he didn't. What do you think that means?"

"It could mean he's being respectful and trying to give you space. Or it could mean he's assumed you can't forgive him and moved on."

My heart constricts. "Do you really think he's moved on? Was he not that into me? Is that why he shared so little?"

Abbie throws her hands up and sighs. "Rach, I don't know. I hope he cares for you and wants to fix the relationship, but he's the only one who can tell you the truth."

I slump back against the couch. "Yeah, I know."

"You deserve to be with someone who respects you and treats you well, someone who's open and honest. If you think that's Tom, then contact him. It's obvious you have deep feelings for him."

"Am I that transparent?"

"You're my twin. I know you inside and out."

"How can I know if he's trustworthy? How can I get him to open up more?"

Abbie shrugs. "I can't help you with either of those."

"I know. It's up to me to decide whether it's worth the effort to find out."

My sister seems to sense my need to think and turns back to the TV. She picks up the remote and finds Ryan Seacrest and friends keeping the crowd hyped up in Times Square. I zone out the noise from the TV, mentally reviewing the past few months with Tom instead. This year didn't end the way I thought it might. Maybe next year will bring better things.

51

JANUARY

Tom

CHARLIE'S CALL HAS me grinning from ear to ear. Not only is my brother engaged, but they're having a small ceremony next weekend in New York City. First it was Jeff and now it's my brother. Is there something in the air? Love, apparently.

Charlie and Serena have been together for less than a year, which seems fast to me. I said as much to my brother, but Charlie convinced me it's a rational, well-thought-out decision. They're a good fit for one another, have a lot in common, and love the life they've created together. I'm definitely letting my own experiences color the relationships around me. Bethany and I didn't work out, but that doesn't mean all relationships are doomed. Besides, my conversations with Bethany and Jeff have changed my view of our relationship. I can now admit to myself that I wasn't the greatest fiancé after the accident.

All these thoughts on love and relationships turn my mind toward Rachel. It's been three weeks since that terrible phone call before Christmas and I still haven't heard from her. I'm second-guessing myself about giving her space via no communication. It felt wrong not wishing her a merry Christmas. Was her holiday as depressing as mine?

It seems wrong not pursuing Rachel. I should be showing her

I want to continue our relationship, not hanging out twiddling my thumbs. Jeff and my sister both agree about giving Rachel space, but it doesn't sit right with me. However, the last time I ignored Jeff's advice, I got into this mess. I really wish I knew what Rachel was thinking and whether she'll give me a chance to make things right between us.

📷

I push the buzzer for my brother's apartment. There's some static and then I hear Charlie's voice. "Hello?"

"It's Tom."

"Hey, little brother. Come on up."

I push the door open when it unlocks and climb the stairs to apartment 201. The door swings open and Charlie pulls me into a bear hug.

"Cutting it a little close, aren't you?" he says.

"Flights from Hawaii to New York take a little time, you know. I'm just glad I didn't have any delays or cancelations."

Charlie grins and slaps me on the back. "I'm just teasing. Welcome to the city. When were you here last?"

"When you moved here for your job."

"So, seven years then?" Charlie clutches his chest. "I'm crushed that I have to get married for you to visit."

I know he's joking, but I could make more effort to see my brother. "Sorry, man."

"I'm glad you're here today, at least. We'll leave for the ceremony in a couple of hours. Grab some food, sit down, and relax."

"Thanks. Where's everybody else?"

"Serena's getting ready with her family, Mom and Dad went out for lunch, and Julie said she wanted to pop over to Kee's Chocolates and compare their truffles with hers."

"For our sakes, I hope she likes hers better."

Charlie snorts. "I know, right? By the way, when you talk to Rachel next, tell her congratulations for me."

"Congratulations for what?"

"She didn't tell you?"

"Tell me what?"

"That she's officially going to be a published author?"

I step back, struck by the news. "She got a book contract?"

"Yeah, for the manuscript she submitted to Pam."

This doesn't compute. Rachel said Pam didn't accept her story. "I thought Pam said Rachel needed something longer than novella length?"

Charlie looks at me quizzically. "She did. Rachel sent her a ninety-thousand-word novel. Surely she told you all this."

I strip off my coat and pull at the collar of my shirt. Is it hot in here? "We had an argument before Christmas and haven't spoken since."

Charlie sits down on the couch and motions for me to join him. "What happened?"

I sigh and plop down next to him. "She was upset that I sent you her story without asking."

Charlie's eyebrows shoot sky high. "Wait a minute. She didn't know you sent it to me?"

I slouch down, wishing the couch would swallow me whole. "I was trying to help Rachel gain some confidence in her writing abilities. I thought if she received some positive comments from a publishing house, it would help her take the next step. Obviously, it was the wrong move and now she feels betrayed."

Charlie nods. "Okay, yes. That was definitely a bonehead move."

"I realize that now. She also accused me of keeping things from her."

"Did you?"

I hesitate. "Not purposefully."

"What didn't you tell her?"

I tick my omissions off on my fingers. "Let's see. I didn't tell her about my surfing past. I didn't tell her about my photography accomplishments. And I didn't tell her about Bethany."

Charlie's face morphs into disappointment. "She didn't know you were engaged? Little brother, that's something you should definitely tell the woman you're dating."

"I told her I'd been engaged. Eventually. I ran into Bethany at a competition last year but didn't tell Rachel right away."

"We'll come back to that later. Tom, that's some major stuff. How did she find out you kept all that from her?"

"The internet maybe?"

Charlie frowns in disbelief at my cluelessness. "*Why* didn't you tell her?"

My body is tight with tension, so my attempt at a nonchalant shrug is a twitch. "I guess I didn't want her to be with me because I have money and success. I wanted her to like me as a person."

Charlie's got his wise-big-brother look pointed at me. "How can she like the real you if you hide things from her?"

"I suppose that's a valid point."

"You apologized, right? Sent her some flowers, made some gestures of contrition, maybe groveled a little."

"No." Charlie's eyes bulge and I spit out my explanation. "I mean, I tried to apologize over the phone, but she hung up on me, so I gave her some space. Now maybe I've waited too long?"

The exasperated look on Charlie's face confirms my fear. "Tom."

"Charlie."

"Do you like Rachel?"

"Yes. Very much."

"Then you should apologize again. And you should make it a big one to show her you're sincere. In person, if possible. She's probably been waiting for an explanation or for you to show her she's important to you."

"Julie said I should let Rachel make the next move."

Charlie rears back. "You took advice from Julie? Tell me, how have her relationships gone?"

I think about it for a second. Since her divorce, Julie hasn't shown one iota of interest in another man. Maybe she'd want to be left alone, but she isn't Rachel. "Good point."

"What do you think Rachel's thinking, since all you've given her is silence?"

My eyes round. "That I don't care about her. Oh man, I've really screwed this up."

"Well, if she still likes you and you do a good job of apologizing, maybe she'll forgive you. But you have to do *some*thing."

"What should I do?"

"Only you can figure that out, but it needs to be heartfelt and personal—both from you and for her."

"It sounds like I've got some work to do. Thanks for your help, Charlie."

"No problem. Now, buck up, little brother. I'm getting married today!"

52

Rachel

MY BOOK CLUB read is lying open in front of me, but I keep staring off into space and forgetting what I've read. *Gert Macabee's Big Year* by Joanna Smoot is the Book Babes' latest pick, but I'm not in the mood for uplifting fiction with a romantic subplot. This cold, rainy day is a better match for my emotions and stirs up a longing for a warm blanket in front of a crackling fire. Too bad my apartment doesn't have a fireplace. I'll just have to settle for a blanket and a steaming cup of coffee when my shift ends.

The front door whooshes open, breaking my latest bout of daydreaming. A man in a navy rain jacket and matching ball cap stops at the counter in front of me and sets down a vase of roses and a small white bag. The pink and white blossoms look quite cheerful on this dreary day.

"I have a delivery for Rachel Price."

I slide the vase closer toward me, inhaling the sweet fragrance of the flowers. It's not my birthday or a holiday, just a dreary January afternoon. If Tom and I were still dating, I'd guess he sent them, but I haven't heard from him in a month. Not that I'm counting the days or anything.

"What are those for?"

My head swivels left, and my shoulders drop when I see who it is. "Brett, I didn't hear you come up."

"I have light feet. Who sent you flowers?"

"Let's find out." I open the small white envelope nestled among the flowers.

Rachel, I'm so sorry for breaking your trust. It was a huge mistake and I regret it deeply. Please forgive me. I miss you terribly. Can we start over? —Tom

Finally, some news from Tom! But why now? Why has he waited so long?

"So?" Brett says.

"They're from Tom."

"It's about time. Is that all he sent?"

"There's a bag too."

Inside is a familiar gold box with another envelope tucked into the box's ribbon. I open the lid to reveal four Blackout truffles then slide my finger under the envelope flap.

P.S. I'm sorry it's taken me so long to contact you. I'm an idiot. Please forgive me.

I grin and pass the card to Brett.

"That's better," he says. "Still, I'd wait to reply. It's one gesture after how many weeks of silence? Let him sweat a little."

"You sound just like my sister."

📖

When I get home that evening, there's a thick manila envelope in front of my door. I carry it inside and tip the contents onto the kitchen counter. Several smaller envelopes and a folder containing some old newspaper clippings slide across the smooth surface. What is all this? I pick up the envelope with *Read Me First* scrawled across the front and open it.

Dear Rachel,

I am so sorry for not opening up to you. I should have been more forthcoming about my past. I'm also sorry for not telling you about seeing Bethany. It was a brief conversation on the beach one day, nothing more. She helped me to see that my perspective of what happened between us was skewed. I experienced some extremely low points after the accident and took it out on my friends and family, including her. I can now admit that I carry some of the responsibility for our relationship ending. I believed for a long time that she was only with me for my status and money and I was concerned that was the only reason women wanted to be with me, even you. I know you're not like that. I was letting my past color my present.

I'm not sure what you want to know about me, but I'll tell you anything. I've enclosed surfing and photography articles about me, so you can learn more about my past.

I'm also very sorry about sharing your work with my brother. I know it was wrong and I promise I won't meddle in your career again. Please forgive me.

In addition to the articles, I've asked my siblings and Jeff to write me reference letters for you. I don't know what they've said. They've known me long enough that I hope you will trust their words about who I really am.

I want to respect you and your feelings so I won't contact you via phone until I hear from you. Take as much time as you need. If I don't hear from you, I'll assume our relationship is over for good. I hope it's not.

Remorsefully, but hopefully still yours, Tom

I'm stunned. I didn't expect something like this from Tom. I appreciate his creativity in reaching out to me, but I'm still not sure why this is happening now. I open the folder and flip through the articles, but my eyes keep drifting to the sealed envelopes. Curiosity gets the better of me. I drop the folder and pick up the three letters. I carry them over to the couch, grab a blanket, and rip one open.

📖

A vase filled with blue and green flowers shows up at work the next day accompanied by a blue box.

These colors remind me of both the water in Hawaii and your eyes. I long to look into them and tell you how sorry I am.0020—Tom

"More flowers?"

I look up. "Yes, Brett, more flowers and a box."

"More chocolate?"

"I don't know."

I lift the lid and pull out a sea turtle stuffed animal with a card tied around one of its flippers.

I'm sorry I left you SHELL-shocked. I think you're TURTLEY awesome. —Tom

I hold the note out for Brett to read. He rolls his eyes. "Terrible puns, but at least he's trying to make amends. And that turtle is adorable."

I cuddle the turtle to my chest, wishing it was Tom instead. "It is pretty cute. There was a big envelope from Tom at my house last night."

"What was inside?"

"An apology letter, newspaper articles about Tom's achievements, and notes from his siblings and best friend."

Brett's eyebrow arches. "That's intriguing. What did the letters say?"

They're too personal for anyone else to read, but I can give him the cliff notes. "They were about their relationships with Tom. They highlighted his good qualities, acknowledged his weak points, and offered insight into having a good relationship with Tom."

"Wow."

"Yeah, I know. I'm still a little blown away by it."

📖

On the third day, six red roses arrive at the store. Attached to each stem is a heart-shaped note.

You have a kind and compassionate heart.
It was fun throwing Frisbee with you.
You have a beautiful smile.

You are a delightful person and a wonderful encourager.

I enjoyed seeing the Winter Lights with you.

I very much enjoyed decorating the Christmas tree with you. ;-)

"More apologies?"

I look up from the last note, heat creeping into my cheeks. "You're very good at appearing without warning. And no, these aren't apologies. They're memories and compliments."

Brett's eyes light up. "Is that so? Care to share them with me?"

I pocket the last note and slide the rest over to Brett. He picks them up one at a time. "Oh, the Winter Lights. I remember that night." He smirks at me and I roll my eyes.

"Throwing Frisbee, huh? Is that what they call it now?"

"Brett!" I smack his shoulder. So glad I was smart enough to hide the last note. The winky face is too incriminating. "That's really what we did. You know I'm not very sporty. Tom gave me a lesson."

"Uh, huh. Sure. You know, I think he really *is* sorry."

"I agree, but I don't know how to respond."

Brett ticks questions off on his fingers. "Do you still like him?"

"Yes."

"Do you believe he's being sincere in his remorse?"

"I think so."

"Are you willing to forgive him?"

"I am."

"Well, it looks like your move because it's obvious he wants to get back together with you."

A package sits in the break room when I return from lunch. "What's this?"

Brett's sitting at a table looking at his phone. He shrugs. "It's for you. I'm guessing it's from Tom."

I open the card first. The front of the card shows a unicorn jumping over a rainbow with the words *I believe in you*. I show it to Brett before opening it up and reading the words out loud. "I think you're an amazing writer who will inspire others with your words. Here's some encouragement and inspiration for you. Tom."

"Oooh, now I want to know what the gift is," Brett says.

I tear into the wrapping paper around the box and remove the lid. When I see what's inside, I hug the box to my body and twirl in a circle.

Brett stands from his seat and tries to peer in the box. "What is it?"

I grin. "Books."

"Books?"

"*Bird by Bird: Some Instructions on Writing and Life* by Anne Lamott and *On Writing* by Stephen King. How thoughtful."

Brett sits back down, his gaze returning to his phone. "I suppose that's a suitable gift for you. I'd prefer more chocolate or some jewelry."

"I think these are perfect. You can never go wrong with books." I thumb through one book.

He shakes his head, but smiles. "You really are a book nerd. I guess Tom knows you fairly well."

"It sure looks like it. Maybe I should call him."

"He'd probably appreciate it."

"I'll do it tonight."

53

Tom

I'M SUPPOSED TO be editing photos from this week's competition, but my eyes won't seem to focus. I've been a bundle of nerves all week. Julie confirmed the deliveries, but I've heard nothing from Rachel. I thought surely the roses with the heart memories would get a reaction from her, but it's been radio silence. Maybe my efforts are too little too late? I sure hope not. I wish I'd been there to see her reaction to my gifts, though it'd be creepy to spy on her. I shake my head and return my gaze to the computer screen, but I still can't concentrate. Maybe stretching my legs will help. In the living room, Jeff's lounging on the couch.

"I'm going to take a walk," I tell him.

Jeff looks up from his phone. "Want some company?"

"Nah. Just need to clear my head a bit."

"Cool, bro."

I step outside and pause, enjoying the sun on my face. I walk across the road and down along the shoreline. I take deep breaths of the salty air and relax my shoulders. They feel tight from being hunched in front of the computer. I let the water lap at my bare toes before turning and strolling parallel to the waves.

My pocket buzzes. My stomach flips and my heart jumps into my throat when I see Rachel's name on my screen. It's the phone call I've been waiting for, but I'm keeping my hopes low in case of bad news.

"Hello?"

"Hi, Tom. It's Rachel."

Her voice is the most beautiful sound in the world. "Rachel, hi."

"Is this a good time to talk?"

I'm not sure I like the sound of that question. "Yes."

"How are you?"

I definitely wasn't expecting small talk, especially since I know how much she hates it. Either she's stalling on telling me bad news or she's nervous. My guard goes up. "I'm doing okay. You?"

"I'm okay." There's a pregnant pause and then Rachel rushes her words. "Um, thank you for all the gifts you sent me this week. The flowers are beautiful, the chocolates were delicious, and the turtle is adorable. Thank you especially for the books. I appreciate the encouragement and support and am excited to read them."

My body relaxes a little. "You're very welcome. Did you receive a large envelope as well?"

"I did, thank you."

I expect her to say more, but she doesn't. "Oh, good. I thought I would have heard from you before now." I wince. That sounds like an accusation. I told her I didn't expect a response, and I meant it. I try to backtrack. "Not that I expected a response, of course."

"I'm sorry about that. I was trying to get my thoughts together."

I'm still not sure what she's thinking, but I have to give this conversation everything I've got in case it's my last chance. The words pour out of me. "No, I'm sorry, Rachel. I was wrong to stay so closed off from you. I was wrong to disregard your wishes and try to force you into something you weren't ready for. I promise I will respect your decisions about your career and everything else in your life from now on. Please forgive me and give us another chance. I've missed you so much."

"I do forgive you, Tom."

The relief is instantaneous. She forgives me!

"I want us to start fresh," she says.

"Me too."

"I have some news."

I'm hoping this is good news, but there's a sense of dread in my gut. Is the other shoe about to drop? "Oh, yeah?"

"Yeah. I submitted a full-length manuscript to Pam Green at Quill Books and received a response."

It's good news. I can breathe again. "What did she say?"

"She wants to publish it."

"Rachel, that's great! Congratulations. I knew you could do it." I pause. This is dicey territory for us. "I mean, *I* think that's great news, but how do you feel about it?"

She chuckles. "I'm excited. And overwhelmed. And a little in shock. I'm feeling lots of things at the moment. Tom, I'm going to be a published author!"

I grin at the excitement in her voice. "I'm so happy for you. How did you celebrate your amazing accomplishment?"

"I haven't yet. I probably should, huh?"

"You definitely should. Go to dinner with friends. If I was there, I'd take you out."

"That's very sweet of you."

A weight lifts off my chest. I'm thrilled she's forgiven me. It feels like a brand new start with endless possibilities. Better solidify the parameters before I get swept away. "Now what?"

"What do you mean?" Rachel says.

"Can I start calling you again? Can I come visit you?"

"Yes, you can call me, and I'd really like to see you. When can you visit Asheville?"

"Let me check the calendar."

I put her on speaker and open my calendar app. I'm already pretty sure of what it will tell me, but want to double-check in case I'm wrong. "I'm working here in Oahu until the second week of

February. Then I have my buddy's wedding. I'll be in Australia for most of March. After that I have a few weeks off."

"Oh, bummer. But I guess we can still talk and text."

A thought pops into my brain. "Unless…"

"Unless what?"

"This may be too forward since we've just started talking again, and please say so." Is this asking too much? I might as well shoot for the stars. "Jeff's getting married here in Oahu after the surfing competition is over and I'm his best man. Would you like to be my date?"

"Wow, Tom. That's quite an offer. Are you sure Jeff would be okay with me coming?"

"Definitely. He's dying to meet you. He's heard enough about you from me he probably feels like he already knows you."

"I've always wanted to go to Hawaii. When's the wedding?"

"It's February 15th. I'd love to show you around."

"That sounds lovely, Tom. Let me ask my boss tomorrow and see if we have anything happening at the store. That's Valentine's weekend, so someone could have a love-themed book coming out to capitalize on the holiday."

She's tentatively agreed! I'm feeling so high I could walk on water. "I'll be waiting with bated breath."

Rachel laughs. "Just don't pass out. I'll call you tomorrow after work."

54

Rachel

WHEN I KICK off my shoe, it flies across the room and smacks into the blinds. The other shoe hits my bedroom door and lands with a thud on the carpet. Huffing out a breath, I fling my body onto the couch, bury my face in a pillow, and scream. The universe is against me! The one opportunity to visit Hawaii and see Tom and I'm thwarted by Doctor Love, which almost seems ironic— Doctor Love keeping me from my love. I can't be too mad, because it's a huge opportunity for the store to host a live segment of his radio talk show. Especially on Valentine's Day, which is his most listened to broadcast of the year.

I can't even imagine the crowd we'll have for him. Actually, I can because we've already sold out of tickets for the event. Plus, I have to admit I'm geeking out a little at the opportunity to meet him. Doctor Love has been around since I was a teenager. He's the go-to guy for relationship advice and even has his own dating app, but at this exact moment, I'd much rather spend a warm, sun-filled weekend in Hawaii with Tom than meet this love guru. At least I'll have someone to share in my misery once I pass along the disappointing news. I pick up my bag and rummage through it until I find my phone. Tom picks up on the fourth ring.

"Hi, Rachel." His voice sounds sluggish.

"Hi, Tom. Were you asleep?"

"You caught me napping."

"I'm sorry."

"No worries. I'd rather talk to you, anyway. Did you find out about February?"

"I did."

"And?"

The hope in his voice pierces my heart. "I was right about a Valentine's Day event. Doctor Love is signing copies of his new book and doing a live radio show from our store on the fourteenth."

"Sounds like an all-hands-on-deck event."

I appreciate his understanding, but I still feel terrible. "It is. I'm so sorry that I can't go to the wedding with you, Tom. I wanted it to work out."

"It's not your fault, Rachel. Fate isn't with us right now."

I lay back on the couch and put my free arm behind my head. "Tell me about it."

"But, hey, Doctor Love? I've listened to his show a few times. That sounds like a big deal."

My heart lifts at the kindness and understanding he's showing me. He's a good guy. "Yeah, it is. I'm curious to see what Doctor Love's like in person. I hope he's as nice as he seems on his show."

"I hope so too. Do you know what his real last name is? Surely it's not Love."

"I'm skeptical about that, too. His first name's Brian and he's a psychiatrist, so the doctor part is real. I'll ask him if I get the opportunity."

"That'd be cool. Since you can't come here, I guess the plan is for me to come to Asheville after Australia like we discussed?"

Ugh. That's so long from now. "That seems like forever, but I guess it's our only option. In the meantime, we'll keep calling and texting?"

"Most definitely. And maybe a video call if you're comfortable with that?"

My face pinches together at the thought. "I hate seeing myself while I'm talking. How about if we text photos instead?"

"Sure, if that's better for you. Hey, if you could ask Doctor Love anything, what would it be?"

His question takes me by surprise, and I think for a minute. "Probably how do I make a long-distance relationship thrive?"

"That's a good one."

"What about you?"

"Well, if I can't use yours, then perhaps how I can support my girlfriend as she pursues her dream."

My heart leaps. *Girlfriend?!* I pretend to be unaffected. "Your girlfriend, huh?"

"Yeah, if you're okay with that."

If only he could see the grin spread across my face. "I'm definitely okay with that. And, if I was Doctor Love, I'd say, 'Ask her about her writing projects and whether there's anything tangible you can do. If she says no, then just let her know you're proud of her.'"

"That sounds like good advice. I'll try it out and see how it works."

My cheeks are starting to hurt from my wide smile. I've missed talking to Tom. "You do that."

"I'd love to keep talking, but work calls. Can we talk again tomorrow?"

I feel a pang of disappointment that our conversation is over so soon. Stupid time difference. "Sure, that would be nice."

55

Rachel

I STEP INTO Little Shop of Sugar and the rich aroma of chocolate wraps around me. I close my eyes and breathe deeply. "Ahhhhh." Someone chuckles and my eyes pop open. Julie's smiling at me.

"I'm sorry," I say. "I can't help it. The smell in here is divine."

"You get used to it when you work here as long as I have, but I'm glad you enjoy it. What can I do for you?"

"Four Blackouts, please."

Julie wraps my purchase while I search for a conversation starter to serve as an excuse to talk about Tom. If I can't see him right now, I can at least talk about him with someone who knows him. "Tom told me your brother Charlie got married a few weeks ago. Did you go to New York for the ceremony?"

"I did. It was nice to spend time with Serena. I'd only met her once before."

"Having family spread out can make it challenging to get together frequently."

"So does working all over the world. How has it been for you with his travel?"

My heart pangs with longing to look into Tom's smiling face and feel his strong arms around me. "It's frustrating not having seen Tom yet this year. I think I'll go crazy having to wait another month and a half until he visits."

"He's in Oahu until the middle of the month. Have you considered visiting him?"

"He invited me to Jeff's wedding, but I have a mandatory work commitment on Valentine's Day."

"Today's only the seventh. What are you doing right now?"

"I have to work tomorrow and part of next week."

"Could you get someone to cover your shifts?"

"I don't know. Why?"

"Maybe you could visit him *before* Jeff's wedding."

Why did that thought not occur to either of us? "How much are plane tickets? Super expensive, right?"

"You might find some last-minute deals. You'll never know unless you look."

"I suppose that's true." Julie's pushing for me to go. Why? "Is there a specific reason you think I should visit him?"

Julie shrugs. "Tom sounded sad when I talked to him yesterday. Maybe seeing you would improve his mood."

I love that Tom's sister is concerned about him. And I can't pass up an opportunity to see him. "Do you think he'd be okay with me surprising him? It's a long way to travel if it doesn't work out."

"It would thrill him to see you. You come up in conversation whenever we talk. I'm glad you two worked out your issues. He was pretty down in the dumps when you two broke up."

"Yeah, it was tough for me, too." My mood sours thinking about our month apart. What's really holding me back from trying to see Tom? A little money? "You know what? You're right. I should go for it. The worst that can happen is that I'll finally visit somewhere I've been longing to go. Should I tell him I'm coming? I don't even know where he's staying."

Julie grins conspiratorially. "I think you should keep it a secret. If you can work out the details, I can give you his friend

Jeff's number. They always stay together in the same house. He can help you figure out the rest."

I chew on my bottom lip while I think about how much fun it would be to surprise Tom. "That sounds great. I'll call my co-workers and, if that works out, find a flight."

Julie hands me a business card. "Here's my cell number. Text me and I'll send you Jeff's info."

I drop it in my purse and grab my wallet. "What do I owe you for the chocolates?"

"My treat."

"Are you sure?" When she nods, I take the bag and head toward the door, pausing and turning back when I get there. "I hope to be contacting you soon."

"I look forward to it."

My heart swims with hope as I exit onto the sidewalk. I have some calling around to do.

📖

I hang up the phone, my shoulders sagging. So far, no one can cover my shifts. My last hope is Brett and who knows what hoops he'll make me jump through if he's even available. The phone rings a few times before he picks up.

"When do you want me to cover for you?"

"Well, hello to you, too, Brett."

"You never call unless you need me to take one of your shifts."

I feel chastened. "I'm sorry, Brett."

"Rachel, I'm teasing you. That's the only time I call you as well. Otherwise, we communicate via texts and gifs."

I exhale, relieved. "I was worried you were mad. Why do you tease me so much?"

He chuckles. "Because it's fun. I love you, but you're an easy mark. What days do you need covered?"

"I know this is super last minute, but is there any chance you're free tomorrow, Sunday morning, and Tuesday?"

"What's going on? Are you high-tailing it out of town?"

"I'm trying to go see Tom in Hawaii."

Brett whistles. "Hawaii, wow. That's quite a trip."

"I'm hoping so. Can you help me out?"

"I can cover your Tuesday shift, but I'm already booked with commitments for the weekend. I'm sorry, Rachel."

I do some quick math in my head. If I leave after my Sunday shift, there's still time for a quick trip. Something's better than nothing. "Tuesday would be great. Maybe I can find a late flight on Sunday."

"You know next Friday is our big event with Doctor Love, right?"

"Yes. I'll have to fly back on Thursday, but I'm willing to be jet-lagged if it means I can see Tom. Thanks so much, Brett. You're a lifesaver!"

"I don't know about that, but you're welcome, at least."

I hang up and pump my fist in the air. This trip may actually happen. I just need flights that fit into my tight budget and schedule. I send up a quick prayer for help and grab my laptop.

Fifteen minutes later, pop music is blaring from my cell phone speakers and I'm dancing around the coffee table in the living room, my hands flailing wildly in the air. I found a flight that leaves Sunday afternoon and arrives in Honolulu the next day. My return flight will get me back home a few hours before my shift on Friday.

This calls for a celebration. I open the box of chocolates I bought earlier and pop one into my mouth, then pick up the card Julie gave me and add her number into my phone.

Rachel: It's happening! Arriving Monday around lunch and leaving early Thursday morning.

I send a follow-up because Julie might not realize it's me.

Rachel: This is Rachel Price, btw. Tom's girlfriend.

I'm too amped to sleep so I might as well pack. I find my suitcase and throw in an assortment of summer clothes. I can hardly wait. Come on, Sunday, get here quick!

56

Tom

MY FACE SCRUNCHES up at the light trying to push in under my closed eyelids. I open my eyes a crack and glance at the clock: nine-fifteen a.m. After submitting my last batch of photos yesterday, I partied late into the night with Jeff and some other guys. I have a few days before wedding festivities start and first up on my agenda is catching up on sleep.

Since I'm officially on vacation, I close my eyes and roll back over. I'm almost asleep again when there's a sharp knock on the door. It bursts opens and Jeff barges in with a coffee mug in each hand.

"Hey, man, get up! You're wasting the day in bed."

I groan. "I'm on vacation. Since when did you become a morning person?"

"Since I won yesterday. I'm still on a high and getting excited to see everyone at the wedding this weekend. I need to burn off some energy so I don't go crazy."

I'm exhausted just looking at Jeff. I reach out for the mug. "At least someone's winning at life. Give me that coffee."

Jeff hands me a cup. "What does that mean?"

"Nothing." I'm embarrassed to admit how much I'm missing Rachel. I take a sip and grimace. "Whoa, are you sure it isn't just the coffee? This is strong, man."

"It'll help you keep up with me. We're going zip lining today."

"Whatever you want, Jeff. Let me get dressed."

Jeff bounds out of the room, and I shake my head. I'm not sure I can deal with him all week if he stays this amped up, but I'll soldier through just about anything for Jeff. Besides, it isn't every day my best friend gets married. My heart twists as a sliver of jealousy wiggles its way in. I'm happy for Jeff and Lisa, but this weekend is going to make me miss Rachel even more.

I haven't seen her in almost two months. If only I hadn't signed on for so many events. The foreign thought startles me. I love what I do, but it's hindering my new love life. Fewer competitions would mean I'd see Jeff even less, but he's going to be married, so our relationship is already changing. Guess I should enjoy this time we have together for the next few days. I take a large slug of coffee and climb out of bed.

📷

The adrenaline-fueled ride through the treetops lifts my spirits. "That was fantastic. I haven't done that in forever."

Jeff smiles and then glances at his phone. He types something and then looks back at me. "I don't know about you, but I'm starving."

"Me too. What's with the face?"

"What face?"

"You look like the cat that ate the canary."

Jeff shrugs. "I'm just having a good day. Let's go find some grub."

"How about a burger place?"

"Actually, Lisa was hoping I could stop by Nani's today to give final approval for our reception food. Would you be okay with that?"

I smirk. "It's Nani's. You don't have to pull my arm. I'd eat there every day of the week. What will you be serving?"

"We're definitely having manapua appetizers. I'd like to have bibimbap, but Lisa's leaning toward a make-your-own poke bowl station."

"Those are both great options. Have you considered tacos?"

"That wasn't even up for negotiation, bro. Everyone who's been to Nani's will come expecting those."

I chuckle. "True."

Jeff clamps his hand down on my shoulder. "My stomach's growling just thinking about eating some kalua pig tacos. Let's go."

57

Rachel

MY LEG'S BOUNCING uncontrollably under the table inside the restaurant. My napkin has become a small mound of paper balls I'm scooting back and forth between cupped hands. My queasy stomach makes me wonder if I'll even be able to eat once the guys arrive.

I've been in paradise for an hour. Lisa picked me up from the airport and drove me to the house so I could drop off my bags and shower. I got some sleep on the flight over, but plane seats are inadequate bed substitutes. I'm thankful Brett suggested picking up a pair of earplugs and a neck pillow, otherwise I'd be totally out of it right now. As it is, I feel like I've got a million ants in my shorts.

Lisa catches my eye and smiles. "The guys should be here any minute. Jeff took him zip-lining this morning to make sure he'd be out of the house when you arrived."

"That sounds a little scary."

"Maybe if you're afraid of heights, but it's pretty safe. I find it quite exhilarating speeding along a cable and getting a bird's-eye view of the island."

"Huh." That doesn't sound like my kind of activity, but to each her own. "Are you excited about your wedding?"

"Very excited. I'm sorry you won't be able to celebrate with us."

"Me too, but I'm glad to be here now."

The front door opens behind me and my body tenses. Is it them? Lisa's eyes light up and she smiles. My heart slams against my rib cage. Without breaking her gaze from over my shoulder, Lisa whispers, "Here they come."

I suck in a deep breath, willing myself not to turn and look. I don't want to reveal the surprise just yet. "Lisa, I'm ready to help you with your reception menu." The sound of Tom's voice is refreshment for my parched soul.

Lisa stands and hugs Tom. "I brought another friend along to help."

Every nerve in my body is on the verge of exploding. My eyes have locked onto Tom and I will him to turn my way. Surprise ripples across his face when he does. "Hi," I whisper, the only sound my tight throat will allow.

The guy with Tom, who I assume is Jeff, laughs and slaps Tom on the back. It seems to knock him into motion. He slips into the booth and wraps me up in a tight hug. "Rachel," he says. I squeeze him back, closing my eyes and enjoying his arms around me. I inhale his scent and my whole body lights up with recognition.

After not nearly enough time, I feel Tom's arms loosen, and he pulls back. Jeff's grinning at us from the other side of the table. "Nice to meet you, Rachel," he says.

"Nice to meet you, too, Jeff. Thanks for your help."

Tom's head swivels between us. "I have so many questions."

I grab Tom's hand, desperate for a reminder that this is real, that he is indeed sitting right next to me. "Ask away."

"First, how are you here? I thought you had to work."

"I still have to work on Friday, but I freed up the first half of the week to visit you."

"That's great! I'm so glad you're here."

"It was your sister's idea."

Several expressions cross his face. "Julie? How many people

took part in this scheme?"

"Just her, these two, and Brett, since he's covering one of my shifts. Julie gave me Jeff's number, and he helped with the details on this end."

Tom grins at Jeff. "So that's why you've been looking at your phone so much. I assumed it was wedding stuff."

Jeff smiles back but doesn't respond.

Tom's gaze returns to me and I feel my cheeks heat under his scrutiny. "How long are you here?"

"I fly out Thursday morning."

"Where are you staying?"

"Jeff said I could stay with you, as long as you agree."

"I think it's a great idea."

"Of course it is," Jeff says. "I'm glad Rachel's here, but I'm also starving. Can we order some food and eat while you catch up?"

Lunch is filled with laughter, funny stories about Tom and Jeff, and a whole lot of hand holding with Tom. Eating with one hand is a bit of a challenge, but I don't mind.

"What's next?" Tom says when our plates are empty.

"Whatever you want to do, Tommy Two-Tone," Jeff says. "You can take my car and give Rachel a tour of the island. Lisa and I have some wedding stuff to do, so I'll ride with her."

Tom looks at me. "What do you think?"

I give him a saucy grin. "I think I need to know about 'Tommy Two-Tone.'" Jeff laughs while Tom groans. "Who's going to give me the scoop?"

Tom sighs. "I guess I will. When we were kids, I fell asleep on the beach one day. I usually wore a rash guard, so my torso was super white from never seeing the sun. This day, I'd taken it off to get some color. An umbrella gave me partial shade, so when I woke up, half of my torso was bright red and the other half was still pale. Jeff dubbed me 'Tommy Two-Tone' and still hasn't let it go."

Jeff chuckles. "And I never will."

We all leave the restaurant and Tom holds the car door open for me before walking around to his side of the Jeep, a bounce in his step. He closes his door, and turns to me, his gaze intense. He leans toward me and I close my eyes just before our lips meet. Fire erupts in my belly and my arms snake around his neck, pulling him closer. A car honk springs us apart. Jeff waves from the passenger seat of a white Jeep, grinning as they drive away. I turn back to Tom in time to see him roll his eyes before he grabs my hand. "I'm so glad you're here. I've really missed you."

"Me too. That's why I came."

Tom's smile crinkles the corners of his eyes and his dimple pops out. I lean over and kiss it because I can. "I've wanted to do that for a while. So, where should we go?"

"You don't want to make out in the car?"

My cheeks flush. I mean, yeah, but… "Err…"

"I'm just kidding. Kind of. What do you want to see?"

I chuckle. "I'm just happy to be here. Show me whatever you want."

"We can drive the circle tomorrow and see the sights. Today I'd like to take you to the North Shore and show you my favorite spot."

"Sounds great."

Tom smiles and leans over to kiss me again. He squeezes my hand when he pulls back. "I'm so happy to see you."

I'm sure my smile is just as wide as his. "Me too."

Tom raises my hand to his lips and kisses it, not breaking eye contact. I bite my lip and force myself not to pounce on him. Tom chuckles and releases my hand. He starts the car and turns out onto the road. My dream vacation with my dream man has begun.

58

Tom

A HORN BLARES behind me. The driver pulls into the left lane and honks again as he passes, shooting me a death glare. I throw up a hand to signal my contrition. I'm driving like a turtle, and getting plenty of honks and sour looks from other drivers, but I'm not speeding up if it means a few extra minutes with Rachel. I hate that she's leaving so soon. It has been a blast being her guide and showing her some of my favorite spots, but we didn't have enough time to see everything on my list.

We hiked to the top of Diamond Head State Park and snorkeled at Hanauma Bay Natural Preserve. I showed her Ko'Olina Lagoons and Maunawili Falls. We ate pineapple soft serve at the Dole plantation and stopped in at a chocolate shop so Rachel could stock up for her flight home. And we talked about anything and everything. She told me more about her soon-to-be-published book which I'm eager to read. I've already preordered a dozen copies, but that's a secret. Jeff and Lisa coaxed us into playing some card games with them. I didn't realize how competitive Rachel is, and I love it. We make a great team, too.

"I've had a great time, Tom," Rachel says. "Thanks for showing me around and making it so special for me. I understand why you love this place."

I hear a slight tremor in her voice, and it makes my throat

tighten. "I'm so glad you came to visit me. It was the best surprise I've ever had."

Despite my slow-as-a-sloth driving, we still reach the departure terminal way too soon. I turn off the car and reach for Rachel's hand. A tear tracks down her cheek and my heart cracks.

"I'm going to miss you, Tom."

I try to swallow down the lump in my throat. "I'll miss you too, Rachel. As soon as my schedule clears up, I'm taking the first plane I can get to Asheville. I promise."

"I'm holding you to it."

She leans toward me and presses her lips to mine. She sighs against my mouth and my heart breaks wide open. I cup her face and caress her cheek with my thumb, yearning for more time together. Rachel rests her forehead against mine, our eyes locked together for a long moment as we communicate everything we're feeling without saying a word.

"I guess I'd better head inside," she says, but the way she's looking at me confirms that she's just as reluctant to leave me as I am to let her go.

Rachel opens the passenger door and climbs out. I also get out, grabbing her suitcase from the trunk and setting it on the curb. I pull Rachel into a hug, inhaling her scent. "You always smell like coconuts."

She smiles against my chest. "It's my shampoo."

"I'll see you soon," I say, willing my arms to let go and taking a step back for good measure.

"Not soon enough."

"You're right. But I hear that absence makes the heart grow fonder."

Rachel's wearing a skeptical frown. "I think we've had more than enough absence already. We need a new phrase, like closeness makes the heart grow content."

"I like it."

"I'd better check into my flight."

"I hope everything goes well with Doctor Love tomorrow."

I watch her until she's out of sight. It takes a fair amount of willpower to drive away from the airport rather than chase her down the terminal for one more kiss.

Jeff and Lisa are sitting on the couch, drinking coffee, and watching the news when I drag myself into the house.

Lisa looks up at me and frowns. "You look miserable. Did something happen at the airport?"

"No, everything's fine. I dropped her off without issue."

"Then why the long face?"

I throw myself down into an armchair. "I'm bummed that I won't see Rachel again until March."

"Yeah, distance is hard on relationships. I'm thankful that part of the journey's almost over for us." She squeezes Jeff's arm and gives him an affectionate look.

"Yeah, bro," Jeff says, "it's tough, but when you care about someone, you do whatever it takes, right?"

"I can't believe you two have done it for three years. That's some dedication."

"Well, I love Lisa. What about you, Tom? Do you love Rachel?"

I open my mouth to give a smart aleck response, but stop and consider the question. Being around Rachel makes me happy. I love her kindness and quirky traits. We have fun together and I didn't once tire of her presence after our non-stop time together on the island. Honestly, it wasn't enough time together. I enjoyed our adventures and want to have many more. It's suddenly very clear how I feel. "Yeah, I do."

"That's great, man! What will you do about it?"

"What can I do about it? I'm here for the rest of the month.

I'm not skipping out on your wedding and we've got our guys' night tonight, or have you forgotten?"

"I haven't forgotten. It's going to be legendary!" He glances at Lisa. "Within reason, of course."

"I've got plenty of time to figure out how to tell her. I just hope she feels the same." Lisa and Jeff pass a look between each other. "What?"

"I don't think you have anything to worry about, Tom," Lisa says. "Trust me."

59

Rachel

IT'S NEARLY IMPOSSIBLE to keep my eyes open. I knew I'd be tired, but now I know the true meaning of the walking dead. I grab my travel mug, put it to my lips, and tip it up only to find it empty. I need energy for tonight's big event, so I duck into the break room for more coffee. Continuous movement seems to be the only thing keeping me awake, so I work on the display for Doctor Love's books in the front window.

"How was Hawaii?"

I perk up and turn around. I wondered where Brett was hiding. I'm dying to tell him about my trip. "It was wonderful! Tom was so surprised. He took me all around the island. It was exhilarating and exhausting, and I wish I was still there." I sigh.

"Don't tell me you miss him already."

I feign nonchalance, but it's true.

"Ha! I see you trying to be cool, but your face is giving you away."

I feel sheepish. "It's only been twenty-four hours since I saw him, but it feels like forever."

"Do you love him?"

My face flushes and I look away.

"Don't feel embarrassed, Rachel. I'm happy for you. You deserve to be in love."

"We've known each other for just a few months. It doesn't seem like enough time to fall in love."

"Love doesn't work on a set timeline. When you know, you know. At least, that's been my experience."

"That makes me feel better. Thanks, Brett."

Joy wells up inside my chest. I'm in love! I can't wait to tell Tom. Does he love me too? My skin tingles with fear that he doesn't, that I've jumped into the deep end alone. I'll worry about that later. Right now I want to enjoy this warm feeling.

Later in the evening, I'm dead on my feet, but the palpable energy of the room is giving me a much-needed infusion. There's not a single vacant seat in the store, and dozens of people stand along the sides of the room. Doctor Love is friendly and personable. His full head of white hair and thin, wire-rimmed glasses give him an aura of wisdom. He insisted we call him Brian, but I can't see him as anything but Doctor Love. I can't wait to tell Tom his last name really *is* Love.

Doctor Love finishes reading an excerpt from his book, *Prescriptions for the Heart*, and it's time to transition to the question-and-answer part of the event. Doctor Love's broadcasting the entire event live and will take forty-five minutes for questions from audience members and callers. There's already a small queue at the microphone near the front.

"We'll take our first question from the audience. Please state your name before asking your question," Doctor Love says, smiling at the woman in front of the microphone.

"Hi, I'm Stacey. I've developed feelings for a good friend. How do I let him know without risking the loss of our friendship if he's not interested?"

"Great question, Stacey."

Doctor Love's answer is well-reasoned. Audience members

and callers ask more questions while I zone in and out. I wish I could ask him my question about having a successful long-distance relationship. After the event is over, maybe I'll get my chance.

I pick up a copy of his book from the table next to me and read through the table of contents. There's a section on long-distance love, so I read the first few paragraphs, nodding to myself. I should purchase a copy to keep on hand for reference.

"Alright, it looks like we have time for one more call."

Doctor Love's words break through my thoughts. I close the book and set it down, making sure the display is still neat. The crowd will head my way next for autographs.

The producer introduces the last caller. "We have Tom from Hawaii."

"Hello, Tom from Hawaii."

"Hi, Doctor Love. Thanks for taking my call."

My heart skips a beat at his voice. It's *my* Tom. What's he going to ask Doctor Love? I search the room for Brett and narrow my eyes. Is he responsible for this? He raises both hands, palms up, and shrugs. Maybe not. I return my attention to Doctor Love, curiosity and anxiety tangling in my chest.

"What question do you have for me?"

"I'm in love with a woman I've only been seeing for a few months. Do you think I'd scare her off if I told her? Is it too soon?"

My mouth drops open. *Tom's in love with me?* I feel elated and scared all at once. What does this mean for us? My mind is going haywire.

"First, congratulations on being in love. She must be remarkable for you to be in love so soon."

"Oh, she is. Whenever we're apart, I count the days until I get to see her again."

There's an enchanted sigh from the audience. I stifle a giggle and look at Brett. He gives me a thumbs up.

"Do you have any idea how she feels about you?"

"My friends seem to think she cares deeply for me. She flew across the ocean to see me for three days."

"That's quite a romantic gesture. I can't be certain about your girlfriend's feelings, but based on what you've told me, I don't think sharing your feelings would scare her off."

"Is that your professional opinion?"

Doctor Love chuckles. "Yes, it's my professional opinion. Good luck with your relationship, Tom."

"Thanks, Doctor Love."

"That's the end of our program for tonight. Next week, we'll be back in the studio with the usual format. My new book, *Prescriptions for the Heart,* is now available for purchase on the website and wherever books are sold, including Page Turner Books here in Asheville, North Carolina. Stay open to love, my friends. Goodnight."

The producer gives the signal that we're off the air. The audience stands and claps. I'm wrapped in a cloud of happiness and only realize that the show's over when Brett bumps me with his shoulder.

"Wow, Rach. Your guy's in love with you."

"Yeah, I heard."

"I know it was a great show, but even I'm not *that* excited about it," Doctor Love says, coming up to the table.

"Your last caller was Rachel's boyfriend," Brett says, motioning to me.

"Is that so? Well, it looks like I gave the right advice then."

I nod, a little embarrassed at how public my relationship with Tom has become.

"Why was your Hawaii trip only three days?"

My lips quirk up into a smirk. "I had to work tonight."

Doctor Love chuckles. "Sorry I cut your trip short."

I wave a hand. "It's fine. I'm glad to be here. Your show was very enlightening."

"I'm sure it was. I wish you and Tom the best of luck."

"Thanks. We should get you set up to sign books. I'm sure you'd like to spend some time with your wife on Valentine's Day."

"We've made plans to celebrate tomorrow when I get home. Tonight I belong to Page Turner Books."

After the event, I'm bone-tired, but the knowledge that Tom loves me is keeping me upright. I pick up a stack of chairs and carry them to the storeroom. When I return to the floor, Doctor Love hands me one of his books.

"A token of thanks for your hard work tonight and dedication to your job."

"Thank you. That's very kind."

"You're welcome." Doctor Love gives me a conspiratorial wink, then turns and walks over to a group of people stacking boxes of radio equipment.

I open the front cover. *To Rachel, I hope you have many years together with the one who's captured your heart.—Doctor Love*

My lips curve up, and I hug the book to my chest. I hope so, too, Doctor Love.

60

MARCH

Rachel

THE BELL TINKLES merrily when I step into the confectionery. I breathe in the glorious aroma of chocolate and my mouth waters. I move over to the glass display and peruse the selection.

"Hi, Rachel."

I straighten up and find Julie's smiling face.

"Hi, Julie. How are you?"

"I'm doing great. Yourself?"

"Can't complain. It's book club night, so I'm here for our monthly infusion of chocolate."

"Do you know what you want? Blackouts, I assume."

I grin. "You know it. Do you have anything special this month?"

"I have some St. Patrick's Day-themed chocolates in the case. There are milk chocolate shamrocks, Irish whiskey truffles, and dark chocolate truffles that look like pots of gold."

"Those all sound fun. I'll take some of each. Anna likes white chocolate. And I can't forget a Jitterbug for Susan. Let's say whatever combination you deem appropriate that equals sixteen."

"I can do that. Your book club sounds like fun. Is it open to new members?"

My eyebrows shoot up in surprise. Is this Julie's way of saying she wants to get to know me? "It is. Are you interested?"

"I might be. What time does it meet?"

"It's supposed to be from seven to eight-thirty, but it often goes until nine because we always get off-topic." I roll my eyes and smile.

Julie scrunches her lips together before answering. "I'd need someone to close the store for me."

"We'd love to have you. It's a lovely group of women."

"I'll think about it. Have you talked to Tom?"

"We chatted yesterday. Why?"

"Just curious. When will you see him again?"

"Only one more long, agonizing week before he comes to visit. I can't wait!"

"I'm sure you'll make it."

I pull my lips into a pout. "I don't have a choice, do I?"

She laughs. "I guess not. Have a great evening and enjoy book club." Julie gives me an odd look I can't quite interpret.

"Thanks. We always do."

📖

I put the chocolates in my locker and return to work. Brett's manning checkout, so I walk around the store straightening up displays and asking customers if they need help.

"These are for Mary V," I say, dropping a small stack of books onto the counter in front of Brett. "She's still looking around."

He smiles. "Great. I'll stick a post-it note on it so I don't forget."

Something about his smile seems off. It's his eyes, I realize. They're intense, like he's trying to communicate telepathically. My mind conjures the idea of someone behind the counter pointing a gun at him. It's a highly unlikely scenario, but just in case, I stretch my torso around the edge of the counter until I have a view of

Brett's shoes. No one there. Maybe he drank too many espressos. "Okay," I say, "I'm going to go see if anyone else needs help."

"You look nice today, by the way."

A compliment from Brett? That's odd. Maybe there's a full moon tonight or something. I shake off the thought and return to the store floor.

I'm getting the coffee maker set up for book club when I hear footfalls in the hall. Lori and Susan appear in the doorway, whispering to one another.

"Hey ladies," I say.

They stop and turn to me at the same time. A shiver runs down my spine at their expressions. They almost look guilty, but that seems silly.

"Hi, Rachel," Susan says. "I have to leave at eight tonight. I have an early appointment tomorrow and need a good night's sleep."

"Oh, okay. No problem."

"I have to leave at eight, too, sorry," Lori says. "Mitch wants me to help him with a project at home."

"That's fine. Help yourselves to some refreshments."

Deb and Anna arrive soon thereafter, both giving their own excuses for needing to leave the meeting early.

It strikes me as odd that they all have to leave early, but stranger things have happened. "I guess we'll just jump right into March's book, *London's Games* by Louis Renault."

The group exchanges a look before Deb speaks. "I didn't like the story. Too many scenery descriptions and not enough action or romance."

"I didn't care for it either," Lori says. "Mr. London toying with poor Elise's heart like that. If you like someone, tell them and see what happens."

I'm surprised at the conviction in Lori's voice. "Susan, did you like it?"

"It was okay. I prefer a true love story where they live happily ever after."

"I agree," Anna says. "Why do people love this book?"

"Well," I say, "I've never known you all to be in total agreement. I guess this one was a dud."

"Did *you* like it?" Susan asks.

"Not really. I like my heroines more proactive. Elise was too meek and proper for my tastes. And Theodore London didn't have any redeeming qualities. Being rich is not enough. I need affection, mutual esteem, fun, and adventure."

I look around the circle. The women are smiling and nodding, but it feels like I'm missing something. "Anyway, enough of my soapbox. How about we figure out April's book together? Then I won't be the only one to blame if it's a flop."

Susan reaches over to pat my hand. "We don't blame you, dear. Not all books can be winners. What about an unusual setting, like a pirate ship?"

I laugh. "That *would* be different. What else should we look for?"

We bat ideas around for a while and settle on our next book selection. We spend the rest of our time catching up with everyone's lives, but it doesn't escape my notice how often Susan checks her watch and Deb peeks at her phone.

A phone alarm goes off and Lori shoots up from her chair. "It's eight. I have to go. See you ladies next month."

The other women also stand, echoing her sentiment. There's a round of quick hugs and then the ladies disappear.

That was strange. I gather my things and head toward the front, shutting off lights along the way. The overhead lights in the main area of the bookstore are already off, but there's a glow near the checkout counter. Did someone leave one of the reading lights on again? Better shut it off to preserve the batteries.

61

Tom

NERVOUS JITTERS HAVE me pacing around the store. I've been here long enough that I've found a loop among the labyrinthine shelves. The book club ladies came through, all giving me encouraging smiles and shoulder pats before shutting off the lights and exiting, leaving me with only the flicker of a dozen candles I've lit for ambiance. I can't believe I'm about to surprise Rachel with my early return. My heart is trying to beat its way out of my chest.

The hall lights turn off and I freeze. It's time. How do I let her know I'm here without scaring her? I can't see her from where I am, but I hear her footfalls and then a gasp. I step forward and Rachel spins around. When she sees me, she drops her bags and lifts her hands to her mouth. "Tom?"

I smile and take another step toward her. "Hi, Rachel."

She takes a quick step toward me and then launches herself into my arms. I pull her to me. "Tom," she sighs, melting into my embrace. "What are you doing here? I wasn't expecting you for another week."

"The competition ended early, so I thought I'd surprise you. I hope you don't mind."

"I don't mind at all."

I lean back so I can see her face. We're wearing matching

grins. "How did you pull this off?" she asks.

"With my sister and your co-worker, Brett."

She rolls her eyes. "That's why Brett was acting so strange today."

"He helped me figure out a plan and got your book club involved."

"So it *wasn't* a coincidence that they all had to leave at eight."

I chuckle. "Nope."

Rachel shakes her head, an amused smile on her lips. We have another staring contest, which is broken when Rachel glances down at my mouth and licks her lips. When she returns her gaze to my eyes, I decide it's go time.

"Rachel…" My voice catches. I didn't expect to get choked up. I clear my throat and try again. "Rachel, I love you."

Rachel smiles. "I love you too, Tom."

My heart feels like it's going to explode from happiness. "It feels so good to say it in person."

"It's wonderful to finally be face-to-face again." She presses a finger into my dimple. "I also love this."

My eyes drop to Rachel's mouth and I lean in. Our lips meet and something explodes in my chest. How does every kiss with Rachel feel so amazing? I end the kiss begrudgingly and rest my forehead against hers. "Rachel?"

"Yes, Tom?"

I love hearing my name on her lips. "Our time together in Hawaii made it clear that I want to be with you. I've decided to make Asheville my permanent residence."

"Tom, that's wonderful!" Her delight turns to confusion. "But won't you still be away a lot for work?"

"I'm cutting back on my travel time. I've already committed to this season of competition but, next year I'm only covering the Hawaii events. It means I'll be here in Asheville for most of the year."

She frowns. "Why are you doing this?"

My smile falters. "Because I love you and want to be with you."

"Tom, that's very sweet, but you can't give up your livelihood for me."

"I'm not quitting, just cutting back."

"Will it be enough for you to live on? I'd gladly support us both if I could, but book selling isn't exactly a lucrative career."

Her pragmatism is endearing. I guess I've still kept one secret from her. Better remedy that now. "I appreciate your heart, but we don't have to worry about money. I invested most of my earnings from surfing and have a sizable nest egg."

Her eyes widen briefly. "Are you sure you want to stay in one place with me?"

I place my hands on her shoulders and hug her against my chest. "It's what I want. *You're* what I want."

Her eyes glisten with tears. "Then yes, definitely do it."

I grin. "Great. What are your thoughts on finding some celebratory chocolate? I do have a key to my sister's store." I pull a key ring out of my pocket and jiggle it so the keys clink together.

Rachel laughs, and the sound is music to my ears. "I can never say no to chocolate."

Epilogue

SIX MONTHS LATER

Rachel

TOM AND I stroll hand-in-hand across Ehukai Beach in Oahu. The beautiful blue-green water is mesmerizing.

"There are hardly any waves," I say, disappointment lacing my voice. I was hoping to see the monsters Tom used to ride like in the pictures I've seen.

"Just wait until next month," Tom says. "The summer months are deceptive. You can't see the true power of Pipeline until fall and winter."

"I guess that means I'll have to come for Christmas sometime."

I smile at Tom, but his gaze skitters away. Nerves twist my stomach.

"I'm kind of hungry," Tom says. "Should we have dinner?"

Tom's fingers are tapping rhythmically on his thigh. He's seemed a little off since we arrived this morning. I hope it's just jet lag or hunger. I force myself to think positively, but there's a noticeable undercurrent of anxiety coming from Tom. "Sure. Where do you want to go?"

"How about right over there?" Tom points farther down the beach.

I squint my eyes. "What are you looking at? I don't see

anywhere to eat? Just sand."

Tom chuckles, but it sounds forced. He leads me to a green checkered blanket with a picnic basket in the middle. "I arranged for dinner on the beach."

The knot in my stomach loosens a tad. "How romantic! Who set it up?"

"There are companies that will deliver meals to specific locations."

Tom sits down on the blanket and motions for me to join him. He opens the basket lid and removes a bottle of wine, which he pours into two plastic wineglasses before handing one to me.

"I want to make a toast," I say, raising my glass. "To us. We're on vacation together in the most beautiful place in the world."

"Here here," Tom says, clinking his glass to mine.

He takes a drink and then pulls several containers out of the basket. "I ordered us poke bowls. I hope that's okay."

"That sounds delicious. I've always wanted to try authentic poke."

"You won't be disappointed. It's from the best place on the island."

I remove the lid from the one in front of me and my eyes soak in the beautiful arrangement of rice, tuna, seaweed, mango, edamame, and cucumbers crisscrossed with unagi sauce. "It's so pretty, like a work of art. I almost don't want to eat it."

Tom hands me a set of chopsticks and a fork. "Look at yours as long as you please, but I'm digging in."

I pull out my phone and snap a picture. "There. Now I can remember it forever."

When we're finished, Tom extracts a square brown box from the basket.

"Do you have room for dessert?"

I smirk and hold out my hand. "What do you think?"

Tom gives me the box, which, when opened, reveals a teal colored interior with nine chocolates in different shapes.

"Yum! Where are these from?"

"Honolulu."

"Oh look, two are heart-shaped! Do you know what flavor they are?"

Tom smiles. "The hearts are strawberries and cream, the squares are triple chocolate, the leaves are mint chocolate chip, and the swirls are dark chocolate."

I look pointedly at him. "I see there are three dark chocolates."

"Of course. Is that what you're choosing?"

"Actually, I'm in the mood for a heart."

I pluck one out of its wrapper and hold the box out to Tom. He's looking at me strangely. "Everything alright?"

Tom blinks and then reaches into the box. "Yes, fine. I think I'll have the same."

I tap my chocolate against Tom's. "Cheers, from my heart to yours."

Tom smiles and takes a bite of the chocolate. I do the same, closing my eyes to focus on the flavors. I hum with pleasure and wiggle my shoulders.

Tom chuckles. "That good, huh?"

"Indeed."

I grab the handle of the picnic basket and move it off the blanket so that I can snuggle up next to Tom. I slide my arms around his waist and rest my head against his shoulder. Tom wraps an arm around my back, resting his cheek against the crown of my head. We watch the waves and the sun lowering in the sky. The ocean turns a shimmery orange.

I sigh. "It's so beautiful. I could stare at this forever."

Tom kisses the top of my head. "*You're* so beautiful."

I smile and turn my face up to kiss him. I press my lips firmly to his, hoping to adequately express my feelings for Tom in one small act. Tom releases my arms from his waist and takes my hand in his. We lock eyes and my stomach clenches at the serious expression on his face.

"The first time I saw you, Rachel, you were pushing a cart of books and humming a song." His forehead crinkles. "I can't remember what it was, though. Can you?"

I smile at the memory. "It was Beyoncé's 'Single Ladies (Put a Ring on It)'. I was so into it I nearly ran you over."

Tom's eyes widen, and then he chuckles. "That's perfect!"

I tilt my head in confusion. "What's perfect?"

He ignores my question, drawing my thoughts back to our first meeting with his next statement. "Then I saved you from being buried under a pile of books."

My lips quirk up and I flutter my lashes. "My hero."

Tom laughs. "I was clueless about how important you'd become to me. I'm thankful for that day in the bookstore and for our next meeting at the park when I learned your name. It hurt me even then to see you cry."

I stick out my lip in sympathy. "Oh, Tom."

"When I witnessed your kindness and compassion for others in Little Shop of Sugar helping Emily with the obtuse customer, I was hooked."

I shake my head. "I was mortified that you witnessed that. But then you gave me the Ancient Treasures truffle."

"And *you* teased me at the park before we threw Frisbee."

My cheeks heat. "We got quite close that day. Literally."

Tom grins. "When I finally worked up the courage to ask you out, I was delighted when you said yes and later horrified when I realized I was going to be late for our first date."

"I thought you'd stood me up."

"I'm so thankful you waited for me."

I squeeze his hand. "Me too."

"I know our relationship hasn't always stayed on the right foot, but I'm grateful for your forgiveness and willingness to see the best in me. You've changed me, Rachel. You've shown me that fresh starts are possible and I should give everyone the benefit of the doubt. Every day I've spent with you has been fun and surprising. I want to spend a million more with you."

My vision is blurry from the tears in my eyes. I swipe them away with my free hand. "Oh, Tom, you're so sweet. I love being with you. You've changed me too, you know. You've helped me get my writing confidence back. I feel more fulfilled now that I'm pursuing my dream. I wouldn't be where I am without you."

Tom smiles and kisses my cheek. Then he reaches into his pants pocket and pulls out a small black box. My heart stutters and a million thoughts flood through my mind. *Is that what I think it is? Oh my goodness! Is he doing IT? He is. Focus, Rachel!* I lift my eyes from the box to Tom's earnest face.

Tom lifts the lid and holds it out to me. Nestled inside is a platinum ring with a large, round blue-green stone in a solitary setting. I look up at him. "Rachel, I love you. I want to spend the rest of my life with you. Will you marry me?"

I let those words wash over me for a minute. Then a huge grin spreads across my face. "Yes, Tom. Of course I'll marry you!"

He removes the ring from the box and slides it onto my finger. I throw my arms around his neck and kiss him thoroughly.

When we break apart, I take time to study the ring on my finger. "It's a beautiful color. I've never seen anything like it. Where did you find it?"

"Here in Oahu, of course. It's a sapphire. I thought it matched your eyes."

"That's so sweet. I love you."

"I love you, too. Let's go back to the house. Jeff and Lisa are waiting for us with champagne."

"They're here? And they knew about this?"

"They set up the picnic for us."

"How sweet. You have wonderful friends."

"And now a wonderful fiancée."

My heart leaps. I'm getting married!

"So what do you say?"

"I've already said yes, haven't I?" I wink and am rewarded with a belly laugh.

"You did indeed."

I smile at my new fiancé. "What are we waiting for? Let's go share our great news!"

Thank you for reading *Take a Chance on Me*! If you enjoyed it, please consider leaving a review online.

Want to stay in the know about future books? Sign up for my newsletter at MeganByrd.net/newsletter

Find additional *Take a Chance on Me* content including recipes and a bonus scene at MeganByrd.net/TACOM

ACKNOWLEDGEMENTS

This book would not be possible without the assistance and encouragement of a whole slew of people.

Racheal Hoaglan, thank you for cheering me on as I embarked on this ambitious project. Your unwavering enthusiasm and willingness to listen to me talk excitedly about imaginary characters and enduring progress updates each time I came into the Y.

Anna Booraem, your wonderful leadership of our Creative Writing Group gave me the courage to attempt NaNoWriMo that first time. Thank you for being my local fellow writer whom I can talk to for hours about reading and writing and for reading through the early version and a few later additions to help me bring out the story.

Heather Gerwing, you have been such a blessing to me as a fellow sojourner in the trenches of writing. Thank you for all of your wisdom and honest feedback throughout this process. Your willingness to share hard truths has made this journey and book better. I hope to do the same for you.

Kristina Lewis, I have been lifted up by your warm endorsement of my writing. I thoroughly enjoyed talking about the stories and characters like they were real. You have provided valuable feedback as well. I'm glad my husband gave a stranger my phone number at open house.

Ben Reed, thank you for providing guidance and your personal experiences regarding surfing and photography. I hope I got it mostly right!

Sherri Wilson Johnson, thank you for going first and offering to share your hard-earned wisdom with me. You are a special friend.

A big thank you to my Beta Readers throughout various stages (Katharine, Susie, Brianna, Erin, Mara, Trish, Katie, Laura, and Kimberly) who provided insightful feedback. It was exciting to find people who enjoyed the characters and book enough to ask about Julie and Abbie. Don't worry, their stories are coming!

Special thanks to my family who has endured countless hours of me sitting at my desk writing, editing, re-writing, graphic designing, learning, failing, and trying again (especially Kaitlyn and Jackson). Your support means everything.

The most thanks goes to my wonderful husband, Adam, who provides a listening ear, practical advice, and plenty of encouragement. I definitely couldn't do any of this without you (also, I wouldn't want to). I love you!

ABOUT THE AUTHOR

Megan Byrd lives in Asheville, North Carolina with her husband and two kids. She hates running, but loves hiking in the mountains toward a waterfall or scenic view and taking a variety of classes including kickboxing, HIIT, yoga, and Zumba. When she's not reading, writing, or chasing waterfalls, she enjoys visiting local bookstores, wandering through thrift shops in search of special finds, listening to live music, and catching up with friends.

Want to be first to know about new books? Sign up for her e-newsletter at MeganByrd.net/newsletter to receive behind-the-scenes sneak peeks at her current work-in-progress, book recommendations, and other fun things. When you sign up, you'll receive a free novella, *Accidentally Yours*, which tells Jeff and Lisa's story. You can also learn more about the inspiration behind her books at MeganByrd.net/my_books

Website: MeganByrd.net
Instagram: @megan.e.byrd
Facebook: Facebook.com/authormeganbyrd
Facebook Reader Group:
Facebook.com/groups/meganbyrdsweetreaders